TRAPPED IN A NARCO-SU
TEN TONS OF COCAINE STC
CARTEL, IT WASN'T THE
CHASE BREWER PI

Praise for Richard Meredith's New Novel THE CROW'S NEST

"Hang on tight as you plunge into this fast-paced thriller that sweeps the reader on a hair-raising ride. You'll be holding your breath until the last page. Hop on board and enjoy!"—*Alexandra Ivy, New York Times Best Selling Author*

"Don Winslow by way of Clive Cussler, *The Crow's Nest* is a fast-paced, action-packed David v. Goliath tale, on land and sea. As terrifyingly intense as a drug runner's voyage in a homemade minisub, with just as uncertain a conclusion. As far as thrillers go, this is literary cocaine."—*Owen Laukkanen, author of Deception Cove*

"*The Crow's Nest* is a frenetic high seas romp, full of explosions, bar stool deals, and dastardly double-crosses. One moment, I felt like I was reading a Clive Cussler maritime adventure, and the next, I was in the dark, gritty world of Don Winslow. Meredith writes crackling dialog and spins out colorful secondary characters with ease and skill."—*Jeff Bond, author of The Winner Maker and Blackquest 40*

"An improbable hero teams up with a wily sea captain to bring down a dangerous drug cartel. A nail-biter climax will keep you guessing whether they will survive. Don't miss this fast-paced adventure."—*Catherine Coulter, author of DEADLOCK*

"*The Crow's Nest* is filled with rich language and breathtaking scenes. Richard Meredith will have you turning the pages in this exciting thriller from the beginning to the satisfying conclusion."—*Barry Finlay, Author of The Marcie Kane Thriller Collection*

i

The gun. Chase saw it. He bent down and picked it up. As if in a trance, he turned it slowly to see all its brilliant facets, admiring the sun's reflection in the bright stainless steel. He wasn't sure what compelled him, but he brought the gun to firing position and slowly aimed with one eye. He lowered the barrel ever so slightly until the sights were centered on the head of the man squirming across the ground to find cover behind his dead compadre. Just as he'd been taught, Chase drew a deep breath, let it out slowly, and inched the tip of his finger onto the trigger.

"No, senor, please."

He was ready—just another two pounds of pull weight. He hesitated; his concentration was broken. He looked skyward, scudding clouds, a bright sun. A calm overtook him. He lowered the weapon.

Chase picked up a cell phone and brought it to the man's face. "What's the code?"

"31881."

Chase turned and walked away.

.

THE CROW'S NEST

Richard Meredith

Moonshine Cove Publishing, LLC
Abbeville, South Carolina U.S.A.
First Moonshine Cove edition May 2020

This book is a work of fiction. Names, characters, places and incidents are products of the author's imagination or are used fictitiously. Any resemblance to actual events, locales or persons, living or dead, is entirely coincidental.

ISBN: 978-1-945181-832
Library of Congress PCN: 2020907179
© Copyright 2020 by Richard Meredith

Cover and interior illustrations by Karen Phillips; cover and interior design by Moonshine Cove staff

Richard Meredith, a Flint, Michigan native, moved to California while serving in the US Navy. After obtaining undergraduate and graduate degrees in Biology, he worked as a marine scientist and wildlife biologist for the federal government and the private sector. His work has taken him to the Eastern Tropical Pacific Ocean, the Amazonian rainforests of Ecuador, the tundra and taiga of the Yukon Flats, the coral reefs of the Caribbean, and St. Lawrence Island in the Bering Sea. *The Crow's Nest* draws heavily on his work aboard commercial tuna seiners and marine research vessels in the Pacific Ocean. His previous novel, *Sky Dance*, was based on his ecological studies in the oil fields of Ecuador. When not writing, Mr. Meredith enjoys travel, bird and wildlife watching, Scuba diving, guitars, rock concerts, and most sports. He is married with two children and four grandchildren.

www.richardwmeredith.com

For the kids; you keep me going!

Acknowledgment

I have so many people to thank in seeing this story finally put between covers. First, my mentor Michele Drier for her long hours reviewing, critiquing, and teaching. I am grateful for the many hours of review and inspiration provide by Karen Phillips, Nuvia Sandoval, and Lynda Markham of my critique group. Karen also prepared the wonderful graphics for the book. Thanks to Laura Garwood of Indigo Editing for an invaluable review of an early manuscript that prevented so many future errors. Special thanks to Lourdes Venard of Comma Sense Editing who took a rough product and molded it into the story you're reading today.

I am forever grateful that Gene Robinson of Moonshine Cover Publishers provided me this wonderful opportunity and for guiding me through the publishing process.

Thanks to the many friends and family that slogged through early versions and provided valuable input: Kevin Guse, Debbie and Larry Yarbrough, Deb and Joe McNamara, Dr. David Spring, Jo Deupree, Sid England, Simon Poulter, Sarah Powell, Kevin Crouch... If I missed anyone, I sincerely apologize.

I especially want to thank my sons Casey and Andrew; daughters-in-law Cassie and Jackie; and the grandkids, Will, Allison, Emily, and Benjamin for their patience in indulging my dream. And, of course, special kudos to my wife, Carol, who patiently sat as I read her passage after passage. With a simple eye roll, I knew more work was required. But, in the end, I take full responsibility for any errors.

High-Seas Tuna Purse Seiner

1 - Crow's Nest ("stick")
2 - Boom
3 - Power Block
4 - Net Skiff
5 - Purse Seine Net
6 - Speed Boat Deck
7 - Speed Boat Davits
8 - Net Deck
9 - Pilot House

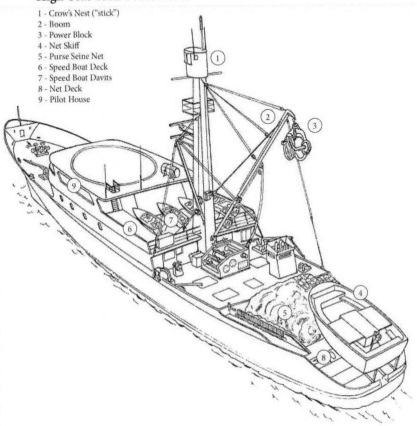

Submarine

1 - Forward Hatch
2 - Top Hatch
3 - Helm Platform
4 - Aft Hatch
5 - Exhaust Snorkle
6 - Forward Fuel Tanks

7 - Water Storage
8 - Generator
9 - Compressed Air
10 - Aft Fuel Tanks
11 - Diesel Engine
12 - Rudder

13 - Propeller
14 - Aft Hydroplane
15 - Flood Holes
16 - Ballast Tanks
17 - Bow Hydroplane

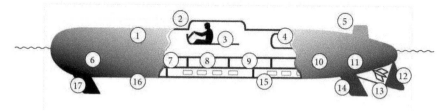

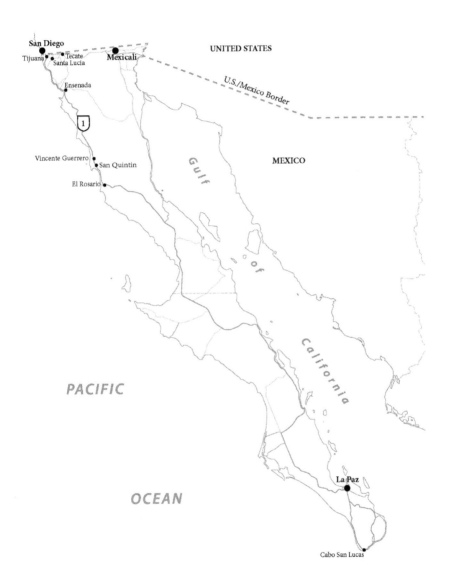

San Diego
Tijuana
Tecate
Santa Lucia
Mexicali
Ensenada
1
Vincente Guerrero
San Quintin
El Rosario

UNITED STATES

U.S./Mexico Border

MEXICO

Gulf

of

California

PACIFIC

OCEAN

La Paz

Cabo San Lucas

THE CROW'S NEST

Chapter One
Eastern Tropical Pacific off Baja Mexico
32°28'41"N, 118°08'06"W

The sea can keep a secret and the night can hide its sins—it's your friends you gotta worry about.

Isosceles LeBeau, Captain Jonny to all but his mama, wedged his short reedy frame through the top hatch of the crude submarine. Steadying himself against the slow swell lapping three feet below, he scanned the darkness, a stingy moon his only light. It was almost serene, but he knew tranquility at sea was an illusion. Like his ex-wife, it could turn fast.

He pawed the scruff of his six-day beard, more out of anxiety than discomfort, before checking his watch. He was early, which should have brought him some satisfaction after a grueling trip from Colombia and navigating blind under the sea half the time, but the sooner he unloaded, the faster he'd get to land and a few days of real sleep before starting again.

It was time. "Get ready below, I'm gonna signal." After a few moments, Jonny heard his two crewmen scramble to their stations at the port and starboard cargo hatches.

Jonny raised his light and sent the signal, praying under his breath it caught the right eyes.

* * *

Lashed together less than a mile away, three speedboats drifted in the empty sea. The six men aboard were silent, their hearing dulled by screeching outboard motors after the two-hour run from Ensenada. They were, however, vigilant, straining tired eyes in the blackness for the signal that would get them home.

Falco, the leader of the small armada, peered again at the GPS screen and looked up. Hopeful expectation was etched in the faces of the men. He folded his arms and shook his head, "Nada."

Disquiet settled over the boats. Falco knew to these men the sea held no allegiance, no allure. It was a job, a dirty job, and if not for the threat of a double tap through the brain, they'd be chugging cheap tequila in some skanky beach bar, not here puking their guts overboard.

The spell broke. "Ten o'clock!" the crewman from Bravo boat shouted, pointing southeast. "Lights. Fifteen hundred meters."

Four long flashes, a pause, and two short flashes.

"That's it, ready up." Falco reached under the console and grabbed the spotlight. Two quick signals, four long.

Two long flashes returned.

The speedboats roared to life, strafing the Pacific on cushions of roiled foam and throttling down just fifty feet short of the beacon.

The boats idled like jittery thoroughbreds in the starting gate, gasping, gurgling, and coughing acrid fumes into the still sea air.

Falco squinted hard, the target was barely visible. Only three feet shone above the surface, her gray-blue skin the color of her namesake—the whale.

A low rumble reverberated through the hulls of the speedboats as hissing air from the whale's ballast tanks erupted in a torrent of bubbles. In slow motion, a shadow rose from the black depths.

A dim light appeared as her starboard hatch opened. Falco gestured to the other drivers. Bravo boat motored over and the crewman jumped aboard. Charlie boat followed, disappearing around the whale's stern before tethering to the port hatch.

At a distance Falco watched as four men, two from the speedboats and two from the whale, struggled to off-load the two-hundred-pound bales. Within fifteen minutes, the two burdened speedboats slogged for shore.

Falco motored Alpha boat into position. At the hatch, he locked his eyes on his crewman. "You know what to do."

The man, his face erased of expression, patted the bulge at his waist.

Jonny was busy in the bilge when the deafening report of a handgun echoed through the cavernous hull. Startled, he hoisted himself from the bowels of the whale to see his two crewmen lying dead on the deck.

Jonny glared at the shooter, his revulsion masked beneath a thousand-yard stare—the face of wounded detachment.

The shooter shrugged, shoved the revolver back into his waistband, and smirked. "No witnesses, no evidence."

Jonny stepped over the bodies of his crewmen and boarded Alpha boat. In only a T-shirt and shorts, the fresh sea air chilled him. The pilot offered his hand. "I'm Falco. Good job with the shipment."

Jonny nodded and moved toward the bow.

Alpha boat chugged away from the submarine for several feet before Falco juiced her to life.

Jonny sat alone, his attention drawn to his watch as he wiped the salt spray from his black, hatchet-shaped face—a testament to his Haitian-Choctaw heritage. He looked up and caught Falco's gaze for a moment, then down at his watch and a silent count. A blinding yellow-orange flash seared the night. Seconds later, a thirty-foot plume of water and debris erupted, followed by a thunderous roar. The men braced against the gunwales as the violent surge pummeled the boat and the salt spray rained.

"Jesus H. Christ," Falco yelled. "They're gonna see that explosion for miles." He jammed the throttle forward and the bow of the twenty-five-foot-long boat lurched upward five feet as the blades of the twin props grabbed the sea. Only when they were safe from the wreckage did he turn to Jonny and ask, "What the hell happened? We lose this load and we're all dead."

Jonny, a drenched cigarette dangling from his lips, shot him a dismissive glare and in little more than a murmur, finally said, "No witnesses, no evidence."

Chapter Two
Nido del Cuervo Ranch, Near Santa Lucia, Baja California, Mexico

The control room was hushed, the silence broken by the whir of air streaming through the vents, the muted clatter of keyboards, and anxious whispers.

Manuel—Manny—Teixeira stared at the center monitor. The subterranean bunker was cool but sweat beaded on the former physics professor's forehead and fogged his wire-rimmed eyeglasses. His fingers drummed the console to a phantom beat.

The two men seated beside him fidgeted in their chairs, exhaling exaggerated breaths in the heavy air.

A fourth man, Fernando Cuervo—the Raven to his men—sat away from the others. With legs crossed, revealing the intricate tooling of his custom three-thousand-dollar Tony Lama boots beneath black trousers, the capo of Baja's notorious cartel, La Hermandad—the Brotherhood, exuded a calm bordering on indifference. If not for an index finger smoothing his white mustache and the nearly imperceptible arch of his right eyebrow, he appeared frozen. Even for a casino sharp it was impossible to read whether he held a full house or bluffed a ten high.

"Here they come," Manny said as three yellow dots converged on a larger flashing green dot at the center of the plasma display.

The technician to Manny's left entered a few keystrokes and zoomed the dots. "About a mile out."

Emotions were on hair-trigger. They'd worked on the plan for two years yet sat helplessly five hundred miles away in the middle of the Baja desert while the fate of the project lay in the hands of the men at sea in fragile boats. Every plan has its weakness.

In ten minutes, the yellow dots surrounded the green dot, and within fifteen more, the yellow dots were heading east, back to shore.

"Damn, they got the cargo." Manny laughed with relief and shot his arms skyward in victory.

The technicians sighed, their smiles visible even in the subdued light.

Cuervo remained still. His eyes were trained on the green dot. In less than a minute, it flashed one last time and disappeared from the screen.

Manny swiveled in his chair. "The whale is down, El Cuervo."

Cuervo rose and exited the bunker. Outside of his men's sight, a ghost of satisfaction crossed his face.

Chapter Three
Eastern Tropical Pacific off the Gulf of Tehuantepec, Mexico
12°05′39″N, 96°43′22″W

Another half night of sleep, another lonely vigil on the cool deserted deck of a sleeping ship. Chase Brenner leaned against the stern rail, gazing at the shimmer of gold peeking above the black sea. Below him, wavelets slapped the steel hull, splashing into thousands of luminescent droplets. His expression was blank, but his moist eyes told a different story—dawn wrenched his soul. To most, the surrender of darkness to light brought renewal, but for him it meant another day away from Maria, another day without his children. Chase reached into his pocket and pulled a creased and fading photograph from his wallet. As he stared at Maria's face in the first moments of day, his heart ached and tears released.

* * *

"Dolphins, one-twenty!" Captain Leo Garza radioed from the crow's nest atop the 215-foot long tuna seiner *Bella.* "Franco, the school's on the move. Cut them off."

The keening outboard engines pierced the quiet of the Pacific afternoon as five chase boats sliced the cobalt sea.

"Roger that, Skipper." The whine of boat's propeller almost drowned Franco's voice.

Like a ballet, the fifteen-foot-long aluminum boats coursed southeast in perfect symmetry.

Garza gnawed the butt end of his Montecristo cigar—his fourth of the day—as he studied the sea through his binoculars. A school of dolphins, a mix of spotters and spinners, erupted from the surface in spiraling contortions, splashing back in shallow dives, and leaping again. Over a thousand animals roiled the sea white in their frantic escape from the fast boats.

But it wasn't the dolphins Garza was after—he wanted tuna, and didn't care if it was yellowfin, bluefin, or albacore. Through a quirk of nature, in this area of the Eastern Tropical Pacific—roughly from Baja Mexico to northern Chile—the tuna shadowed the dolphins. The scientists speculated about a symbiotic defense against sharks and killer whales but weren't sure. Garza knew if he saw dolphins, it was a good bet tuna were close.

But dolphins are almost impossible to spot at a distance. Instead, the fishermen searched for birds. Again, nature conspired against the poor tuna. The birds, dolphins, and tuna fed on the same baitfish, usually sardines, sauries, and anchovies. Flocks of high-flying birds were easy to spot, even at two to three miles, and if they were diving, they were feeding. The *Bella* would motor toward the flock, searching for splashing dolphins. If dolphins were there, Garza, high up in the crow's nest—the "stick" to the crew—looked under the dolphins for tuna. If he saw them, game on.

Garza lifted the intercom mike and hailed his navigator in the pilothouse. "Hey, Denny, the boys seeing anything?"

On the bridge wing outside the pilothouse, two crewmen were scanning the sea through huge binoculars. Coined "Big Eyes" by the Navy, the two-foot-long, twenty-power lenses were capable of spotting birds as far as three miles out.

"Just flippers," Denny said, transmitting the fishermen's tag for dolphins over the radio. "No fish yet."

"Keep on 'em." Garza replaced his binoculars with his aviator sunglasses and rose to relieve the cramps from sitting for most of the day. What he really wanted was to walk around the deck, but the sixty-foot climb was getting more difficult, and nearing his forty-fifth birthday, he wasn't getting more limber or lighter. He was a big man, not tall, maybe five ten, but a solid two hundred and fifty pounds with thick, squat legs and bulging arms.

Garza peered down at the thirty-foot-long net skiff, *Bellita*, secured on the angled stern of the seiner, and radioed his assistant engineer. "Chase, what's the word on the skiff? Good to go?"

Brenner peeked from under the skiff's engine hatch and looked up at the skipper. He swiped his hands over his oil-stained coveralls before reaching into his pocket for his VHF radio.

"I don't think it's a shaft bearing. It sounds okay to me. Maybe Jerome was just hearing things," Chase said, his broad smile visible even to Garza in the stick.

"Why don't you stay on board during the next set and see if you can hear anything while it's under load?"

"Sure thing, Skip. You'll have to break it to the chief, though. He'll need to keep an eye on the engine room, and you know how grouchy he can get when he misses his nap."

"I heard that," Gus Furtado, the chief engineer, grumbled over the radio. "You're a real Tom Sawyer, finagling me to do your work while you are on a little pleasure cruise in the skiff. Hey, don't forget your cribbage board, you worthless dreg."

"Sorry, did I wake you?" Chase asked. "You should have known I was a slacker when you hired me."

Garza fought to contain his laughter. "Boys, boys, boys. I'm trying to run a fishing boat here. Can't you two ever agree on anything?"

"Cold beer and hot women," Gus said.

"Copy that," Chase said.

"How about agreeing on one more thing? Like maybe taking orders from the captain?" Garza asked.

"As long as it doesn't become a habit and you make that young buck pull his weight. I'm not Atlas—I can't shoulder the entire load," Gus said.

"What? With your bad knees and that supposed hernia you're always bitchin' about, you need two deckhands to carry your coffee cup. Quit your grousing." Chase's laugh blared through Garza's speaker.

"I'll show you bad knees when they are halfway up your butt—"

"Okay, everybody, fun's over. Let's see if we got any fish. And Chase, no more fights on my boat. You almost broke Tommy's nose last week," Garza said.

Like cowboys wrangling stray doggies, the chase boats corralled the dolphins into a tight circle. Exhausted after the intense chase, the dolphins lolled on the surface loudly, exhaling a fine mist through their blowholes.

Garza raised his binoculars and squinted hard at the murky ball of fish only tens of feet under the dolphins. But were they tuna? This was the captain's moment because once he gave the order, there was no turning back. If he was wrong, not only would they have wasted valuable fishing time, they'd be pulling sharks and trash fish from the net for hours while the money fish swam elsewhere. And if there was one thing that ruffled a crew, it was a skunk set.

As the seiner approached, Garza had what he needed. A tuna broke the surface, its scythe-shaped pectoral fin and crescent tail gleaming yellow in the sun.

That's it. He picked up the loudspeaker mike and looked below at his anxious crew. "Let her go!" From his perch, Garza guided his team like a symphony conductor. Each movement precise, timely, harmonized.

The deck boss, Tommy Beagle, strained at the shackle lanyard until it released, and the net skiff crept slowly off the stern on its thick, steel skegs.

Once clear of the seiner's propellers, Jerome flipped the ignition switch to the skiff's diesel engine. Its exhaust coughed until it finally turned over and Jerome backed it away from the seiner. Garza laughed as Chase raised his head skyward and clasped his hands in mock prayer.

The skiff headed in one direction while Denny steered the seiner in the other, each attached to the opposite ends of a mile-long braided-nylon net. The two boats encircled the school of tuna and dolphins as the chase boats kept them corralled.

After fifteen minutes, the two boats converged at the port side of the seiner. Jerome passed the purse line to Tommy. His job done, he carefully backed the skiff away. The dolphin and tuna were contained within a 1,700-foot-diameter nylon mesh cylinder.

Garza's voice bellowed over the PA. "Tommy, close up the net."

Tommy returned a two-finger salute and started the hydraulic winch. The purse line was slowly spooled aboard, cinching the bottom of the net. The tuna and dolphin were now trapped on all sides but one.

In another hour, the dolphins were released from the net and the tuna were hauled on board. It was a good haul—forty tons.

Garza sat back in his seat, relaxed for the first time in two hours. He rolled his cigar to the side of his mouth and picked up the mike. "Another set like that, boys, and we can hit the beach. Get things ready for tomorrow and call it a day."

* * *

The mood was electric when the crew queued in the galley an hour later. After ninety days at sea, the boat was almost full. Garza poured each man two fingers of Jack Daniel's for a job well done.

Fresh from his shower, Chase grabbed his bourbon and returned to his bastion at the stern just as the sea extinguished the sun in a blaze of red and yellow. He raised his glass to the horizon. "To you, CeCe." He downed it in a single tug. It was time to call home.

Chapter Four
Eastern Tropical Pacific off the Gulf of Tehuantepec, Mexico
12°05'39"N, 96°43'22"W

Chase ducked his six-foot-two frame through the squat passageway, closed the hatch, and was instantly slammed by the 110-degree heat as he descended the ladder into the engine room.

Santos, leaning back in a swivel chair with his legs propped up on the console, sighed in relief at the sight of Chase.

"You look beat."

"I am," Santos said, removing the headphones designed to protect his hearing from the ninety-decibel din of the rumbling equipment. "Bouncing on the waves all day, stacking net, cleaning my boat, and then evening watch, I barely had a chance to eat dinner."

Chase turned his attention to the engine room log and ran his index finger down the recent entries. "How's everything?"

"Good. The temperature in well-seven started to rise, but I gave it a shot of ammonia and it's been okay since. Better keep an eye on it. Also, I lubed and oiled auxiliary-two. It was due tomorrow anyway."

Chase looked up from the log. "Skipper's got a drink for you then, hey, hit the rack, you're gonna need it. We've got some heavy fishing for the next few days. At least I hope so."

"Me too—almost home."

Chase checked the console and signed the watch list. He turned and checked the clock on the bulkhead and decided to conduct his hourly inspection after he made the call. He inhaled deeply; the smell of oil, diesel, and all manner of solvents was comforting. In spite of the raucous clamor and commotion, this was his redoubt. Unlike other boats he'd worked, this engine room was spotless. Gus demanded it. He would not tolerate any spills on his floor or on the equipment, and you had better be damn sure everything was in order when you finished your watch. All tools secured on the pegboard, no trash or abandoned coffee cups on the console, all glass and metal surfaces wiped clean, and the deck mopped. At any time, some portion of the engine room was being scrapped, stripped, and repainted. As Gus would say: "This is our home more than half the year, and I ain't livin' in a damned sty."

Chase took out his wallet and gazed at the picture. Against the backdrop of a dark blue sea meeting a cloud-dappled sky at Ocean Beach, Maria lay buried up to her neck in sand. Grinning with delight, Denise and Kevin piled even more sand with their toy shovels and pails. It always brought a smile. Most crewmen kept their wallets in lockers while at sea, but Chase wanted the picture close. He never knew when he needed a fix to relieve the monotony of ship's life, if only for a moment.

Chase inserted the earbuds, opened his laptop, and saw he had a strong Wi-Fi signal even within the bowels of the boat. The range extender he had installed eliminated the dead spots in the steel-shielded confines below the main deck.

He clicked the videophone icon and dialed his home number in San Diego. He knew it was late, but he called every Saturday and Tuesday night, and Maria would struggle to stay awake.

After a couple of rings, Maria's beautiful, albeit tired, face appeared full screen. Even without makeup, her deep brown eyes, full lips, and flawless skin were as seductive as the first day he had seen her in high school fifteen years ago. Chase watched her slight frown dissolve into a full smile when his face appeared on her screen.

"Well, hello, stranger," she said.

"It hasn't been that long, has it?"

"Ninety days and counting. How's the catch? Any chance of coming home soon?"

"We're doing great. Another day like today and it's Ensenada here we come."

"That's great. The kids miss you. Maybe you can get home for some of their games."

"The skipper says we'll be off for at least a month. The boat will be in the yard for some work. I'll be there for a few days when the new gear is installed, but otherwise, I'll be home."

Chase didn't mind the eighty-mile commute between Ensenada and San Diego. Most of the route was on Mexico's Federal Highway 1D, a four-lane toll road. It normally took him two hours with his usual stop at the Pemex fuel station in Rosarito, where he filled the truck's tank with fuel and his belly with fish tacos.

He kept his 2004 Nissan Frontier pickup at the Pescadero Baja office for a quick getaway when he "hit the beach." He traveled light, a single suitcase and truck bed free of any cargo for quick border inspections. Only his laptop and cell phone sat in the front compartment.

"What have you been working on?" Maria asked. "Anything interesting?"

"No, same routine. I've had to fix the chase boats. They take such a beating that the welds split. I had to untangle some line on the rudder and got to use the hookah again—reminded me of our scuba trip to Puerto Vallarta. And I'm trying to fix some vibration in the skiff. Other than that, just long days. I remain a bored and lonely guy."

"What about all those mermaids I'm always hearing about?"

"They were old wives' tales—no offense—and were just manatees, you know, sea cows."

"No way. I saw the movie. Daryl Hannah is no sea cow."

"Well, if she surfaces, I promise I won't be lonely."

"Watch it, big guy. You're a happily married man, remember?"

"Oh, I suppose if Brad Pitt miraculously showed up at the front door, you wouldn't—"

"No comment."

"There, goose-gander, I rest my case. Hey, did you just yawn? You know, I can see your face."

"Sorry, it's not you. The kids are running me ragged. You'll see when you get here. We spawned two perpetual-motion machines. Maybe I can catch up on sleep when you get here."

"I think not, CeCe. It's my vacation and I plan to languish on the beach for long hours with a case of longnecks and a longboard to catch a wave every now and then."

She laughed. CeCe was their little code, short for "cupcake," and only used in their private moments, mainly because she hated it, and Chase loved to goad her.

"I may be tired, buddy, but you're the one dreaming," she replied.

"Only dreaming of you. Why don't you get to bed? I'll call on Tuesday. Hug the kids."

"Love ya."

Chase disconnected. He leaned back in the chair, his head braced from behind by his interlaced fingers. It was moments like this, just after calls, when the loneliness squeezed the hardest, and he still had another three hours on watch. He missed them and longed for a job on the beach, but the fishing money was too hard to pass up. No way he would earn anything close working the docks. Even shipping out on a freighter, the union money was good, but not the same. He knew the only antidote to his loneliness was work, and so his night began.

Chapter Five
Eastern Tropical Pacific North of Colombia
10°33'49"N, 97°28'46"W

Glazed with sweat, Captain Jonny reveled in the cool Pacific breeze for a few seconds, long enough for two satisfying drags before he flicked the butt into the wind. It'd be another half day before his next smoke. It was his second cruise in less than a month, and he was spent.

"Okay, boys, break's over," Jonny shouted in his Cajun patois as he took his seat at the helm. "We're goin' down."

To his left, Joaquin rose from the makeshift berth and wormed his way aft, edging around the bales stacked four feet high that engorged the sub.

Benji was already at the port hatch, on his knees, retching his last meal of canned peaches and tuna into the ocean.

"Benji, when you're done there, dog this one," Jonny said, jutting his pointy chin toward the top hatch above his head.

"Got it, boss. Ain't you worried we'll be spotted? It's already daylight."

"Yeah, but I needed more light to check the hull. We took a beatin' from that storm. This thing ain't like those steel and titanium nukes prowling the ocean. She's just a lumbering fiberglass turtle."

"Everything okay?"

Jonny crossed himself and kissed the silver crucifix around his neck. "Yeah, she's holdin' up pretty good. She may be ugly, but she's tough."

With the hatches sealed, the hold was veiled in darkness. Jonny flipped a switch on the helm panel and a ribbon of small LED bulkhead lights flickered to life. He strained to read his watch; the time had to be exact. He'd be dead reckoning for the next twelve hours—the GPS was worthless under thirty feet of ocean. The squall had set them back and he had to make up for lost time.

"Damn, it's like a coffin in here," the bearded Joaquin moaned as he hunched like a gangly Quasimodo toward the helm, just clearing the low-hanging spars. He was already dripping with sweat in his running shorts and tank top.

"Ya gotta be kiddin'," Jonny said. "A coffin is dry and cozy. This is more like a sewer. I'll say this, though, you don't do your job and this could be a crypt for all of us. Just keep it together for a few more days."

Submerging was the worst part of the day. Ten hours of breathing the fetid air. The stench of mildew and diesel mixed with vomit and piss burned their lungs. The heat was barely tolerable, and the humidity was stifling. All they could do was wait until night to surface and open the hatches. Until then, it was misery, and they still had another four days.

Benji clawed at the heat rash on his legs. "Yeah, yeah. I know, just a few more days. You keep telling us."

Benji and Joaquin were scared, especially after the storm. They weren't seamen—they'd been shanghaied from the Cali barrio and hadn't held down a full meal since. Jonny felt for them. Even after a life at sea, he was nervous on his first run from Colombia, never imagining a homemade submarine was possible. He feared every groan and creak meant the hull was imploding, that every wave would flip them, and that each dive would be their last. Thankfully, it didn't happen; she held tight.

But Captain Jonny couldn't waste time stewing about the boat, weather, or the crew. If he was gonna worry, it'd be about the cartel thugs waiting for the ten tons of cocaine crammed behind him—the shipment he was about to lose. Instead, he secretly grinned in the dark.

Chapter Six
Eastern Tropical Pacific North of Colombia
10°33'49"N, 97°28'46"W

Jonny's face twisted into a scowl and he swore under his breath as he struggled through the narrow top hatch. Sweating from the exertion, he slicked back his curly hair before wringing the sweat from his hand. It took him half a minute to adapt to the sliver of light from the crescent moon.

The night was silent, disturbed only by the muffled diesel drone and the sea pounding his boat.

Jonny drew hard on the Lucky Strike. His nostrils expelled tendrils of smoke as he crushed the butt against the hull and watched the embers tumble like kamikaze fireflies into the sea.

He had set a new course—his course—one not programmed into the GPS, one closer to the shipping lanes. He grabbed his binoculars and scanned the dark.

To the north, maybe a mile out, white running lights bobbed with the swell. Finally, dammit. He slipped back down to the helm and readied himself.

He looked back at his men. Both were asleep in painful contortions atop the bales, their snoring almost as annoying as the diesel. The best chance for sleep was at night when the sub motored on the surface, its hatches open to the cool sea air.

He drew a breath, mopped his brow with a forearm, and blew his fingertips dry. Gripping the port ballast tank handle, he pulled back in a slow, gentle motion. As the seawater surged into the tank, the boat rolled slightly to port.

Careful, Jonny boy. He grabbed his flashlight and illuminated the port hatch. Another couple of inches.

The boat continued to heel. Jonny eased back on the throttle until the boat slowed.

He shined the light again. The sea rippled at the open hatch. Just a tad more. Jonny jiggered the ballast handle an inch.

Water spilled into the hold. Jonny waited until a half foot swirled around his ankles before he closed the valve.

Benji bolted upright and knuckled his eyes. "What are you doing?"

Jonny turned and screamed, "Oh my God! Get up, we're sinking!"

Joaquin woke in a panic. "What...what's happening?"

"The ballast tanks are filling. We're taking on water," Jonny said, straining at the valve handles.

The water was now a foot deep.

Jonny rose and ran toward the stern. "Joaquin, start unloading the bales. Benji, get the lifeboat overboard."

Joaquin sprung from his berth, ran aft, and began muscling the heavy bales into the ocean. Benji joined him, heaving bales out the starboard hatch.

Benji turned. "At least we're gettin' out of this hole."

Joaquin arched an eyebrow and with a snide laugh replied, "Yeah, the hard way."

Jonny returned to the helm. "I gotta empty the tanks before the batteries die." He actuated the air pumps and began purging the tanks. Slowly, almost imperceptibly, the boat righted.

The three men worked with fervor and within ten minutes the bales were out of the sub.

Jonny inspected the empty hold. "Quick, get that damn lifeboat inflated."

His hands dripping with sweat like the rest of his body, Joaquin fumbled for a grip on the slick plastic release cord. He yanked hard and the canister mushroomed as its pressurized cartridges inflated the raft. Benji dove in first, grabbed the tether line, and brought the raft back toward the starboard hatch. Joaquin followed.

Through narrowed eyes, Jonny stared at the Sig Sauer 9 mm at the bottom of his bag. He knew the procedure; if a sub was scuttled, there could be no witnesses, except the captain, who would know all the cover stories if rescued. But Jonny needed the men; he needed an alibi.

He zipped his bag shut and stashed it in the sub.

Jonny double-checked the timers on the explosive charges in the bilge and sloshed aft to the lifeboat.

Benji handed him the third oar.

Jonny rowed with a ferocity that belied his skinny frame. "We got three minutes to get the hell out of here."

He looked around and sighed in relief. The sea was empty—all the bales had sunk as planned.

Though he hadn't designed them, Jonny marveled at their engineering. Each bale was waterproofed with three layers of shrink-wrapped plastic and encircled with an air bladder. They were supposed to sink between seventy-five and a hundred and twenty-five feet, invisible from the surface. But Jonny had to be sure—and now he was.

The men huddled in the raft.

The explosion scorched the dark night, but the running lights continued in their direction. Plans change.

Chapter Seven
Near Tecate, Baja California, Mexico

Cuervo knew he looked silly in his housekeeper's frilly apron as he prepared breakfast for his son, Ramon. The six-year-old wiggled in his chair for his French toast, a meal he had first tried at the Pancake Circus in San Diego. It was love at first taste and now a routine breakfast at the Cuervo home.

"Papa, I'm so hungry. Could I have more juice?"

Cuervo poured his son a second glass before returning to the stove. "They are almost ready, but you will have to eat fast. Donte needs to get you to school. Father Simon will be upset if you are late." He had just flipped the egg-soaked bread in the skillet when his cell phone rang. Wedging the phone between his ear and shoulder, he loaded Ramon's plate.

"Hola."

"El Cuervo, this is Manny. I thought you should know right away. One of our boats had a problem. We're not receiving a signal. It might be lost."

"What about the cargo?"

"We're getting signals, but they are all coming from different locations. It's overboard."

Cuervo's face tensed. He walked to the stove, turned off the burner, and placed the spatula in the sink. "I'll be over in a short while. In the meantime, call Cuda and have him meet us."

"Yes, El Cuervo." The call ended.

Cuervo looked over to Ramon's imposing bodyguard. "Better get him to school."

Donte nodded and grasped Ramon's tiny hand, hurrying him through the garage door and into the custom-armored Escalade.

"Don't forget your bag. I don't want any calls from Father Simon," Cuervo said as the door to the garage was closing.

Ramon's voice faded. "I have it, Papa."

Cuervo shook his head in wonder. It was Ramon's passion for sharks that started it all. If not for the documentary his son begged to watch, Cuervo would never have thought to use underwater satellite transmitters to track his shipments. He removed Estrella's apron and sat for a moment, concentrating on his next move. He knew a lost boat was a possibility; contingencies would now be tested.

Chapter Eight
Near Tecate, Baja California, Mexico

The ring jolted Cuda from a deep and deserved sleep. He fumbled for the phone on the nightstand, staring bleary-eyed at his wristwatch. He cleared his coarse throat and answered. "What is it?"

"It's Manny. The boss needs you, pronto. A shipment is missing. Meet at the ranch."

"When?" Cuda asked as a lithe, tanned leg coiled serpent-like around his waist and sharp manicured nails gently traced the contour of his spine.

He playfully slapped the hand away and mouthed, "Trouble."

She rolled away at the affront.

"As soon as you can," Manny said.

"No, I mean when was the shipment lost?"

"About four hours ago."

"Tell El Cuervo I'll be there in two hours." Cuda dropped the call.

He shifted and stared, lost in her deep brown eyes. "A shipment is missing. El Cuervo needs me."

She yawned and turned onto her side, a tangle of raven hair hanging across her face. "See how important you are to him. He needs you because you know so much. You do the things he cannot."

Cuda smiled back, marveling at her beauty and, even more, his luck. She lay naked, confident, no pretense of modesty. "I must leave."

Her bent elbow propped her head. "How long will it take to get there?"

"An hour or so."

"So, I have you to myself for a while." She swept the hair from her face, straddled him, and braced her locked arms against his shoulders.

His response was predictable, even after a full night of lovemaking.

After a satisfying twenty minutes, she rolled away and slipped under the covers. "You have to get moving. If it's to work, El Cuervo cannot suspect anything. We must bide our time."

Chapter Nine
Eastern Tropical Pacific

Gus stood on his toes, stretching his stubby frame to its limit, his head barely clearing the side of the skiff. "Hey, Navy boy. What's the word on the net skiff? Jerome's bugging the skipper, he's on my ass, and I'm on yours. Don't ya just love the pecking order?"

"Jesus, you want to try to squeeze your fat ass in here and fix it?"

"No, remember why I hired you? Well, this is why."

Chase laughed silently as he recalled his first encounter with Gus. Nico had introduced him to Garza in the pilothouse as the *Bella* took on supplies at Pescadero Baja's company dock. Garza had taken one look at his papers and said with a smile: "Nico, he is fine with me, but you got to get him by Gus. I'm only the captain, he's the boss."

Nico escorted him down the two decks to the engine room, where Gus was sitting behind the console. Chase noticed the chief engineer was about average height, but stocky. Not fat, more like linebacker muscle bulk. The top of his head was bald but fringed with snow-white hair on the sides, draping down over his ears and almost to his collar. Though he was only fifty-eight his ruddy complexion and hair made him look ten years older. He wore an old Hawaiian-print shirt, cutoff jeans, and plastic flip-flops. If any safety inspector had been aboard, the boat would have been gigged for numerous violations just from Gus' apparel. Chase immediately thought he was trapped in some space-time vortex and Gus was some geriatric parrothead at a Jimmy Buffett concert.

Looking up, Gus scowled as he set down his midmorning crossword puzzle.

Without prompting, Nico yelled out over the din of the engine room: "Got an assistant for you."

"Oh, do you now," Gus replied.

He stared at Chase over the half-frame reading glasses planted at the tip of his bulbous nose. Chase stood silent as Gus eyed the tall and skinny kid, twenty-five, well dressed in a light blue short-sleeved button-down Oxford shirt, tan khaki slacks, and brown loafers.

"Hey, those clothes don't hide that tan. Surfer, huh?" Gus started reading the papers Nico handed him. "Um, Navy...four years...machinist's mate...discharged. You ever work on the nukes?"

"No," Chase said.

"Good, 'cause we ain't got none."

Gus flipped through the pages. "Hold on. What's with this Captain's Mast? Pay docked for two weeks and confined to the ship for a month. What the hell did you do?"

Chase's face reddened, and he tugged at his collar. "I had a disagreement with another sailor."

"Uh huh. That how your nose got so crooked?"

Chase half smiled. "Naw, that's from a misunderstanding at the beach over a wave."

"I knew it, a damn surf bum. Any others brawls I should know about before I let you loose on the crew?"

"A few, but not for a long time. The Navy shrink said I had anger control issues. I told him I'd get pushed so far and it was like a red cloud falls over me and I'd go a little crazy. Shrink said he was worried I'd lose it with my wife or family someday. That was the slap in the face I needed. No way would I ever hurt them, so I learned control. Now I just rag on people."

Gus cocked his head slightly and in theatrical motion swept his right arm around the engine room. "Okay, Navy boy, tell me what you see here."

Chase paused, took a good look. He read off the banks of controls, gauges, and switches on the panel. He called out the array of diesel engine gauges and controls, the electrical generator, environmental systems, the hydraulics, the refrigerator system, the works.

"Not bad, if you're the chief. But you'll be my assistant. And your job will be to scurry like a wharf rat though all the areas I can't fit. All I can say is you better have a lot of coveralls because your skinny-ass body will be getting dirty in places you didn't even know existed."

Gus was finished with the interview and returned to his puzzle.

Nico gave Chase a nod. "Let's get your gear on board before he changes his mind."

Gus looked up a last time. "No fights."

Gus was true to his word and Chase did worm his way through all the compartments from the lowest claustrophobic bowels of the bilge through the refrigeration pipeline raceways to the top of the mast. The ship's equipment inspections were the assistant engineer's prime responsibility. And dirty he had gotten. Most of his overalls had been deep-sixed, way beyond soap.

Gus pounded at the side of the skiff. "I didn't hear an answer."

Chase jerked back to reality. "It's almost done, boss. A few more hours."

Gus huffed. "You're treating that damn boat like some kind of yacht. You plan on sailing it somewhere?"

"Don't you have a nap to take?"

Chapter Ten
Nido del Cuervo Ranch

Cuervo drove to the ranch alone. He had no fear for himself and figured a bodyguard and entourage would attract more attention. Besides, he had his little Uzi, Suzie, in the passenger seat. And if Suzie failed, he had his trusty Glock, Rocky, right under his seat. Suzie is sweet, but Rocky packs the punch.

The Ford Focus was his added element of stealth. No one expected the CEO of one of the largest criminal enterprises in the Western Hemisphere would drive himself in such an unassuming car.

As he sped toward the ranch, he did the math. Fifty bales at two hundred pounds are almost four thousand five hundred kilos of product. That's over $125 million on the street. But Cuervo was not a retailer in the US—too much trouble, too much exposure. The wholesale value was closer to $85 million, which amounted to over a month of lost revenue. He could absorb the loss—what did they say in business schools? It was "the cost of doing business." But if he could recover his lost inventory at a low risk, so much the better. It was at times like this that his investment in a tuna fleet seemed prescient.

The old ranch, nestled in an oak-pine woodland valley of the Sierra de Juárez range in north-central Baja California Norte, was over two miles beyond the nearest public road.

Cuervo had purchased the property for its isolation—there were no neighbors for miles. The previous owner surrendered to nature. While it was considered cattle range, it was arid and rocky, and the vegetation was sparse and scrubby. The ten-thousand acres could only support a couple hundred head. Roundups were difficult through the deep canyons and steep ridges, but to Cuervo, it was perfect.

The operations center was in the ranch house. The generator and all electrical equipment were housed in the main barn. A stable with

Cuervo's prized horses was separated from the barn by a small corral. The satellite receiver was disguised as a television dish. Even the technicians added to the illusion by dressing as ranch hands and doing occasional chores. But it was Cuervo's cousin, Tomás, who was the vaquero and did the real ranch work.

Cuervo stepped from the car and leaned against the locked cattle gate with one boot propped on the low rail. A hand-carved sign, Nido del Cuervo, hung from a fence post. The morning stillness was broken by the rustling leaves of the two hundred-year-old oaks standing sentry beside the gate. In the distance an old windmill in need of oil rattled with each gust. Such moments were quite rare in Cuervo's bustling life. Over the rise, a dust trail signaled his cousin's approaching pickup.

"Good morning, Tomás," Cuervo said as his younger cousin, dressed in dusty jeans, sweat-stained denim shirt, and scuffed cowboy boots, unlocked the gate.

"And you, my cousin, I'm sorry to be late. It's so good to see you. Are you here for a ride? El Diablo is in need of exercise."

"Maybe later. I have been called. It appears we may have a problem. Enrique should be here shortly. Can you let him in when he arrives?"

Tomás's smile disappeared, replaced with a brow laden with concern. "He is already here waiting for you. The man puts fear of God in my soul."

"He has that effect on many people, and it's a valuable asset in his occupation." Cuervo paused. "But he knows who our friends are."

"Why do you call him Cuda?"

With a wry grin, Cuervo asked, "Do you really want to know?"

Tomás immediately changed the topic. "Is there anything I can help you with, my cousin?"

"No. Not yet. But let us have lunch before I leave. I'll invite Cuda, er, Enrique. You'll get to know and like him as I do."

Tomás chuckled haltingly. "It's going to take more than one lunch."

"You may be correct." Cuervo laughed in return.

"Just let me know if you have time and I'll saddle El Diablo. At least come and see him in the stable. He is a magnificent animal and is excited when you visit."

"I'll try. I can never thank you enough for finding him. It's you he should love after all you have done for him."

"But there is only one El Cuervo."

"You flatter me, Tomás. I better leave before my head grows too large for this hat."

Cuervo saluted with one finger as he watched his cousin close the gate through the rearview mirror. It's good to have family.

Cuervo arrived at the front door. The weathered ranch house was surrounded by brittle shrubs battling to survive the parched landscape. He inhaled the mountain air; the scent of the barnyard carried the memories of his childhood, a time and place now so distant.

He strode, catlike, into the small kitchen. At five nine and a hundred and sixty pounds, Cuervo's build was sleek but powerful. With the slight misalignment of his nose from youthful indiscretions, he looked like the prizefighter who quit the ring just in time. More rugged than handsome, his piercing brown eyes were eased by a convincing smile. His close-cropped black hair, peppered in gray, contrasted with his thin, snow-white mustache.

"Good morning, El Cuervo," Manny said. "I'm very sorry to have to bother you at your home, but—"

"No, Manny, you did the right thing. Do not apologize—besides, it's good to see you and to inspect our operation. Cuda is here, correct?"

"Sí, he is out back. I didn't know if you wanted him in the bunker."

"I'll see him after we're done." Cuervo opened the warped wooden door and he and Manny descended a flight of creaking stairs to the musty basement. At the far end of the cluttered room, a rack of floor-to-ceiling wooden shelves stored canned goods and house supplies. Manny reached behind the far-left shelf and depressed a latch. A section of the shelf sprung open to reveal a two-inch-thick steel door. He tapped a series of numbers on the door's keypad and it, too, opened.

They walked into the harshly lit twenty-by-thirty-foot subterranean bunker excavated under the old ranch house. The reinforced concrete control room was plated with armor along the walls, ceiling, and floor. It was not impenetrable, but it would take considerable effort to breach its security, by which time all sensitive information would have been destroyed.

Along one wall was a console with four large video screens, radio and satellite communication equipment, and keyboards and computers.

Two men, seated in high-back leather chairs, were monitoring the myriad activities on the screens. Both leapt to their feet at the sight of El Cuervo.

"Please sit. Where's the boat?" Cuervo asked.

The large center screen had an outline of the coast of northern Colombia northward to Point Conception in California. Three illuminated red dots, each a half inch in diameter, were scattered along the coastline. Each flashed on and off at five-second intervals. A group of much smaller white dots, clustered off the coast of Tijuana, blinked faster.

"Señor, the last signal we had was right here," the first technician said, pointing to the white dots. "Then it was gone. You can see we have good signals from the others." He pointed to the red dots.

The subs had no radios, so they could not be tracked by fugitive signals. Instead, they sent periodic and highly encrypted location signals to the satellite. All rendezvous points, times, and alternate sites were detailed for each trip. There was no need for superfluous communications.

"No satellite transmissions?" Cuervo asked.

"Nothing. We think they scuttled the boat; otherwise, we would not have the signals from the bales," the technician said, now pointing to the white dots. "The telemetry indicates they are still underwater and are beginning to drift apart."

The bales could not communicate below the surface—the water blocked the weak signal. So, when they reached a prescribed depth, a small, fist-sized antenna buoy was automatically deployed to the surface.

The buoy, attached to the bale by a thin, hundred-foot cable, transmitted the bale's location to the GPS satellite.

The second technician entered a few strokes on his keyboard and the far-left screen flashed to life. It reenacted the time sequence of the white lights as they morphed from a single bright spot to a mosaic of smaller lights distributed over a two-mile area. "This is the time sequence over three hours."

Cuervo studied the screen. "What have we got in the area?"

With a couple more taps on the keyboard, the center monitor displayed a series of blue lights, mostly located between the southern tip of Baja California and northern Panama.

"Nothing closer?"

"Not at sea. A couple of boats are unloading in Ensenada, but they can't get out for a few days," the first technician said. "They just got to port and are provisioning."

Cuervo pointed to the northernmost boat located off the coast of Tehuantepec. "How quickly can they get there?"

"It's about six hundred miles; two, maybe three days if they have the fuel and are not loaded."

"Send them. Let me know when they get there and keep a close eye on those bales."

Cuervo was pleased with himself. He knew he was smart, but he was also lucky. What had Father Simon said: "a charmed life"?

He had bought the tuna fleet as a means to launder his money. Most tuna fleets had relocated to the western Pacific, where the tuna were more numerous and the labor cheaper, but Cuervo wanted his boats closer. He needed them for another use and this was it.

He knew the fishermen would be displeased when they were diverted from fishing. The tuna boat might lose $15,000 a day when idle, but it would be recovering over $85 million of product. It's a cost-benefit hardly worth calculating.

"Anything from the crew?" he asked.

"Nothing. It's Jonny's boat, and he would only scuttle it if they encountered the authorities. Maybe there was an accident? The crew is either dead, drifting in the raft, or in custody," Manny said. "I don't know what happened, but this is the second time for Jonny. He scuttled his first boat too early, almost taking out one of the speedboats, and now this."

"Could it be something else? Maybe Jonny has his own plan. It wouldn't be the first time," Cuervo said. "You remember the crewman who stole a bale to sell it on his own? It was a bad career move, and he was very surprised when Cuda tracked him to his cousin's house." Cuervo paused and shook his head in wonder. "I still don't know how he found the man in a small hovel outside Sedona, but that's Cuda. He recovered most of what remained of the bale and took photographs of what remained of our entrepreneur and his family. He posted them on the darknet—thought everyone should see the results of the failed business plan. So, we must always consider a rogue operation."

The men were silent.

Cuervo left the bunker and climbed the steps to the kitchen.

Cuda was sitting with a bowl of soup and tortillas. He made the table and chairs appear to be children's toys. He barely fit—the chair's back was invisible behind his girth. He stood over six four, but his huge chest, arms, and legs contrasted with his narrow waist and made him seem much taller. His coal-black hair was the second thing people noticed. It was cut perfectly straight and hung just over his ears, a wayward Beatle.

"Buenos días, El Cuervo," Cuda said, standing quickly in respect to his capo.

"El Barracuda, good to see you, my friend. Please sit. How's the soup? Tomás always favors us with the best meals. He paid attention to our grandmother when she cooked, and we're all thankful he did."

"I, too, appreciate his efforts. Please, El Cuervo, sit and let me get you a bowl. It's liquid heaven."

"I can manage, but thanks."

Cuervo placed his bowl on the table and sat across from Cuda. He poured a glass of water from the pitcher and crossed himself in silent prayer before his first spoonful.

"What is the problem? Why do you require my services, El Cuervo?"

"We lost one of our subs. It was scheduled to off-load near Tijuana in two days. We will try to salvage the cargo, but it will take several days. I need you to inform our buyer, Señor Martinez, of the delay and tell him how long it will take to remedy the problem. He will understand we're serious about fulfilling our obligation if you are my emissary. And if things do not go as I expect, well, I want you there."

"El Cuervo, it's an honor you have selected me. When should I leave?"

"As soon as you can. Manny here and Nico in Ensenada will keep you apprised of the situation. I'm sorry that I must go now, but Tomás says I need to exercise El Diablo."

"I'll leave immediately, El Cuervo."

Chapter Eleven
Eastern Tropical Pacific off the Gulf of Tehuantepec, Mexico
12°27'33"N, 99°27'36"W

Leo Garza was not a man to easily submit to fear, but a chill of dread fell over him. He tried to swallow but his throat resisted. He sat, silent, snuffing the remains of an unsatisfying cigar. Cuda was on his way.

He climbed down from the stick and walked over to Tommy. To his right along the port quarter, the net was teeming with fish leaping, squirming, trying to escape the ever-constricting noose. "Get these in the hold. We have to move fast. Any trouble let me know. I'll be in my cabin."

"You got it, Skip."

Garza strode through the hatch into the galley, where he filled his mug from the ancient urn that had been percolating almost continuously for fifteen years. By this time of the day, the coffee was a thick bitter syrup after stewing for hours. The fishermen joked about the sludge at the bottom, and that nobody had the guts to clean it out. The rumor was EPA was about to declare it a Superfund site.

"Man, you look like you saw a ghost," Chase said.

Garza looked over. Sitting in the corner of the rear curving banquette, his assistant engineer was sipping a cola. "Huh? Sorry. I didn't see you. Got some things to work out."

Chase nodded toward the deck. "Looks like a good catch. What do you think, eight tons?"

Garza scratched at his wiry beard. "Pretty close, I'd guess."

"One haul closer to home."

"Fingers crossed." Garza exited the galley into the passageway leading forward. He passed the pantry, the walk-in refrigerator and freezer, and then the series of crew cabins. He climbed the forward ladder and entered the pilothouse. With his right index finger, he pushed his sunglasses onto his forehead and stared at the navigation screen to check the boat's position.

He handed the sat phone to Denny. "Gotta call from Nico. We're gonna be moving out in a few minutes. They're sending me the coordinates now."

Garza opened the door to his cabin off the rear bulkhead of the pilothouse and tossed his tattered San Diego Padres ball cap on the bed, releasing a tangle of sweat-soaked curly gray hair. He walked to the table and lifted the cover on his laptop and opened the company's proprietary communication software. The thirty-two-key encryption system was next to impossible to break unless the full resources of a country's intelligence services were activated. As an added layer of security, each boat had a secondary codebook. Even if the electronic message was intercepted and decoded, the characters would mean nothing without the boat's key.

Garza transcribed the message from the laptop onto a yellow legal pad. He then retrieved a copy of John Steinbeck's *The Log from the Sea of Cortez* from the bookshelf—it was the secondary cipher he had been given—and began to decode the message.

After ten minutes, he had the message. He was to make haste to the location and stay on station until the service boat arrived. He was to look for any signs of the wreckage of a small vessel and its survivors. Most important, if he saw any cargo floating in the ocean, he was to retrieve it and secure it safely below deck. He was to engage in fishing operations, if necessary, to keep other vessels out of the area. At the end of the message was a series of eight-digit numbers. Garza was puzzled. He could not make them out—they were not geographic coordinates because they didn't match any latitude and longitude on the globe.

His hands shook after he put down the pencil and even in the air-conditioned cabin, beads of sweat streamed down his face. Only a few in the entire Pescadero Baja company understood the real purpose of the fleet, and he was one of them. He had made his deal with the devil, and now he had to hold up his end.

Chapter Twelve
Ensenada, Baja California, Mexico

Jonny restrained a laugh when he was saw an expression of surprise mixed with a little anger crawl across Nico's face. Seconds before, Jonny and his crew, battered and disheveled, had ambled unannounced into Pescadero Baja's Ensenada office.

Nico glared at Jonny. "We thought you were dead or in jail. You'd better have a damn good reason for losing your boat. El Cuervo wants his cargo."

Jonny sat almost lost in the large armchair across from Nico's desk. In a tone thick with indignation, he said, "Not exactly the greeting I expected. Hell, we almost drowned. You guys sitting high and dry in your cushioned chairs got no idea what we deal with."

"My job isn't to listen to your excuses. My job is to get the product to market, and you set us back weeks. So, what happened?"

"There was a problem with the port ballast tank. You're just lucky I survived to fix it." The pique in Jonny's voice was staged. "The valve opened, and seawater rushed into the tank. It was jammed; I couldn't close it. We were listing and started taking on water from one of the hatches. I got the pumps blasting air to purge the water, but the batteries were running low. It was just lucky I could keep the boat from sinking until we got the bales out. Otherwise, the whole cargo would be at the bottom of the ocean right now, maybe with me and the men too. I think we got a big problem."

"What do you mean?"

"It could be a design flaw. If it happens again, a whole shipment could be lost. I need to get back to Colombia to check the other boats."

"In time. First, how the hell did you get back to shore?"

48

"We got picked up by a squid boat. They saw the explosion when I scuttled the sub. By the time they got to us, everything had sunk. I told 'em our fuel tank exploded."

"They bought it?"

"Yeah. They said they didn't know we were even around—we didn't have running lights. Anyway, they dropped us off here on their way down the coast. They don't know who we are."

"Did they report the sinking?"

"No. I told the captain I could get in big trouble because I was fishing illegally."

"What about the crew? How'd they make it back?"

"It happened so fast. Benji tossed out a bale that had my duffel bag attached. I had no weapon, and I was not big enough to take them on without one. Look, I need to talk with Manny. We gotta fix the subs."

"No, you hold tight. I'll call Manny and tell him what happened. Cuda will be coming in to handle the recovery. He may have questions for you."

"Cuda, shit. You gotta help me get back. Everything went down, even my papers."

"Yeah, but it'll take a couple of days." Nico swiveled in his chair, reached into the credenza, and grabbed a small cashbox. He counted out four hundred dollars and handed the money to Jonny.

"This should be enough for a few days. Get a couple of rooms on the east side of town, away from the tourists. Try to stay out of Cuda's way, comprende? And get some decent clothes. You look as bad as you smell."

"Got it, and you hurry with my papers."

Jonny left the building with his two crewmen in tow.

* * *

The more Jonny tried to control the men, the more they resisted. He now questioned his decision about the 9 mm.

"This can't happen again. Stay in the room—I'll get the meals and whatever else we need, understand?" he said to Joaquin and Benji, who had just returned sloppy drunk after midnight.

49

"We almost died in that stinking boat. We deserved some time off," Benji said, slurring every other word and glancing over to Joaquin for support.

Joaquin laughed heartily. "Yeah, it has been a long time since we have even seen a woman. What's the matter with you? Are you some kind of monk? Did you take some vow of chastity?"

"You found women who would talk to you?"

"The talk was free, but that was all." Joaquin giggled.

Jonny wanted to slam the bedside table but held back. He'd been trained early in life by his second stepfather that displaying emotion only brought pain. "Hookers? You were with hookers? You gotta be messin' with me. What did you use for cash?"

"Our dinner money."

"What prostitute would work for that?"

"They took pity on us when we told them how we were stuck on a boat for a month before it sunk," Benji said. "Plus, they said we were the best-looking hombres they had seen all night."

Jonny tensed, but kept the anger in his voice low and controlled. "I told you from the day I hired you, you do not tell anyone about the boat. You know what could happen. If the boss hears about this, well, just stay in the room, understand? Only I'll go out. Get to sleep. You will not be feeling so good in the morning, and even worse if the boss finds out."

* * *

When Jonny told him about his crew's night on the town, Nico sat for a few minutes and calculated his next move. Manny and El Cuervo would be livid the crew were still around—Jonny should have taken care of them; he knew the rules. Now two more people knew way too much about the operation and they were out running their mouths. A security breach like this could expose everything and cost La Hermandad countless millions. And they would lose confidence in Jonny by bringing the crew back to shore, let alone to the office. Jonny was trusted but the crew wasn't; they were expendable.

Nico faced a tough choice. If he told Manny too much, he would be in trouble for not controlling Jonny's crew, but if Manny found out on his own, it would be worse.

His finger shook as he punched the number to the ranch. After three rings, Manny picked up. "Hola."

"Manny, the crew arrived a little later than expected," Nico said, hoping Manny would understand.

"Hmm," Manny said and paused. Nico heard a long exhalation. "All of them?"

"Yes. I'll send more information when I get it."

"Please do. Has our friend arrived?"

"No, but I expect him shortly."

"Perhaps he should handle the crew? I shall speak with the boss."

Nico's stomach was churning as he hung up.

* * *

Cuervo was in his office when the call came, the thick wooden door closed from the curious ears.

"El Cuervo, I just had a call from Ensenada. Jonny and his crew are at the office," Manny said over the open line.

Confusion fell over Cuervo's face. With an index finger, he stroked the crown of the bronze statue of a raven atop the desk. "At the office? This is a surprise."

"I don't have the details yet. Nico will send a secure message."

"But his crew is still with him? This is not good. Make sure they speak to no one."

"Nico knows."

"This is unfortunate. Why would Jonny bring them back, and what does he know of the cargo?"

"Do you not trust Jonny?"

"It's not a matter of trust—it's a matter of need." Jonny was valuable to the operation, but Cuervo knew he was a weak man. It would not take much to push Jonny over the edge with the alcohol and cocaine again. If he doesn't have self-discipline in his personal life, can he be trusted with our plans? He could never be part of La Hermandad.

51

Much like the Italian Mafia, where all "made men" must have direct Sicilian lineage, La Hermandad required specific blood ties to assure loyalty and servility. Membership was only open to those who could trace their ancestry to the ruling families of "New Spain"—the conquistador class.

Though time, distance, and intermarriage had greatly complicated modern Mexico, those in this class always knew who they were. Their stories were well documented in oral histories, but also in the impeccable records of the Catholic Church, where every high birth, baptism, marriage, and death was painstakingly documented. Jonny's heritage, however, would challenge even modern genetics.

"How shall I instruct Nico?"

"Let us keep a close watch on Jonny, keep him with Nico in Ensenada until Cuda has completed his work. It will give us a chance to see how the other captains perform. Maybe it's time we conduct a performance review on Captain Jonny."

"And the crew?"

"Cuda knows."

Chapter Thirteen
Ensenada, Baja California, Mexico

It was nearly midnight when Cuda stormed into Pescadero Baja's headquarters. Nico, tired and apprehensive, met him at the sprawling port complex. In addition to the tuna processing plant, the company had repair facilities, warehouses, and the administration building. It was a one-stop shop for the fleet. El Cuervo had constructed a similar facility in Panama.

Surly from the late-night trip, Cuda shoved his travel bag at Nico. "Is the service boat ready?"

"It's fueled and supplied. The captain should be here in a couple of hours," Nico said quietly.

Cuda glared through pinched eyes. He knew Nico thought the trust El Cuervo had in him was misplaced. Nico and most others had misread him, but it was not their fault entirely.

Cuda had secretly crafted his persona as carefully as El Cuervo did his own. Anyone who looked at him immediately assumed he was a dullard, a lummox, all muscle and no brains. He never changed his appearance and was blind to fashion. He looked like he had just been released from prison—or, more likely, a mental hospital—with a cheap haircut and institutional clothes. He spoke haltingly in a slow cadence, seemingly searching for, but never finding, the correct word. His strength was everyone else's perception of him. They often talked of sensitive issues as if he weren't even in the room—he was invisible. He was only needed when intimidation or violence was necessary.

His facade served him well, and he was acutely aware of his effect on others—he cultivated it. He was always calculating, analyzing, and designing, but silently. He had the gift of echoic memory, the ability to remember the tiniest detail of whatever he heard. He remembered names, addresses, telephone numbers, bank accounts, dates, and geographic coordinates—just about everything needed to run La Hermandad. He never used a computer and seldom wrote anything down; he never left a trail.

He shared one important attribute with El Cuervo—the ability to read a room. He picked up on nuance, a change of tone, mendacity. He could sense someone's true motivations and not reveal he knew he was being manipulated. He just played his role.

"Can we trust him?" Cuda asked Nico.

"The skipper knows the score."

"What about his crew?"

"We have the men from Jonny's boat. Manny says they have a debt to pay."

"What about the crew on the tuna boat?"

"Other than the captain, none of them know about our business. They've all been handpicked. They are very experienced and paid the highest rates in the industry. On most boats, the profits are distributed on a share system. After all expenses were paid, the company keeps five shares and the skipper four, followed by three for the navigator and chief engineer and two for the assistant engineer, deck boss, and cook. Each of the eight crewmen draws one share except for new hires, who got a one-quarter share until they had learned the ropes. So, for a typical catch yielding a net profit of $400,000, each of the thirty shares is worth at least $13,300. And that's for a two-month deployment. To entice the best crews, El Cuervo insists that Pescadero Baja takes only one share so the crew gets more. In addition, he pays retention bonuses. It keeps the crew and their family's content and dependent. Plus, we have detailed dossiers on each fisherman and his family."

"And they will stay silent?"

"That will not be a worry."

Cuda's cold, angry eyes bored into Nico. "You better be right."

Chapter Fourteen
Eastern Tropical Pacific off the Gulf of Tehuantepec, Mexico
14°48'55"N, 101°22'56"W

The crew was huddled in the mess for breakfast at the three long tables arranged in a U-shape and bolted firm to the deck. A large serving island separated the tables from the galley. Atop the end of the island was the coffee urn, a requisite stopover in and out of the mess.

Eduardo, the cook, had set out the day's breakfast on the island—scrambled eggs, chorizo, rice and beans, pancakes, biscuits and gravy, and a bowl of sliced fruit—and the crew was already queued. Rafael, the young galley hand, was busy at the sink cleaning the deep fryer from the past evening's fried shrimp. The experienced men knew if fresh oil was going into the fryer, odds were strong that donuts would be on the menu in the morning.

Chase bounded through the passageway into the mess. "Hey, you started without me."

Gus looked up from his crossword puzzle book and rolled his eyes at his assistant. "You done with your watch already?"

"Yup. Time for a warm meal and about six hours of sleep."

"That engine room better be spic-and-span or it's a twelve-hour watch for you."

Chase grabbed a plate and filled it with what remained of the breakfast offering. "You can eat off the deck if you want to test it. And the boat's running like a fine Swiss watch."

"Watches run in circles; a boat tries to avoid that. As a US taxpayer, I'm not impressed with the education you conned from the Navy. Maybe you need a refresher course in engineering, maybe start out with a speedboat and work your way up to a big-boy boat."

Garza entered moments later. The crew's conversations lowered to an indecipherable grumble.

Always ready to challenge anyone, Tommy Beagle called out across the room and asked the question on everyone's mind: "Hey, Skipper, where the hell we heading? We're leaving a damn good spot."

Chase half-turned toward Garza. A sense of gloom was masked beneath the captain's smile.

"I know, Tommy, and I'm pretty pissed off about it, but we got orders from the company to head north. They're seeing some anomalies on the satellite we should check out," Garza responded, his eyes locked on the galley deck.

"No closer boat?"

Garza worked his way to the head of the table. "Nope, we're it. We'll get there in another sixteen hours. This will give us a chance to get some repairs done, especially the net."

"I'll get the men on it. Hey, Rafael, bring me another coffee."

Eduardo looked up from the island. "Leave the kid alone, he ain't your servant."

"If he wants a share of the catch, he's got to do more than wash a few dishes."

Across the table, Franco held a hand aloft with a forefinger and thumb an inch apart. "Man, we were this close to going home."

"Tell me about it." Santos raised his arms in frustration. "I got a pregnant wife and promised I'd be there for this one."

"She don't need you anymore. You've done your part," Franco said. "She delivered the other three without you. Just make sure she gets your paychecks."

Santos rose and hurled a piece of toast, missing Franco by inches but splattering butter over the bulkhead. The tension broke. Jerome almost blew a mouthful of coffee through his nose.

Eduardo shot a cold look at Santos. "Hey, none of that in my kitchen. And don't expect Rafael to clean your mess."

Chase resumed his goading of Gus. "Hey, Skipper, I'd like to lodge a complaint against your chief engineer. You know, if we were working under the US flag, I could sue the company for this hostile workplace, maybe even get a settlement out of the old fossil."

56

Garza shook his head and issued a mirthless laugh. "Why don't you get up and take your breakfast over there next to Gus. If you two can't work this out, it will be a timeout for both of you. After that, I'm gonna have to call your mothers."

"Make 'em sit in the corner," Denny said.

"Yeah, with those pointy hats," Jerome added.

"Naw, their egos are too fragile already. We don't want to push them over the edge. Sooner or later, we may need them to fix something," Garza said.

Gus muttered just loud enough for all to hear. "What an ungrateful bunch of ingrates. I have this boat working so flawlessly you don't even realize it. Just think how much better it would hum if you got me a decent assistant."

"I believe that's a redundancy, Gus," Chase said.

"Oh, look at you, one online course and now you're an English professor."

Without a word, Garza rose, grabbed his coffee mug, and left the galley.

Chase raised his eyebrows at Garza's abrupt departure. "Good job, Gus. You've cost us another captain, and this one could find fish."

"Dime a dozen. You want a good boat, invest in a great engineer."

"Yeah, sure be good to find one."

"Go check on the prop shaft in the skiff. Your little cruise yesterday was a waste of time. I knew what it was from the first time Jerome told me about it."

"Oh, to learn at the feet of the master—"

"Enough of your guff, get the hell out of here, and no more video calls to your wife when you're on watch. I've heard about this 'sexting' thing. No tellin' what you're showin' each other. And I want no immoral behavior in my chapel."

The crew burst out in laughter.

"You caught me, you old sea dog. I'm out of here." Chase left with a troubled smile on his face. Something about the skipper wasn't right.

* * *

Cuda leaned over the deck rail and retched violently. He had been on the ocean before, but not much, and this time it was no different.

Joaquin frowned as he handed Cuda a wet towel to wipe his face.

"Here, señor, we have another two days. You will start feeling better in a few hours," he said, passing him a bottle of carbonated water.

Cuda rose from the side of the deck still clutching the railing with a death grip against the three-foot swells. In the bright midday sun, his face was a ghostly bluish-white as if only bile pulsed through his veins.

"Is there a place to sleep?" he asked.

"Yes. Down below, but better for you stay topside in the wind. Just don't look at the water. Focus on the sky. Everybody gets seasick at some time. It will pass."

Cuda walked from the rail and sat on the padded bench at the stern of the forty-foot long service boat. The aft deck was cleared of all equipment except the permanently mounted winches on the port and starboard quarters and the crane in the center of the deck. Forward of the deck, a passageway led to a small galley and a ladder up to the even smaller pilothouse. A second ladder accessed the lower deck with an engine room at the stern and crew quarters in the bow. The open bow deck contained another small crane, anchor winches, and mooring lines.

Cuda removed his jacket, loosened his collar, stretched out on the bench, and stared skyward, squinting under his sunglasses. His head was spinning and his stomach was rolling. He tried to focus on a cloud but could not keep his eyes open. He knew he was vulnerable, and he didn't like it; he could not muster enough energy to fight off the smallest of the crewmen. If he had to draw his pistol, he wasn't sure if he had the strength to hold it up, let alone to pull the trigger. At this point, he couldn't give a damn about all the bales of cocaine in the world. He didn't care if El Cuervo sent someone to kill him for his failure; in fact, right now, he would welcome the bullet.

Joaquin interrupted Cuda's suffering.

"Señor. Let me put this behind your ear. It's a seasick medicine. I used it on the sub. It will take an hour or so, but you will feel better."

Cuda nodded and Joaquin applied the patch.

Using his crumpled jacket as a pillow, Cuda rolled onto his side into a fetal position and prayed the medicine would take effect.

Chapter Fifteen
Ensenada, Baja California, Mexico

Jonny kept the agitation out of his voice when he entered Nico's office, but he couldn't disguise the rage on his face. "I just left the motel. Joaquin and Benji are gone. I can't be held responsible for those idiots cutting out. We need to start searching the bars."

Nico looked up, squinting at the far door. A half smirk crossed his lips. "Ahh, but you are responsible. You should have taken care of them at sea, remember? But, not to worry, Captain Jonny. They're in good hands. Cuda needed a crew to recover the bales and who better, right?"

"They find the bales?"

"Yup. We got one of our tuna boats on station. Manny's tracking them by satellite."

Jonny exhaled a relieved breath. "How much time to salvage the load?"

"Let's hope it's less than a week. We have very impatient buyers awaiting delivery."

"You should have sent me out. I'm better at sea than those guys."

Nico nodded in agreement. "No doubt about that, but we may need you to pilot another sub. El Cuervo wants you available."

"I'm gonna need more cash. I'm running pretty low. And how about my papers? It shouldn't take this long."

Nico slapped his right hand on a six-inch stack of papers his desk. "I'm working as fast as I can." He turned, retrieved the cashbox, and counted out three hundred dollars in bills. "Here, this should tide you over."

"Look, I'm going stir crazy sitting in that stinking motel room. There must be some work here I can do. I can repair just about anything. Let me work in the shop."

"I could sure use your help. I've got another boat coming in tomorrow. But El Cuervo doesn't want you mixing with the regular crews. That's how secrets get out in spite of your best efforts. Just lie low. It shouldn't be much longer. Keep checking in here daily. I'll let you know what's happening."

There was nothing Jonny could say. He shrugged and left the room.

It was Nico's turn to breathe a sigh of relief.

Chapter Sixteen
Point Loma, San Diego, California, USA

Maria lay in bed semiconscious after her late-night call from Chase. Her eyes were still shut. She knew as soon as she opened them the morning sun would revive her, and she'd lose the valuable sleep she cherished. But she felt something—a presence. She strained one eye open. Staring at her was Kevin, her four-year-old son.

"Mom, Mom, you awake?"

"Almost." It was at times like this, and there were many in the day, Maria longed to have Chase home to get just a few more minutes to sleep.

"I'm hungry."

"Not before I get a hug."

"Oh, Mom." Kevin sighed, then wrapped his arms around Maria's neck and kissed her solidly on her cheek.

Kevin's cheeks were soft and warm, and his baby-like breath was the tonic she needed.

"Okay, I'm getting up. Where's your sister?"

"In the living room watching TV."

Maria noticed Kevin had again, with little success, dressed for the day: Ninja turtle pajama bottoms, a Chargers jersey emblazoned with "Kevin" across the back, and his soccer shoes worn without socks.

"I see you're dressed for success, kiddo." She grinned. "Very GQ."

The eight-year-old Denise was a quicker study. She learned early to let Mom sleep a little longer. She could entertain herself for a few minutes until Mom got up. The television didn't hold his attention as much as his growling stomach. Just like his old man, Maria thought.

Maria sat upright and wiggled her fingers through her unruly hair. It took a moment to clear and regain her equilibrium.

"Okay, kiddo, what will it be?"

"Fruity Pebbles."

"Ah, the gourmand in the family."

"What's that?"

"Oh, nothing. Just a joke."

In the bathroom, Maria peered into the mirror and blew a wisp of hair from her cheek. The small dark circles under her eyes stared back. This is going to take a little work.

In her pre-caffeinated condition, she made a mental note of the day's tasks. There was much to do, and only herself to do it. But she was from a long line of fishing families, and knew, like her mother and grandmother before, the suffering of long absences.

Maria had been sure her life would be different because Chase was not from a fishing family—his father had sold insurance and his mom was a secretary for a local accountant. She expected he would have a career on the beach. She knew he loved the ocean and when he wasn't working on his '68 'Stang Fastback, his homage to Steve McQueen—now under a tarp in the garage with a blown head gasket—he was surfing. But she was still a little surprised when he joined the Navy. He hadn't wanted to go to college, at least not right away, and he'd told her he didn't want to get stuck in some futureless job.

He had trained as a machinist mate, which made sense because he was always tinkering with some kind of motor, someone's car, the lawnmower, or even his dad's golf cart. He completed a full four-year stint, which included three tours on the guided missile frigate USS *Gary.*

Maria was grateful the ship was home ported in San Diego. They could be together almost every day when he wasn't on one of his eight-month deployments, or the time he was confined to the ship for a month over some ruckus. She knew that Chase, usually easygoing and friendly—fast with a quip and a smile—when pushed too hard, could explode.

But she didn't blame Chase for his absences—it was her father's fault. It was her dad who offered Chase the job on his fishing boat. After he was discharged, Chase had no prospects, but even more important he wanted to please her father, knowing sooner or later they'd have a man-to-man talk about the future.

Maria padded into the living room, where Denise was sitting lotus-legged on the floor watching television.

"Morning, sweetie pie, thanks for letting me sleep in. I talked with your dad last night, and he wanted me to give you a big hug and kiss and tell you he loves you more than the moon, sun, and the universe."

Balancing a bowl of cereal on her knee, Denise barely looked up. "Did Kevin wake you up? I told him not to, but he never listens. He said he was too hungry."

"That's okay. I needed to get up. We have oodles to do today. Do you want to go grocery shopping this morning, or do you want to stay with Grandma?"

"Can't I stay here? I'm almost nine."

"In a couple of years, you'll be able to, but not yet. You're still my little princess."

"Yech. Gross. I'll go with you. What about Kevin?"

"I'm dropping him with Grandma. He always fills my cart when I'm not looking. Better get dressed."

Chapter Seventeen
Eastern Tropical Pacific
31°54'22"N, 121°23'08"W

Denny looked out the salt-glazed window of the pilothouse to the dark gray-green seas over the bow. A slight northwest breeze rippled the surface, and the bright blue sky was dappled with wispy cirrus clouds. Fishermen liked it calm; it was easier to spot birds and catch fish. Next to Denny, lookouts on the "Big Eyes" were focused on finding something, anything resembling either.

They'd been on station for about three hours in the exact location the front office had identified but hadn't seen anything yet.

The port door to the pilothouse opened and Garza burst forth.

"Hi, Skip. What's up?"

"Denny, tell the boys to rest their eyes and help out with the net for a few minutes."

"Sure thing."

Through the glass, Garza watched as Denny spoke to the lookouts. Almost simultaneously, they both covered their binoculars with the vinyl hoods and walked aft from the pilothouse.

Denny returned. "Why the intrigue?"

"For the time being, only you and I can know what I'm about to tell you, understand?" Garza said, lifting the frame of his aviator sunglasses with one finger to meet the eyes of his navigator.

"Sure."

Garza walked over to the sonar unit and switched it to "ON." It took a few seconds to warm up, but finally the screen glowed bright orange. Garza carefully fingered the controls, adjusting the resolution, magnification, and contrast, until a few yellow blips were visible.

"Those don't look like fish to me," Denny said.

"They're not. Those are the packages the company wants back."

"What are they?"

"Don't ask."

"How do we get them, they're pretty deep." Denny ran his index finger down the graduations on the screen. "What, maybe seventy-five to a hundred feet?"

"We're not to recover them, at least not yet. We're to keep this area clear of other vessels. The company is sending out a boat. It will be their job to get the...whatever they are."

"When?"

"Tomorrow morning. Until then, we'll just keep searching in large circles and look for fish. I'll stay in the stick and keep watch. Keep the pilothouse clear and leave the sonar off. No sense in getting the crew's curiosity raised."

Denny scrunched his face.

Garza sensed Denny's bewilderment. "Any problems?"

"No, Skip."

* * *

Secrets are impossible on a boat, and the rumors were flying. The crew even brought it up to the skipper a couple of times, but his answer just didn't make any sense. All were experienced fishermen and had never heard of fishing this far north at this time of the year. Maybe if it had been an El Niño year, when the warmer currents force the fish north, but it wasn't. Sea temperatures were cool.

The crew also questioned the skipper's search pattern. It was not his normal routine. But what really raised eyebrows was that everyone but the helmsman were kept out of the pilothouse. It was a long-standing tradition that a few crewmen congregated in the pilothouse to keep the helmsman alert and to catch up on the radio chatter, but not now.

Tommy told Santos he had tried to get a sonar reading but noticed the fuse had been removed from the panel. Denny told him the unit had been overheating and blowing fuses constantly, so he was only using the unit when they were near fish.

Garza sat alone in the stick most of the time with nothing to do but monitor his own sonar unit while he waited for the service boat. The yellow blips were still present but drifting apart. He searched the water with his binoculars, but the objects were too deep.

He knew the crew was uneasy. They were very close to finishing the trip, and they should be fishing, not circling aimlessly. He'd have to make it up to them, but he wasn't sure how.

He hadn't seen many vessels; most were container ships bound for Central and South America. A few smaller ships appeared on the radar, but too far to see. They weren't fishing boats because they cruised too fast and didn't stay long in any one location. This pleased Garza because, if a vessel approached, he wasn't exactly sure how to keep them away. All he could do was hoist the single triangle flag and illuminate the mast lights to signal his boat was fishing. If a ship got too close, Garza figured he would blast the horn, but that was about all he could do. He certainly would not fire on another vessel under those conditions. Besides, what firepower did he have? The AR-15 carbine, Remington 1200 shotgun, and a few handguns stashed in the gun safe were far from intimidating.

* * *

On the morning of the third day of endless circling, the service boat arrived and Garza was summoned aboard. When he exited the small cabin, his face was ashen, his brow deeply furrowed, and his gaze was focused a thousand miles away. He walked slumped-shouldered to the deck and climbed into the chase boat to return to the *Bella*. He looked back at Cuda on the deck. It wasn't a smile on the big man's face, more the satisfaction of terrorizing another human being. Garza doubted the man experienced anything close to happiness.

He started the motor and accelerated at full throttle without looking back.

Garza had no alternative. He considered just ramming the chase boat full speed into the seiner and ending it all. But that would not protect his family, nothing could. Unless he complied, the Garza line, from San Diego to the Azores, would cease except for photographs and in the memories of friends. It was something Cuda had stated with relish.

Maybe El Cuervo would reconsider if his crew did the job well. It was a possibility that kept him going.

* * *

While Garza waited in his cabin, Denny mustered the crew to the mess.

The men were talking among themselves.

"I hope he tells us what's been going on for the last days," Jerome said to no one in particular.

"Maybe the skipper's gonna tell us there ain't no fish up here," Gus said, topping off his cup at the coffee urn. "I could have told you that. We don't need to waste any time in a meeting."

"What, like you're too busy?" Chase said from across the room. "Or were you disturbed from you pre-midmorning nap?"

"If you ever catch me sleeping while on duty, it's a bottle of Jack Daniels for everyone."

"How we gonna tell? You sleepwalk during the day with your eyes open. And just because your nose is in a repair manual doesn't mean you're reading those big words."

"You should try it sometime—the reading part—then this here big boat wouldn't be such a great mystery to you."

"By the way, glad to see you dressed for the occasion." Chase pointed at Gus's torn and grimy coveralls, which hadn't seen the laundry room in years.

Garza could hear the banter from the galley as he descended the ladder to the main passageway. He hesitated and drew a deep breath. Be commanding, he reminded himself. He was, after all, their captain.

"Good morning, men. Sorry to take you away from your work—or your nap," Garza said, looking directly at Gus.

The room erupted in laughter, and Gus stared at Chase. "Friggin' teacher's pet."

Garza stroked his beard and turned slowly as he addressed his crew. "I won't keep you long, but I wanted to explain our current circumstances, and what you can expect for the next few days. Judging from all the scuttlebutt, you believe this is a bad place to fish. You are correct. That wasn't why we diverted. We were sent here to help retrieve some packages the company lost a few days ago. I was directed to wait on station until the service boat arrived. Our job is to help with the recovery."

Santos raised his hand. "Recovery of what?"

"I'll get into the details, but first a couple of general orders. First, until I say otherwise, there will be no communication with the shore. No telephone, no radio, no email, no chat rooms, nothing."

"I hope that includes porn sites," Chase said. "Gus's hand could use the break."

"I still got Miss Michigan here," Gus said, holding up his right hand with the thumb extended. "And hey, it's more action than you've seen, you little choirboy."

"Okay, okay, it's only for a day or two," Garza said, refocusing the crew. "I'm sure Gus can abstain for a while. Anyway, I had Denny shut down the transmitter and dish. Our only communication will be to the office. Is that clear to you all?" Garza paused for emphasis.

"Second, the company knows this is a burden and not something you signed on for, so they have decided to match your share with a bonus.

"Third, as soon as the packages are recovered, we're heading home!"

The tenor of the room changed in an instant. All were smiling, nodding and buddy-punching at the fortuitous change of events. Even Gus broke out in a smile and said: "Better alert the clubs in Ensenada, Uncle Gus wants a pole dancing marathon."

"Well, that's one way to spend your bonus," Garza said. "But I was hoping you'd think about your retirement fund. What is it now...forty bucks and climbing?"

Gus turned up his nose. "I don't trust the market, they're all crooks."

"Maybe you should save for a liver transplant. I'm sure it's long overdue," Chase said.

"Now the hard part," Garza said. "The packages are contraband and worth much money. And if we're caught with them, well, the Mexican government would not be pleased."

"What are we talking about here, skipper?" Santos asked. "You know I can't afford any more trouble with the federales. I got a baby on the way."

"There are a number of packages in the water. Our task will be to locate them and, with the chase boats, drag them to the service boat, where they will be loaded. None of them will be aboard the *Bella*. Denny and I'll monitor the radio and radar, and if any boat approaches, you will be directed to drop your loads and return here. You will never be seen in direct possession. Is that clear?"

"Skipper, I've been on the 'Big Eyes' for the past hours and I haven't seen anything," Rafael said.

"You will soon enough. I must also impress upon you nothing leaves this boat. You tell no one—not family, not friends, not other boats—no one. Is that clear? The men we're dealing with are not the understanding type. If the word gets out that one of us talked, we're all in jeopardy, as are our wives, children, and other family members. Are you reading me on this? They know us all," Garza said.

"When do we start?" said a voice from the back.

"This afternoon if there are no vessels approaching. Until then, get lunch and finish up what you were doing. Tommy, make sure all the boats are fueled and ready. Throw some towlines in the cockpits. Okay, men, thanks." Garza turned and left the room. He had pulled it off, but now it was all he could do to make it back to his cabin before his legs buckled.

* * *

"What was that all about?" Chase asked Gus as they headed to the engine room.

"I like the money and the time off, but, damn, I do not like being threatened. Anyway, I ain't gonna rile anyone. I'm gonna keep quiet, do my work—that's what I'm gonna do."

"Sage advice as always, boss."

* * *

Cuda stood on the deck of the service boat and watched as the chase boats from the *Bella* were lowered from their davits. He was relieved the sea was calm, as was his stomach, with nothing but small wavelets stirred by a three-knot wind.

The sonar of both boats confirmed the presence of the yellow targets between the vessels. Cuda picked up his radio and called Garza, who was up in the stick to direct his boats. "You ready?"

"Yes, let's get going before anything shows up on radar."

Cuda flipped a switch on the custom-made remote-control box in his hand and extended its two antennas. A keypad allowed him to enter the discrete radio frequency assigned to each bale. He watched as the three lights sequenced from red to yellow and, finally, to green. The signal was locked on and ready. Cuda depressed the "ENTER" switch and the signal was sent.

Sixty-five feet below the surface and three hundred yards to his left, a microreceiver with a small antenna floating at the surface picked up the radio signal. It instantly sent a small electric current that activated a solenoid valve on the flotation collar. The pressurized gas cylinder slowly filled the bladder and the bale began its ascent.

Just as the bale broke the surface, a photo sensor activated a white strobe light.

From his high perch, Garza saw it first.

"Santos, six hundred feet off your port quarter," he called over his VHF radio.

"Got it, Skipper," Santos said as he accelerated to the pulsing light. He stopped ten feet short and allowed the boat to drift to the package. With a short gaff, he brought the bale alongside his boat and secured a line through the shackle on the bale. He then moved forward slowly, letting the slack play out from the line, and towed the bale to the service boat.

Joaquin and Benji waited beside Cuda on the service boat. Joaquin passed the cable from the boom to Santos, who inserted the cable's hook into the shackle. Benji, operating the winch, lifted the bale to the deck. Both crewmen dragged the bale to the forward end of the deck.

Cuda inspected the package and switched off the strobe. He then cut the nylon straps securing the satellite transmitter pack to the bale. He placed it a locked box away from prying eyes. All anyone saw was a small watertight plastic box the size of a large book. It housed the satellite transmitter, a battery pack, and the hundred-foot wire antenna.

Cuda walked back to the rail and entered the next numerical sequence into the control box.

Garza was, again, the first to see the strobe and directed Santos to the second bale.

After about an hour, the sonar had no more targets nearby and Garza radioed to Cuda, informing him they needed to head farther south as the remaining bales were drifting with the current.

* * *

Arms folded, Chase slouched against an empty boat davit and watched the first half-dozen recoveries. All he saw was what looked like black hay bales with some kind of tube around them. He decided he had better things to do with his time. If a boat needed repair, they knew where to find him.

He climbed down two flights to the well deck. Eight wells were arranged on both sides of the deck with a wide working aisle between them. A single well was located at the stern. Each of the seventeen wells could hold about seventy tons of fish.

Leaving port, a couple of wells were filled with drinking water and a couple of others stored extra diesel fuel, while the rest contained a highly concentrated brine solution. The brine wells were kept at just above zero degrees by the on-board ammonia refrigeration system. Once caught, the fish slid down chutes from the net deck into the brine wells, where they were instantly frozen. This flash freezing method kept the delicate tuna meat firm until it reached the cannery.

When a well was filled, the brine was pumped out, leaving a solid block of frozen tuna. The well was then covered and sealed.

Walking the center aisle, Chase counted twelve full wells. Two were still open with the churning brine awaiting the next big catch. He smiled. This could be a very profitable trip. He couldn't wait to tell Maria tonight. His mood darkened when he realized it was a call he wouldn't make.

Chapter Eighteen
Point Loma, San Diego, California, USA

Maria woke at seven. It had been a long night; she had waited until after midnight, then fallen into a grudging sleep hoping to not miss Chase's call.

She checked her laptop to see if he'd emailed her but found nothing. It was curious because he tried never to miss their Tuesday calls. If he knew he couldn't call, he'd send an email. But this time, nothing.

She sent a quick note: Missed you. Everything okay?

She closed her laptop just as she heard the kids beginning to stir.

She rolled her eyes back. Well, there goes my day. What I'd give for just two more hours.

Once she got Denise off to school, she planned to drop Kevin off at her Mom's house, so she could get some work done. She had an appointment with a mortgage broker to refinance the house. Maria had convinced Chase that with a lower interest rate and a slightly longer loan, they'd have enough cash to make some needed improvements. While she loved their location in Point Loma, it was still a small 1930s bungalow. She wanted to bump out the master bedroom, add a drastically needed second bathroom, and a long overdue facelift for the kitchen. Fortunately, Chase had no objections with her taking the lead. In fact, he more than welcomed it. It was one less worry for him. They'd managed to squirrel away about $36,000 and the additional $70,000 from the refinance would more than cover it.

Maria had worked in real estate before Denise was born, but it had been too difficult to continue work and raise a family with Chase gone for so long. Maria was so thankful she wasn't a single working mom. Even though he was gone for half the year, she wouldn't know what to do without Chase.

Chapter Nineteen
Eastern Tropical Pacific
31°48'43"N, 121°17'58"W

Spirits were high at dinner, possibly because Garza poured four fingers of bourbon to celebrate the successful recovery.

Gus wrinkled his forehead and whispered into Chase's ear, "You think the skipper's a little out of it?"

Chase told him he was full of it, but that was Chase's usual response to most things out of Gus's mouth.

Garza leaned against the galley door. "You did a good job today, and hopefully we can finish tomorrow. We're heading a little south because the cargo has drifted."

Franco grinned wide and rubbed his hands with excitement. "How many more, Skip?"

"The crew on the service boat believes it's around fifty, and we got over half of them today."

"So maybe we'll be heading home on Thursday or Friday?" Santos asked.

"Keep your fingers crossed." Garza's smile hid his fear.

"So, what are going to do with your bonus, Skipper?"

"I hadn't thought much about it yet, but I've been promising my wife a vacation to the Azores for the years now, but never had the time off. What about you?"

"Diapers," Jerome said. He looked over at Santos. "Hey, you play, you pay."

"I've had my eyes on a new Camaro," Denny said. "ZL1, fire engine red, 650 horses, black leather, paddle shifters, the works."

Tommy scoffed. "You're out at sea three hundred days a year."

"Yeah, but you'll see nothing but a red streak when I'm home."

Franco grabbed his collar daintily with a forefinger and thumb of each hand and shot a toothy grin. "Threads, man. A whole new wardrobe. No more smelly T-shirts and bloody shorts. What about you, Rafael?"

The slight, fifteen-year-old looked up with sad eyes. "My mama. I'm all she's got now. She needs the—"

"What a mama's boy," Tommy shouted.

"Hey, leave him alone," Chase said. "Pick on someone your own size."

"Like, maybe, you?" Tommy said.

Garza saw the storm brewing in Chase. He'd seen it before and it wasn't pretty.

"If you want to try again, be my guest. I almost broke your nose last time. You should never lead with your face," Chase said and laughed.

Tommy jumped from the table toward Chase. Before he got two steps, Gus wrapped his huge arms around him from behind.

"Settle down there, bruiser. You may be mean, but you ain't tough," Gus said. "I can't have you provoking my able assistant here into any more fights. You know he's got a mean streak."

Tommy struggled against Gus's hold to no avail and finally went limp. He fixed a cold stare at Chase. "Just wait until we're off his boat."

Chase stared back. He hadn't made a move. Just stood straight with his arms at his side.

Gus saw Chase's face relax. The anger had passed. He released Tommy. "Maybe you should use your bonus for boxing lessons when you get home."

Tommy turned to Gus and sneered before walking from the room.

Garza caught Chase's attention. "Way to maintain your cool. Thought you were going to blow it again."

Chase shrugged. "Hey, Captain, any chance of using the satellite tonight? I missed my call home last night."

"Sorry, not yet, Chase. We're still on shutdown."

Gus goaded Chase to defuse the tension. "Poor baby, still need to check up on the little lady? Worried she may have found a real man this time, not like the soft sensitive guy she landed on her first cast? Maybe you should be on Oprah or Dr. Phil to work out these role reversals."

Chase smiled at the provocation. "Hey, I'm at ease with my feminine side. It makes me so much more tolerant of mouth-breathers like you, Gus."

"I find my companions at the finest clubs along the eastern Pacific, not some cake decorating class or encounter group."

"How's that working for you, Gus? I find cooking classes are a target-rich environment. But if you want to frequent those tittie bars with a thousand other guys, have at it and good luck. I'm sure the girls are lined up to follow you home."

"Home? The backseat will do fine. No muss, no fuss, no hurt feelings."

Chapter Twenty
Eastern Tropical Pacific
31°53'3"N, 121°10'46"W

As the evening approached, Cuervo stood on his back patio and watered the plants surrounding the pool. Though he had a very good gardener, he took special interest in the flowerbeds he and Ramon had planted on their own. He was, after all, only one generation removed from the soil. In fact, his father remained on the farm where Cuervo was born, and continued to raise corn, tomatoes, peppers, and avocados, as well as chickens and the holiday goats. His father sometimes helped Tomás at the ranch.

His cell phone rang. He put down the hose and walked to a teak chair under the arbor leading from the kitchen door. He sat in the shade of a lush coral vine ensnaring the wrought iron structure with its twisting stems, curling tendrils, and bright orange flowers.

"Hola."

"El Cuervo, it's Manny. I have news from our friend. Thirty so far, and more are expected tomorrow."

"Wonderful. How many more days?"

"Only one. If they can finish tomorrow, delivery could be in as few as three days."

Cuervo was pleased. He would not miss his deadline by much. The speedboats would meet the service boat at an isolated transfer point offshore of La Mision along the Baja coast. The bales would be taken ashore and transferred by trucks to a small warehouse just south of the US border in Tijuana. The warehouse was connected to a larger warehouse in San Ysidro by a very sophisticated half-mile tunnel.

Cuervo was always relieved when the shipments reached Señor Martinez because they were then his problem and the contract was completed. The remaining fifty percent of the fee would be transferred to an account in the Caymans, and he could begin the next shipment.

"Cuda knows what to do, right?"

"Yes, El Cuervo. We have talked."

Cuervo returned to his watering. He lived discreetly, the owner of a successful food distribution business, Alberto Foods—named after his dead older brother—and a commercial fishing fleet. No one could imagine the true source of his wealth.

The family lived outside Tecate. Cuervo said it was for the quiet and solitude, but the security of his family was the real reason. Tijuana had become a lawless frontier, and while his drug industry was the cause, he shielded his family of its brutal criminal element. He did not want to subject Serena and Ramon to the savagery.

The house was the definition of understated elegance. Almost invisible from the street behind the wall and a small coppice of jacaranda trees, it was a typical neo-colonial Spanish white stucco structure with a red tile roof. Approaching through the gate to the semicircular driveway, it looked like a small one-story home typical of the area. However, past the dark mahogany double-doors with their black wrought iron adornments, the home opened into a sprawling and inviting abode. While 4,500 square feet in size, it felt much larger, with the fifteen-foot high ceilings, whitewashed walls, and banks of floor-to-ceiling windows on all but the street side. The furniture was traditional, but covered in the palette favored by Serena, whose taste Cuervo considered impeccable, and borne of the hundreds of fashion and design magazines she consumed.

The backyard had a small guesthouse now used by Estrella, over Serena's strenuous objections, to eliminate the stress and indignities of the long daily bus trips to and from her apartment.

Next to the guesthouse was the pool area. An open area was maintained behind the back wall of the property for security purposes.

While the house and landscape looked like any upscale suburban home, it was a fortress. The windows created the airy ambience but were three panes of bulletproof polycarbonate plastic. The rustic doors were reinforced with steel and ballistic fabric. Security cameras were hidden throughout the grounds and monitored from the house next door, which housed Cuervo's security detail. Pressure sensors were placed at strategic locations to detect intruders stupid enough to try to scale the eight-foot walls, and if they did, infrared detectors would trigger banks of floodlights and alarms. The area behind the house had no cover and would be the "kill zone" for any trespasser. As for as neighbors, they were all La Hermandad or their immediate family, and their homes were equally protected.

Cuervo checked his watch. He expected Ramon to return from school shortly, but he had no clue when Serena would return from her perpetual shopping spree.

He raised his nose. The aroma of Estrella's roasted pork wafted through the kitchen window.

"Is that what I think It's, Estrella?" Cuervo asked.

"Oh yes, Señor Cuervo. Your very favorite meal."

He sighed. "You are much too kind to us, Estrella."

Half embarrassed by his praise, Estrella giggled. "Oh, señor."

It would be good to have the family together tonight. Tomorrow he was needed at the ranch, and he didn't know for how long.

Chapter Twenty-One
Eastern Tropical Pacific
31°54'22"N, 121°23'08"W

Denny stood watch in the pilothouse, his eyes fixed on the calm black ocean. The *Bella* was quiet, drifting in the open sea. The slight breeze carried the heavy salt air through the open door.

Garza stepped from his cabin and walked to the helm. He nodded to Denny and handed him a sheet of paper with the new coordinates. "Keep the radio off. You and I'll handle the helm until we arrive."

"When do you want to get underway, Skipper? It'll take about an hour to get there," Denny said, looking up from the navigation monitor after entering the new position.

"I want to be there first light. Let's depart about 0430."

"Roger. I'll let the engine room know."

* * *

It was a short trip and Garza manned the helm most of the time. Denny returned from the galley, struggling up the steep ladder with two mugs of coffee.

"Anyone stirring?" Garza asked, blowing a gray cloud of smoke from the cigar locked in his jaw.

"Eduardo and Rafael are in the galley." Denny handed a mug to Garza. "I told them to have breakfast ready at five thirty. I'll muster the crew at six. I figure we should have the boats in the water around six forty-five. Picking up anything on the sonar yet?"

"No, just a few balls of fish I'd sure like to bring on board. I'm gonna grab something below and head for the stick." Garza left the pilothouse.

Reaching the crow's nest, Garza radioed his plan to Cuda.

"Any boats on the radar?" Cuda asked.

"Nothing close. A couple of targets twenty miles out. By their speed, I'm guessing empty containerships hauling ass back to Asia."

"Good. Let me know when you get a hit on the sonar."

Garza signed off. He looked eastward toward a dim glow barely visible on the horizon. He checked his watch but didn't need to—another twenty minutes until sunrise.

* * *

"Skipper," Denny said over the radio. "Check out your sonar. I'm getting some weak blips."

Garza turned to the sonar screen at his small console. He adjusted the range and contrast. After several seconds, he saw them.

"You're right, get the boats launched."

The announcement over the PA cleared the galley and the boats were in the water in less than fifteen minutes.

"Okay, let's get some packages," Garza said to Cuda over the secure sat phone.

Cuda punched in a new code.

Fortunately, it was not full daylight yet, because the first bale surfaced a distance from the vessel. Garza detected it by its pulsing strobe about three-quarters of a mile out.

"Franco, I got something behind you," Garza said over the radio.

"I don't see it."

"Just head two hundred and seventy degrees and I'll guide you."

"Aye." Franco threw the throttle forward, spun the wheel ninety degrees, and accelerated at full speed, rooster-tailing the calm early-morning sea into a churning froth.

After a few minutes, Garza saw Franco was headed toward the strobe. "You on it, okay?"

"Got it."

Garza radioed Cuda and told him to let another one go, which he did.

This package surfaced a little closer and was retrieved before Franco's boat got back.

The work continued the rest of the day. When no more targets were seen on the sonar, Cuda would direct them to another location. It didn't take Garza long to surmise Cuda knew the location of the submerged packages. He knew the packages were tracked but wasn't sure how.

At about four p.m., Cuda phoned the bunker.

"Manny, we've got forty-eight, are you seeing any more signals?" Cuda asked.

"No. That's all we have on the screen."

"Could the others just be out of range? Maybe a little farther east?"

"Maybe, but we've got the whole area covered."

"I can think of two possibilities," Manny said. "There were two malfunctioning satellite transmitters, which is possible. Or the bales never made it out of the sub and didn't inflate. You should stop searching and get the shipment ashore. Our buyer is getting impatient."

"You will tell El Cuervo It's not possible to find the last two?" Cuda said with some trepidation.

"I will. He will be pleased with your success. You only have one more task before heading back."

"Yes, I know."

Chapter Twenty-Two
Eastern Tropical Pacific
31°54'22"N, 121°23'08"W

The day broke bright and clear the next morning when Cuda and the two crewmen boarded the *Bella* to reward the crew.

Gus looked down the hatch at Chase, who was crammed into the bilge of the net skiff working on the propeller shaft rattle. "Hey, the skipper wants us in the mess."

"Why don't you go? You can tell me what they say. Otherwise, we're gonna have oil all over the deck."

"Yeah, but you better get this thing fixed. We may have to go fishing someday." Gus rose from the hatch. Just to piss off Chase a little more, he lowered the hatch cover, cutting off the sunlight.

All Gus could hear as he jumped from the skiff to the net deck was the muffled voice of Chase: "Screw you, asshole, but I got a work light in here."

Gus grinned as he walked across the deck to the galley.

* * *

"Are they all in there?" Cuda asked Denny in the passageway.

The shouts and laughter of the excited crewmen grew louder as they approached the mess room.

"All except the skipper. He'll stay in the pilothouse."

"I want you to go in there and let them know we want to thank them for their efforts. We have the reward your captain promised."

"Just listen. That's the sound of a happy crew." Denny smiled broadly at the three men from the service boat, two of whom were holding daypacks containing the bonuses.

Denny opened the door to the mess and walked to the center. *Bella*'s crew was sitting at the tables, except Gus, who stood in the galley pouring a coffee from behind the island.

"Men," Denny said. The crew quieted. "The guys from the service boat want to talk to us and have a big surprise for—"

He was interrupted by a commotion. Two of the men from the service boat were standing in the entryway. Each man tossed a melon-sized object toward the tables and immediately slammed the galley door shut.

Before Denny's attention was diverted back to the crew, a searing white flash enveloped the galley, followed a moment later by a deafening explosion. Denny stood for a second or two until the full effect of the white-hot metal shrapnel ripped the life from him and most of the others in the confined metal-plated crypt, his body collapsing to the deck.

The concussion had sent Gus reeling backward into the galley, where his head slammed against the oven door, knocking him semiconscious. The island took the full brunt of the flying shrapnel, but a few shards ricocheted off the metal walls and rained around him.

Pressed tight against the safety of steel bulkheads, the assassins waited for a few seconds to open the door. A cloud of atomized blood, combined with the RDX-TNT vapor of the anti-personnel grenades, hung over the room. As it slowly cleared, they witnessed the carnage. Blood and tissue bathed the walls and deck, severed limbs littered the tables, and the bodies of the fishermen lay in perverse contortions. The room was eerily silent except for the plaintive moans from Santos, who, while hemorrhaging from a missing left leg, clung to life. Cuda walked to the mortally wounded man, gently lifted his head, and fired a bullet from his 9 mm Ruger pistol into his skull, silencing him forever.

"Make sure they are dead," Cuda said. "I'll take the captain to set the charges."

Joaquin and Benji were far less experienced in such matters. When they entered the mess, they covered their mouths and noses and wretched at the sickening sight. When Cuda left, they both ran to the head.

Gus, gagging on the smell of burning flesh, slowly regained his senses and remembered the explosion. While still down, he heard the gunshot and the words of Cuda. He knew he had to do something, and he had to do it fast.

He got on his hands and knees. He was shaky, and his head ached from his encounter with the steel oven. He stood and was horrified by the gore confronting him. Minutes earlier this room had been alive with the cheer and excitement of getting back home and having their best payday in years. These were his friends, his shipmates, and now, what— a bitter nightmare of lost hopes and dreams. There would now be kids raised without their dads, wives forever brokenhearted. It was too much for Gus. He ran out the door, into the passageway, and onto the net deck.

* * *

Chase had not heard the explosion but felt the skiff shudder from the blast. He wormed his way from the stern of the propeller shaft raceway to the hatch cover Gus closed fifteen minutes before. He pushed it open and it fell forward. He saw Gus with the skiff release lanyard in his hand and was about to shout for him to stop when Gus looked at him. His face was taut in a determined grimace, but his mouth curled into a slight smile when he saw Chase.

In the next instant, Chase saw the blurred outline of the big man from the service boat backlit by the sun standing on the bridge deck. The man fired four shots. Gus fell to his knees and mouthed the word "GO." He pulled the lanyard with all the strength he had left before he fell dead, face first, onto the cold steel deck.

Chase was shocked. This can't be happening, he thought, but immediately ducked from view behind the engine cover, praying the shooter wouldn't see him. He felt the skiff sliding into the water. It was drifting from the *Bella*, but the bulky net still shackled to the bow slowed its progress.

Chase waited a few more seconds and peered over the cover to see if the shooter was still there or, worse, walking toward the skiff.

Gus's body was motionless on the deck. Chase didn't know what to do, other than to hide until he could work out what had happened.

* * *

Hearing the shots, Garza ran to the rear of the bridge deck and stood next to Cuda. He saw his old friend, Gus, lying in a pool of blood on the deck below. This was the first realization of the horror he had brought to his crew. He had heard and felt the explosion, but he didn't have the guts to enter the mess.

"Look, the boat is drifting away," Cuda said. "Get it back."

"Don't worry, it's still connected by the net. We got work to do below."

As instructed the night before, Joaquin and Benji had affixed the pliable C4 shape charges to the ship's hull just a few feet below the waterline in the lower engine room. The charges were placed at fifty-foot intervals on hull support beams. A detonator was inserted into each charge and timed to go off at precisely 8:35 a.m.

Garza and Cuda worked in different areas. Garza placed charges on the ammonia refrigeration tanks and pipes, while Cuda placed them on the diesel fuel tanks. Both were set to go off at 8:20 a.m., minutes before the hull charges.

The men sprinted to the net deck, where the launch from the service boat was tied off. Joaquin scrambled down the ladder and steadied the small craft against the hull of the *Bella* for Cuda's entry. Benji followed and started the engine.

Garza ran back to the bridge and placed a Mayday call. "This is the tuna purse seiner *Bella*. We have had an explosion and are taking on water fast. Our position is 32 degrees, 12 minutes, and 46 seconds north latitude and 122 degrees, 10 minutes, and 15 seconds west longitude. Repeat Mayday, Mayday, Mayday," he screamed into the microphone and waited.

"*Bella* do you read me, over. This is the freighter *Robert D. Walls*. We have received your message and are transmitting it to the Mexican authorities. We will continue to alert all vessels in the area," Garza heard over the speaker.

"Roger that, *Robert D*..." He stopped in midsentence and turned off the radio. The coordinates he had given were seventy miles northeast of their actual position—it would give them plenty of time to escape.

He returned to the net deck and hoisted his right leg over the rail and was about to step onto the first rung of the ladder when Cuda looked up and said, "Isn't there a tradition that the captain must go down with the ship?"

Garza turned and looked into the cold half smile on Cuda's face and the black barrel of his 9 mm. In an instant, he knew the promises of new identities, relocation to a place of his choice, the two-million-dollar bonus, and the safety of his family were nothing but lies. He took a deep breath and realized his own betrayal to his crew, sighing knowingly as the two bullets sliced through his brain. The impact sent his body tumbling backward onto the net deck, not fifteen feet from Gus's lifeless form.

"Get out of here. We only have thirty minutes," Cuda said as the launch sped toward the service boat.

* * *

Chase heard the second volley of gunshots, followed by an outboard motor revving at full speed. He crawled out from behind the engine cover and, on his hands and knees, crept forward, hidden below the skiff's gunwales. When he reached the bow, he carefully raised his head and saw the furious wake of the departing launch.

The skiff was drifting from the seiner. He was three hundred feet away, but he could now see a second body on the deck. The rest of the vessel was silent—no voices, no engine or equipment noise—a ghost ship. Chase waited alone, exposed and afraid.

* * *

Cuda paced the deck of the service boat, rubbing his palms together in expectation. Except for an occasional glance at his watch, his eyes were fixed on the *Bella.* At the prescribed time, the small charges set by Garza exploded, breaching the anhydrous ammonia refrigerant tanks. The gas quickly dissipated through the boat. A minute later, the diesel tank exploded, sending a fine vapor of volatized hydrocarbons to mix with the ammonia gas. Finally, after what seemed to Cuda an eternity, but only fifteen minutes later, the shape charges went off, sending jets of water skyward around the entire hull as each explosion opened a two-foot hole in *Bella*'s steel skin.

As the sea rushed in and filled the lower engine room, the real excitement for Cuda was about to begin. The super-heated vapors of the TNT ignited the diesel-ammonia mix, and the ear-shattering reaction launched a fireball one hundred feet into the air, vaporizing everything within the sealed metal can. The thunderous shockwave almost knocked Cuda off balance. It wasn't a smile on his face; it was a reaction more base—limbic.

The other crewmen could only stare in shock as the smoke cleared and the hull of the once-proud seiner sunk below the surface. Cuda watched too, his black soulless eyes not looking away until the crow's nest finally disappeared into the Pacific.

"Let's get out of here in case someone gets curious about the smoke trail," Cuda said.

"What about the skiff?"

Cuda smiled again. "It's tied to the seiner. It'll be dragged down."

* * *

Chase was crouched in the bottom of the skiff dazed, disoriented, and temporarily deafened by the explosion. The blast wave sent molten gases over the skiff, which singed the back of his clothes. Fortunately, the following shockwave sent a stream of water over him, snuffing the fire. He was showered with debris, but uninjured.

He looked over the side and saw what was left of the *Bella* and his friends; a slow eddy of bubbles as the cold seawater flooded the compartments and displaced all the air in the submerged hulk. Moments ago, what had been a thriving industry of men and equipment, of friendships and animosities, of plans and dreams and desires, of fathers, sons, uncles, brothers, and friends, was gone—lost forever except in memories.

Chase was too numb to react. In front of him, or what wasn't in front of him, was too much to process. It was as if his brain switched off its emotional center to shelter him from the pain. But it wouldn't be off for long.

Chase looked east and saw the faint silhouette of the service boat in the distance. He worried they could see him but realized he didn't care. After all, if it weren't for the propeller shaft and, more importantly, the heroic actions of Gus, he too would be sinking to the bottom. He asked himself, like all survivors, why me? If they came back to kill him, it would only be fair. The more important question would come later: Why?

Chapter Twenty-Three
Eastern Tropical Pacific
31°53'22"N, 121°17'08"W

Chase curled into a ball on the wet deck, his arms clasped around his head, shielding him from the horror as a torrent of emotion swept over him. The tears wouldn't stop. The skiff drifted with the current.

The high sun at noon warmed Chase's face. He opened his eyes to a bright blue sky peppered with cottony clouds. The deafness was gone, replaced by a loud and incessant ringing, and he heard waves against the skiff.

He remembered his last image of Gus's final furtive smile when he pulled the lanyard. It was Gus telling him: If you escape, my sacrifice was worth it. I beat 'em!

Vintage Gus, Chase thought with a slight grin, revenge from the grave.

He drew a long and deep breath, gathered himself, and decided to survive.

He walked around the skiff and assessed the damage. The paint was charred and debris was strewn everywhere, some displaced from the skiff when buffeted by the explosion and some from the *Bella*. He could find no breach in the hull, as the bilge was dry. He looked at the bow. The net was still attached, several hundred feet of it floating on the surface and the rest submerged. Chase realized how lucky he was. If the ocean floor had been another 1,500 feet in depth, the skiff, with him in it, would have been dragged under. He leaned over the bow and unscrewed the shackle pin securing the net to the skiff. The net sunk into the ocean, severing his last physical connection to the *Bella* and his crewmates.

He inventoried his resources. The skiff was rated as an auxiliary lifeboat and had a small provision of survival food and gear. Jerome, the skiff's pilot, always made sure he had plenty of water available during the long fishing sets under the hot semitropical sun.

Chase walked to the control console, which was Spartan at best. It had the steering wheel, engine control unit with its gearshift and throttle levers, a small instrument cluster with a speedometer, tachometer, fuel gauge, oil pressure gauge, voltmeter, and a compass. There was no sonar unit, no radar, and no communication gear except the small, short-range VHF radio used by Jerome to communicate with the *Bella.*

He turned the key and checked the fuel level. The gauge read full, at least two hundred gallons of diesel. He thought about starting the engine but was afraid the diesel exhaust would be spotted, or he'd be detected on radar. He decided to wait.

With its blunt brow and open hull, the net skiff looked like a barge or an old personnel landing craft from World War II. It was designed to only float and pull a heavy load, not to travel long distances, nor endure heavy seas; it had the hydrodynamics of a brick. With its flat bottom and small rudder, it was a slow, unstable, and lubberly brick, and never intended to be piloted by an inexperienced mechanic.

Chase knew, as did the rest of the crew, what they had been salvaging—there was no doubt. Otherwise, why go to such extremes? But what he couldn't wrap his mind around was why kill the crew and destroy the boat? It didn't make sense. The crew would have kept quiet; the money was more than a sufficient motivation, and they weren't choirboys, anyhow. Like all fishermen, they resented authority. They didn't like the government telling them when to fish, what they could catch, and how to run their business. Many had their brushes with the law, so they weren't exactly inclined to run to the police. There had to be some other reason, he thought, and when the answer didn't come, he became more enraged.

The mental anguish and physical exhaustion finally overwhelmed him, and he fell into a deep, fitful sleep. Images of Maria soothed his broken dreams.

Chapter Twenty-Four
Eastern Tropical Pacific
32°12'46"N, 121°10'15"W

The M/V *Robert D. Walls* was fifty miles west of the position Garza had radioed and could not reach the *Bella* in time to mount a rescue. It was, however, successful in hailing the Mexican Navy, which deployed several BO-105 helicopters and Polaris-class patrol interceptors to the area. The search reported no signs of the ship or survivors. Even if they had searched another seventy miles west at the actual location of the explosion, their efforts would have been fruitless. Before the charges had been set, the exterior of the ship had been sealed, hatches dogged, and windows covered; the debris field was minimal.

* * *

The Navy contacted Pescadero Baja of the ship's distress signal. It was Nico's responsibility to inform the families.

When the call came, Maria was so busy getting the kids ready she almost let it go to voicemail. But something about the insistent ring moved her to answer.

There are only a few moments that are truly life changing—events that delineate "before" and "after." This was one.

She locked herself in the bedroom, sparing the kids from her breakdown. They watched television, unconcerned about being late for school, unaware how their lives had just changed.

After less than half an hour, Maria garnered the poise to call her mother, and spoke through her tears.

Her mother, a fisherman's wife, immediately knew what to do. She arrived in minutes, arranged for the children's care for the next few hours until the news could be broken to them, and informed the church to send over a priest. Last, all the wives of the fishing families were informed through their exclusive pipeline, and at least a dozen were in Maria's living room when her mother gently led her from the bedroom. It had been a dizzying and painful few hours.

Maria, her doleful eyes red and swollen, walked to each woman, hugged her tightly, accepted the condolences with grace. Most, too, were in tears and knew instinctively: There but for the grace of God...

All tried valiantly to comfort the inconsolable; Maria appreciated the outpouring.

"What have you been told?" One woman asked the question the rest had been afraid to broach.

"They said a ship had received a distress call that the *Bella* was on fire and taking on water. The Mexican Navy sent out helicopters and rescue ships, but they couldn't find anything."

"Are they still searching?"

"Yes, they even expanded the search area."

"What about the distress beacons? All the boats have them," another asked.

"The man from the company didn't say anything about any signals."

"When did it happen?"

"The day before yesterday in the late afternoon. The helicopters searched until dark, and then the rescue boats arrived."

Another woman gently stroked Maria's hair and said, "It's still early in the search. The men on the *Bella* are very experienced and they have the speedboats and the life rafts. Surely they had time to launch them. They are just not searching in the right places, that's all."

"Let's pray Teresa is right," Maria's mother said. "We must have faith. Father Brian, will you lead us?"

Father Brian's prayer was warm and comforting, hit all the right notes, and was expressed with deep love and sympathy, but it had little effect on Maria. She was numb. Her mother led her back to her bedroom to rest while the other women began organizing the difficult tasks for the next weeks. Maria would need her the strength.

* * *

The service boat arrived at the rendezvous point on time. Three speedboats were waiting.

Cuda and the service boat pilot assisted off-loading the bales since Joaquin and Benji had gone missing after meeting Cuda on the stern the previous night. The pilot was now watching his back constantly and hoped for high seas on the return to Ensenada to disable the big stranger. The pilot sighed deeply when Cuda boarded one of the speedboats.

Cuda looked at his watch. If this current schedule could be maintained, the bales would be through the tunnel in ten hours.

* * *

"This is, indeed, good news," Cuervo said after Manny relayed Cuda's report over the phone.

"Cuda has done well," Manny said.

Cuervo, though, lamented for the lost crew. "I pray their deaths were quick and painless. They certainly deserved a better fate, but it's most important to everyone, including their families, that we succeed, and our enterprise remains secret. If the police or our competitors learn our methods, it would not be long before they, too, would find a way to track and steal our shipments."

"Yours is the curse of leadership, El Cuervo. You must sacrifice the few for the good of the many," Manny said. "Politicians and generals face grave situations every day. But, for you, it's never a decision made without careful consideration and empathy."

"But I think of my poor brother and light a candle at every mass. He, too, was an innocent victim, so I grieve for our men."

"Yes, it's difficult, but we have made a considerable investment and we must take advantage of this opportunity. We know every smuggling scheme is eventually discovered and countered. Just as the cigarette boats replaced the fishing boats, someday our subs will be discovered and replaced. But for the time being, hundreds of millions, perhaps billions, in profits are at stake. It's much easier to replace a tuna boat and crew than to develop a more advanced smuggling system, And Nico has arranged generous compensation for all the families—it's the least we can do."

Chapter Twenty-Five
Eastern Tropical Pacific
31°53'38"N, 121°08'57"W

A rogue six-foot wave bucked the skiff, jolting Chase to consciousness. He shook his head to revive himself, and instantly the haunting image of the *Bella* consumed by the towering fireball jarred him back to his new reality.

His body was cold and stiff from the hours on the steel deck. He sat up, surprised it was already night. The silence was broken by swells slapping against the skiff. From the waxing moon, a glint of light was all that was visible as the distant breaking waves fluoresced white in the black sea. The cool northwest breeze was gathering.

Without a sea anchor, the skiff bobbed randomly. It was at the mercy of the wind and waves and would pitch and yaw as it was attacked from the stern, bow, and quarter. Chase knew a large wave could roll him and his best chance was to head directly into the waves, but that was the wrong direction. He'd have to chance running with a following sea. It would require more steering and he and the skiff would take a pounding, but he'd reach shore faster.

He shook his arms and knotted his fists back to function as he stumbled to the console. He started the engine and nudged the throttle until the tachometer read 1,500 rpms. He let it warm up. He shifted into gear, eased the throttle forward, and began motoring southeast into what would be a long, empty Pacific night.

He had a vague idea of his position. The *Bella* was headed toward Tijuana when she met with the service boat. He knew if he continued on the east-southeast course, sooner or later he would encounter the Mexican coast. He just hoped it would be the Baja peninsula and not the mainland coast.

The skiff had only two running lights, one on the bow and one on the stern, but the vessel sat so low in the water, it would be nearly impossible for any nearby ship to see them. It had a few signal flares, but no spotlight.

No, Chase thought, it's up to me to spot other vessels.

It was then that the realization hit him: I can't be found. If I am, it will be reported to the authorities. Whoever did that to the *Bella* does not want any witnesses. And what about Maria and the kids?

He had been optimistic about his chances for rescue; he was sure there was enough fuel to make it to shore, but now the foreboding enveloped him and jarred him into reality. Not only could he not be rescued, but he also had to avoid other boats—a difficult situation because a lone skiff in these waters would be a real curiosity. He had to stay hidden. He didn't know what to do, but for the sake of his family, he had to be dead.

The wind was at his back, but Chase could feel its intensity. Storm clouds shrouded the moon and stars. Except for the whitecaps now crowning each wave, the sea was a frothing pewter cauldron. Chase was steering the best he could, but the skiff's small rudder was no match for the growing sea.

A large wave knocked Chase from the pilot's chair and against the hard steel gunwale. Crawling on hands and knees, he struggled back to the helm. Afraid of washing overboard, he tied a rope around his waist and secured it to the console.

A lightning bolt flashed in the distance and Chase could taste the charge in the air. In minutes, the squall was on him. The ocean, at least the little Chase could see, was now a roiling maelstrom with waves smashing from all directions, and all seemingly bound for the small vulnerable skiff.

A ten-footer pummeled the port quarter, heeling it hard to starboard and almost swamping the boat. The skiff was floundering, and Chase was flailing. He'd steer hard left, then right. Nothing worked. It was the sea, not Chase, in command.

The open hull provided no cover, and Chase was soaked, shivering, and standing in at least six inches of water. He searched the controls for the bilge pumps. He wasn't sure how much more water the skiff could take on before sinking, but he wasn't about to find out.

Over the tumult of the tumbling seas, Chase could hear a steady mechanical whir. Just keep it up, baby, he willed the pumps.

At least for now, he was in the moment—no time to think of his family, his shipmates, or the men who caused it all. Nothing mattered unless he survived.

* * *

Awake the entire night, Chase watched as the final glow of moonlight struggled against the early dawn. The seas had finally calmed, and Chase rested the engine and himself for a few hours. He had survived.

He wiped droplets from the instruments and peered at the compass. The current was taking him in approximately the right direction, but he wasn't sure how far off course the storm had taken him. He would try to correct by motoring due east later.

The port tank fuel gauge read "1/2," but the starboard tank was still full. He guessed he'd traveled fifty miles in the last ten hours. It was about the best the skiff could do, even with the storm's assist.

Chase removed his shirt, wrung it out, and set it to dry on the engine cover. He did the same with his trousers and shoes.

He stretched out on the pilot seat, basking in the emerging morning sun with his legs draped over the console and his hands locked behind his head. Then he felt the churning. His stomach was growling after two days without food. He could take it no more and opened a survival kit.

It contained about twenty foil-wrapped biscuits, cans of water, matches, first-aid supplies, and miscellaneous gear, most still dry. He read the label on the biscuit. Hmm...all the nutrients necessary for twenty-four-hour period...supplied a full 2,000 calories.

Chase took a bite. It was like a bland energy bar. The label assured him there was enough food for one person for ten days.

I'll drown myself if I have to eat these for three more days, he thought, forcing another bite. He silently lamented all the great meals Eduardo had prepared that he'd taken for granted.

He fumbled through the gear and pulled out a cellophane-wrapped box about the size of a deck of cards. Survival Gear; Fishing. In smaller print: hooks (5); nylon line (50 feet); painted metal lures (2), weights, lead (2).

"What the hell," he said aloud.

He ripped the cellophane and unspooled a fifty-pound test nylon line and tied one end around a rope cleat on the starboard aft quarter. He then tied one of the metal lures and sinkers to the opposite end. He had no bait and doubted the effectiveness of the shining metal to attract much, so he ran the hook through a survival biscuit.

He laughed as he tossed the rig overboard. "Let's see how desperate these fish are."

He watched halfheartedly as the line played out. The sea was calm with just a slight ripple, but he thought he saw a wave break. Hope the wind's not picking up again.

He continued to stare. There it was again. But it wasn't a wave. It was more like a reflection, but it was bobbing. Where are the "Big Eyes" when I need them? Maybe it's something I can use. He reeled in the nylon line, looping it around his left hand.

He started the engine while trying to keep the object in view. He motored about five hundred yards when he finally recognized it. It had the same plastic box and long trailing wire as the others, but the strobe wasn't working. A part of the flotation collar was deflated so the package sat lower in the water than the others recovered by *Bella*'s chase boats.

You're as far off course as I am, he thought, amazed at how far the storm had carried the bale.

Chase edged alongside the bale and saw the wet glistening black plastic wrapping that had been reflecting the sun. He put the skiff in neutral and walked over to the side. He grabbed the nylon strap around the bale and began to pull. It was heavy, two hundred pounds of dead weight, and Chase couldn't lift it over the gunwale. He found a length of line and secured it fast to the bale. He then walked the bale to the stern, where a two-foot-wide dive platform was welded to the transom just above the waterline.

Chase stepped out of the skiff and onto the platform. Grunting loud from the effort, he lifted the bale six inches and edged it onto the platform. He then hoisted the bale until it was sitting on its end. He got back into the skiff and grabbed the nylon straps again. With all his strength, he lifted the bale until it balanced precariously on the stern gunwale. With one final tug, the bale tumbled into the skiff as Chase scrambled out of its way.

Unlike the speedboat drivers, he had not been able to see any of the bales up close and was impressed with its cover. Shrink-wrapped in thick plastic, the bale was watertight, and there was not a mark on the cover. Chase decided to investigate a little deeper. He cut the nylon straps securing the plastic box to the top of the bale. The box had a lid, which was glued, and a seam filled with a waterproofing epoxy. A thin wire came out of a single sealed pinhole.

Chase grabbed a box cutter from his toolbox and sliced through the epoxy with the razor. He pulled the two pieces apart.

What have we here? He peered into the box at a small circuit board with a number of chips connected to an array of nine-volt batteries. The coated wire through the box was securely soldered to the circuit board and also connected to a small spring attached to the box. Chase fingered the spring curiously and determined it was to take up a shock or slack, so the wire wouldn't become disconnected from the circuit board. *Clever.*

He picked up the box to get a better angle in the sun and read the small lettering on the chips. One read: "GPS, 45234" while the largest chip read: "Sat-Trans 11-0030-54, ver. 3a."

"It's a damn tracking device!" *Holy shit, they know where I am.*

He was about to heave it overboard and get the hell out of there when he noticed the battery pack. The small cable was still attached to the board but was disconnected from the batteries.

Chase sighed with relief. They lost this one.

He then examined the flotation bladder. It, too, had a control box. Chase pried it open and found another circuit board, battery pack, a couple of compressed air tanks, and a small antenna. Chase hadn't seen the big man with the control box but surmised the service boat remotely actuated the air bladder.

He turned his attention to the bale. With the box cutter again, he carefully sliced a thin four-inch slit in the outer plastic cover. With his fingers, he spread the wrapping wide to reveal a second layer of black plastic. He sliced the second layer, and beneath was a small clear plastic-covered, brick-shaped object. He cut a half-inch slice to reveal a tightly compressed white powder. He swiped the brick with a wet finger and placed the residue against the tip of his tongue. An astringent taste hit him, followed soon with a numbing sensation. He recognized both from some earlier, reckless years.

Chase was impressed. This was not an organization resorting to stuffing coke under the spare tire of a truck crossing the border or forcing young girls to swallow cocaine-packed condoms and flying to the States. No, this was big time. And the technology meant big money was behind it. Chase wasn't sure how much the bale in front of him was worth, but he knew to someone it was more valuable than a tuna boat and thirteen of his shipmates.

Chase sat and contemplated what to do. More than ever, he had to elude detection and get to a beach unseen. But now a fire burned. Someone would pay.

He stood, walked to the control console, and set the course due east.

Chapter Twenty-Six
Coast Near San Quintin, Baja California, Mexico

Chase plowed through the biscuits and most of the survival water, but he still had Jerome's private stash. The skiff had no cover and Chase was totally exposed. His face and arms burned red from the baking sun and his skin was crusted with salt. His eyes were swollen to mere slits from the constant squinting.

He had motored off and on for a day and a half since he found the bale, stopping only to rest a few minutes before proceeding east. It was now ten o'clock at night and he was approaching the coast. Just before dusk, flocks of gulls flew over and a small tight formation of brown pelicans glided across the bow just inches off the sea.

He wanted to beach at night to avoid detection, but knew it was too dangerous. He had no idea how the skiff would handle in the surf, but he was not optimistic about it after his experience in the storm. At least during light he would have a chance to find an opening in the break. He decided dawn would be best, before the fleets of local fishermen set out in their long, narrow pangas for their day's catch. With light, he could maybe locate a deserted stretch of beach. He had to lay low. If word got out that he had survived, he was sure teams of killers would be on his trail.

He peered over at the bale and understood why they—whoever they were—wanted no witnesses.

Chase knew he would have to scuttle the skiff—it was traceable back to the *Bella*. Not only was "*Bellita*" emblazoned on her transom, but also registration numbers were painted on her bow. It would take a ten-minute call to track her provenance, and anyone with knowledge about the tides and currents would know it would have been impossible for the skiff to drift such a long distance on this course. They would know it had been under power and someone had escaped the sinking of the *Bella*.

In the darkness, he thought long and hard about whom was behind the sinking. He knew Garza was in on it because he was the one who diverted them to the north. It was Garza who cut off communication with the beach, and it was Garza who met with the big man on the service boat.

Chase knew Garza would only take orders from the company. No one else would have the authority to have the vessel move so far from the successful fishing grounds. It would have been the company that dispatched the service boat. Chase wasn't sure, but the most logical port of departure for the service boat would have been Ensenada, the company's headquarters. But Chase had never seen anything remotely suggesting drug smuggling. If the *Bella* had been used, he would have known because, other than Gus, nobody, not even Garza, knew all of her compartments, passages, and holds as well as he did. If fact, he knew the boat better than even Gus. So, how were the bales transported? He hadn't seen signs of a shipwreck or flotsam.

* * *

As dawn broke, the blurred sawtooth silhouette of the coastal foothill peaks, backlit by the earliest rays of the morning sun, came into view. There was probably another ten miles to the coast. The sea was flat, and Chase made a run for it. He started the skiff and threw the throttle back full, as it crawled at the breakneck speed of eight knots.

After two hours, he was just a few thousand yards off the beach. He had traveled parallel to the coast looking for a deserted place to land. He found a small cove flanked by two high rock outcrops. He had not seen the lights from any villages as he had sailed in the dark, and now he saw no fishing boats or other signs of activity. *This is it.*

He spotted the long, thin, and continuous white line of the wave break at the beach. He looked for the telltale signs of turbulence and overspray from a submerged outcrop or reef but saw none. Still, he knew it was dangerous because he had no way to judge the height of the surf. As the squall had taught him, if he encountered anything greater than three feet, the skiff was unsteady.

Chase had misjudged the surf. While the speed and direction of the wind and distance it has traveled affect the height of a wave, It's the sea floor that determines the intensity of the break. On a gradual sloping shore, a wave breaks more gently and in deeper water, but on a steep bottom or a reef, its breaks more violently and in shallower water.

He couldn't see the steep approach. He gunned the engine, but the skiff hit the peak of an eight-foot wave just as it crested. The skiff was momentarily suspended on the wave with both the bow and stern exposed. The propeller whined as it sliced impotently through the air. In the next instant, the wave effortlessly rotated the skiff ninety degrees until it was parallel to the shore, exposing the largest and most vulnerable face of the boat. The skiff slipped into the trough and before Chase could gain control, the next wave cascaded down into the open hull. With water up to the gunwales, the skiff lost all maneuverability, and it was all Chase could do to just hold on. The third wave finally flipped the floundering boat. Chase felt himself rolling over. He tried to hold tight to the helm, but his grip was no match for the power of the ocean. He was hurtled violently to the bottom and tumbled uncontrollably beneath fifteen feet of eddying surf. He couldn't see anything but felt the thunderous impact as the skiff hit the bottom not four feet away.

Chase tried with all his might to swim to the surface, but the force of the crashing waves was too much. In a last-ditch effort, he turned and swam at an angle to the oncoming surf. As he did, he felt his body being lifted as the next wave pounded the bottom, displacing both the water and Chase from below. He kicked vigorously and, on his last molecules of air, surfaced. He was inside the break. The foaming white water roiled him. Treading on the surface, he gasped and inhaled as deep as he could. It was another two hundred yards to the beach, where a second break was forming.

He had a long hard swim ahead, and he was exhausted. He hoped he could stay afloat for just a few more minutes, but another wave crashed over him. This time he surfaced quickly. He'd been blindsided and coughed a lungful of sea.

He tried to float on his back long enough to catch his breath but with his saturated clothes and shoes he was too heavy. He swam a few feet, but his energy was ebbing. The cold was taking its toll. Then, out of the corner of his eye, he saw it. It could still float, even with a partially filled bladder.

With the last of his reserves, Chase swam over and grabbed the bale. He kicked hard three times, each time inching closer to the top. He lay motionless and exhausted. His arms and legs dangled over the sides of the bale as the surf washed them toward the beach.

The bale finally bottomed out and Chase rolled off into the shallow water and wet sand as the dying waves washed against him.

After a few minutes, he had enough strength to crawl onto the dry, sunbaked beach.

Safe, but drained, he took stock. He had his clothes, but not much else. Everything was drenched. He took off his shoes and socks and laid them out to dry. He did the same with his shirt. He took out his wallet and looked at the wet photo of Maria and the kids. He had seventy dollars and another two thousand pesos, worth about one hundred and fifty dollars, and two credit cards. He removed his belt and took off his trousers.

Waves were washing over the bale at the waterline, and it was already accreting sand. Chase studied the beach. The wrack line was just landward of where he sat. A high tide would refloat the bale, and he didn't want to lose it.

He rose and walked to the bale. There was no way to carry it any distance; maybe he could drag it, but to where? There was nowhere to hide it. He decided to take the bale apart—it would be far easier to carry the individual bricks.

He took his knife from its belt sheath and cut along the two slits he made almost two days before. He removed the two layers of black plastic and found the thirty-six individual bricks, each nine inches long, six inches wide, and four inches tall, stacked three rows high, three rows wide, and four rows long.

He scanned the cove. There was no vegetation to conceal the bricks. He looked up the cliff's rocky face and knew he didn't want to climb it even one time.

He decided burial was his best chance. He walked to the edge of the south cliff. It was deep sand and easy to dig, and well above the high tide.

There wasn't much chance of anyone sunning themselves this far from the beach. He grinned at the thought.

Using his hands, Chase dug until he reached the firm moist sand about eighteen inches below the surface. He widened the pit and placed six bricks into it. He then covered it and tamped the sand with his feet. He spread more top sand over it and with a piece of dried kelp brushed the surface to blend it with the adjacent undisturbed areas. With a small rock, he etched a line into the cliff face to mark the location of the pit.

Chase repeated the process five more times, but in the last pit, only five bricks were buried—he'd need the sixth, along with the tracker box.

Chase shook the sand from his now dry clothes and dressed. He placed the brick and the small tracker box under his waistband and started his climb. It was steep, but the only way out.

* * *

With stops to catch his breath, it took him an hour to scale the 1,500-foot granite escarpment. His hands, worn and blistered from clawing the rocks, clenched the trunk of a sagebrush plant to hoist himself up the last few feet. His clothes were dirty and stained from the soil and sweat; his bare arms scraped and bruised from the dense prickly pear and agave shrubs. He looked like he'd been living off the land for months.

With his hands shielding his eyes from the sun, Chase scanned his position. To the east, a large sediment-laden estuary flowed to the sea. To his south and west was ocean. He'd landed on a narrow peninsula, and the only way out was north. He was tired, hungry, and thirsty when he started north.

The little used crest trail spiraled through the hills. He looked down to the cove where he had beached and could not see the skiff, completely sunken under the surf. He continued a few miles until he encountered a primitive road, which he followed as it wound east around the upper estuary.

Agricultural fields lined the road. In the distance, a brown dust cloud spiraled as a farmer disked under what was left of his crop.

After a few more miles, he arrived at a highway outside of the small town of San Quintin. He walked north toward town, past a Pemex station and a small cluster of stucco houses, until he found a cantina. He looked down, dusted off, but realized he looked just like the farmworkers milling around the street after a morning in the fields.

The cantina had five booths along one wall under a set of windows shaded from the intense sun by thick, frayed, and sun-blanched crimson drapes. Small tables and chairs dotted the opposite wall, and a large counter separated the dining area from the kitchen. The floor was a checkerboard of worn dark green and white linoleum tiles, and long, buzzing florescent lamps lit the faded white plaster walls.

It was almost noon and the cantina was half full.

Chase immediately walked to the restroom. He locked the door and reached under his shirt and removed the brick and plastic box and placed them on the windowsill next to the sink.

He stared at his haggard reflection in the mirror and realized it had been three days, four if you included the morning on the *Bella*, since he had shaved.

He opened the faucet and washed his hands with a half-used soap bar, splashed the cool water onto his face a few times, and slicked down his oily hair. After drying himself with a few paper towels, he stuffed the brick and box under his shirt and returned to the cantina.

He chose a small booth near the rear and a young waitress approached, casting a slanted look at the brown-haired gringo.

Chase looked up and flashed a smile. "Do you speak English?"

"Yes," she said as she handed him a menu.

"Could you get me a water while I look over the menu? I just had a long walk. Oh, and do you have a small bag I could use?"

She nodded.

The waitress returned after a few minutes with a glass of water and a small plastic takeout bag.

He ordered carnitas with beans and rice before he drained the glass in a single chug. Water had never taste better and his parched throat begged for more.

It was a few more minutes before the waitress returned with his plate and a plastic container filled with hot flour tortillas. She refilled his water glass, which he promptly gulped down.

"Is there a bus station nearby?"

"Up the road three blocks," she said and left.

* * *

Chase finished his meal and pulled out his wallet. He was lost for a moment as he gazed at the moist and faded photo of Maria and the kids and wondered if he'd ever have such happy times again. He looked over to his California driver's license in the clear plastic pocket with a photo of a man five years younger. He knew he had to get rid of it and any other identification. For now, he was a dead man, and had to stay dead for a while. He scanned the room before he slipped the brick and plastic box into the bag.

He paid in pesos and strode revitalized to the bus station. He could catch the bus to Ensenada and Tijuana in an hour, or an earlier bus to La Paz and on to Cabo San Lucas. He opted for the earlier bus. He wasn't ready to head north yet, and what he had to sell had a better market in Cabo.

Chapter Twenty-Seven
Point Loma, San Diego, California, USA

It was wrong for so many reasons, Maria thought from the front pew at St. Roberts Church. It wasn't fair that Chase was dead, and it wasn't right to have a memorial service without a casket.

Kevin and Denise were sitting next to her, each clutching a hand. They were dressed in their Sunday best on that Tuesday morning, and Maria in her dutiful black dress and scarf. Any other time, this was the day she'd get Chase's call.

Father Brian comforted Chase's family and friends, preaching that Jesus was sometimes a fisherman and he, too, died an untimely death. And, like Jesus, it was these brave and caring men of the sea who risked their lives so we could be nourished in body and spirit.

Maria tried hard to focus, but her mind kept returning to the phone call from the company, and the visit from Nico a day later.

Nico had tried to console her, but the fact was the Mexican Navy was calling off the search. They had found nothing after three days.

Nico said the company was processing all the insurance papers, and she could expect payment in a few weeks. But he gave her five thousand to help until she received the settlement.

Maria was grateful and took the money, but in doing so she felt guilty that she was giving up on Chase and was accepting his death too easily. She didn't know what else she could do but would never stop hoping.

* * *

The ride was Chase's first chance to rest, something he'd missed in the last days, but the bus was hot and crowded.

Between his short and grudging naps, Chase had a chance to think and plan. His first thought was Maria. He knew she would put on a brave front for the kids, but late at night, in her solitude, she would suffer. He wanted to call to ease her pain, but he could not risk it. If word got out he was alive, they would come looking for him. Worse yet, they could try to use his family and friends to get him. They wanted no witnesses, no one to tell the tale of the *Bella*. He had to find out who they were.

He thought about how his family would fare without him. There was plenty of money squirreled away for the work on the house, and if Maria had signed the new mortgage papers, she would have additional cash. Then there was the life insurance. More than enough to cover expenses for a year. But, hopefully, it would not take that long. Too long to do what? His plan needed some more work. But first things first. Chase Brenner was gone, but who would he now become?

* * *

He found a small hotel well off the beach. It was not a tourist hotel, more like the kind used by truckers for short stopovers where a guy like him wouldn't get a second look. It was clean, they accepted cash, and no questions were asked. That was all that mattered.

After he cleaned up, he headed for a local mercado. He purchased some turista clothes—a pair of shorts, leather huaraches, a couple of tropical print shirts, T-shirts, and underwear. He topped it off with an "I HEART CABO" ball cap and sunglasses. He needed to slip in, unnoticed, among the tourists. He got some grooming items and a box of small envelopes.

At a park three blocks from the hotel, he retrieved the brick that he'd stashed in a small hole amid the landscape plantings. He couldn't be caught carrying the drugs. He stashed the brick in a paper bag and headed back to the hotel.

On the small table in his room, he carefully measured four spoonfuls of the powder into the envelopes. He scanned the room for a place to hide the brick. Under the bed was too obvious, as was the chair, or the toilet tank. He checked the air register, but that was the first place he would look, and figured the police would too. The ceiling was solid. He opened the closet. Then he noticed the baseboard along the tile floor. It was a three-inch-wide piece of wood molding nailed to the wall. He took out his knife and gently pried the board from the back wall of the closet. He stuck the blade between the drywall and the board and worked his way along the wall until he opened an inch-wide space. He reached his fingers in the gap and pulled. Slowly the board separated from the wall with four finishing nails protruding. There was a narrow one-inch space between the floor tile and the bottom of the dry wall. With his knife, he cut the drywall until he enlarged the gap another inch and a half. He placed about twenty of the envelopes into the space between two wall studs along with his old identification and the plastic tracker box. He then aligned the baseboard so the nails were reinserted into their holes and, with his shoe, pounded the board back into place. The paint covering the nail holes had come out, so he went to bathroom and grabbed his toothpaste. He refilled the holes and smoothed the surface. He picked up the small pieces of drywall he had cut and placed them in his pocket, and with a damp washcloth, cleaned the dust from the floor. He stepped back and admired his handiwork.

If anyone can find it, then I deserve to be caught.

Chapter Twenty-Eight
Near Tecate, Baja California, Mexico

Cuervo stood in the parking area watching his son on the field with pride. On the sideline, Donte stood with his arms folded urging Ramon, "Nice pass. Get down the field." It was fortunate El Cuervo had selected him to guard his son because he loved fútbol as much as the six-year-old.

Cuervo knew Donte spent hours in the side yard instructing Ramon. Before every session, Donte had the boy run the agility course, do the strength training, and a little stretching before his foot was allowed to touch the ball. Then it was another half hour of dribbling around the pylons, first with the left foot, then the right, and then alternating with both feet. Finally, the last hour were shots on the net with Donte, a better-than-average goalie, rejecting ninety percent of the boy's attempts. Donte was not easy on the Ramon, but the boy was even harder on himself.

Cuervo knew Ramon loved the training, loved the routine, and it best showed when he went to regular practice because he was years ahead of the other kids. There was even talk of moving him up a league, but Donte convinced him that Ramon would get more playing time at this level, and there was less risk of injury playing with boys his own size.

"Someone is always the best, and why not let it be Ramon," Donte told El Cuervo, insisting his training sessions would keep the boy humble.

"Sorry I'm late," Cuervo said as he shouldered next to Donte.

"I didn't see you coming, El Cuervo. I'm sorry." The bodyguard gazed down at the oversized Adidas athletic bag at his feet. With El Cuervo present, he now had extra reason for quick access to the MAC-

10, spare clips, and diversionary concussion grenade hidden in the bottom compartment below Ramon's sweats.

Cuervo panned the field for his son. "You seemed focused on the game. How is he doing?"

"Good. He is clearly outplaying the others, but he needs to concentrate more on technique. We will continue to practice it until it's second nature. It's just a matter of time. He has the tools and the desire."

"And I thought I had assigned you as his bodyguard. I didn't know you were such a good coach. I know Ramon cares for you. He talks about what you two do together all the time. And when you bought him the Cruz Azul jersey for Christmas, he did not take it off for three weeks. Finally, I said 'Enough.' We have to wash it sometime."

Donte smiled. "He's a good boy. You have raised him well. He tells me all the time he can't wait for the next game because you always come. He loves it when you kick the ball with us at the house. He laughs and says It's funny watching you in your dress clothes dribbling. He does ask about the Señora sometimes."

Cuervo loosed a hearty laugh. "Well, fútbol is not her sport. If Ramon wants quality time with the Señora, he will have to learn to shop."

The halftime whistle blew and the kids ran to the sidelines. Ramon spotted his dad next to Donte and sprinted, leaping into his arms at the last second. Cuervo hugged his son tight with a father's fierce love.

"Papa, did you see me score? I did just what Donte told me to do and it worked."

"I'm so sorry I missed it, but maybe you can show me again in the second half. Donte has the camera and we will record it. Okay?" Cuervo lowered his son to the ground and rustled his hair with vigor. "You better get back to the team, the coach is saying something."

"I hope I don't have to play goalie."

"It's important to learn all the positions," Donte shouted at the sprinting boy. "When you know how hard it is to play goalie, you become better on defense to help your goalie."

Ramon turned, nodded eagerly, and ran to his teammates.

"Coach and psychologist?" Cuervo said.

Donte shrugged. "Full service."

Cuervo wasn't well educated in a formal sense, but he was intelligent. He thought of himself as better than average at most things, but not expert at any—except for two things: reading people and instilling admiration and loyalty.

Cuervo could walk into a room of ten accountants or ten thugs, all of equal skill and experience, and select the one. In the course of two or three months, he would have the person so devoted to him they would willingly sacrifice all to please him.

He was a presence, but never loud or extroverted. He evoked a calm, almost Zen-like quality that inured him to others. They wanted to be around him—to bask in his reflected glory. He would only ask you once. If you refused, you were no longer within the circle. You may be too valuable to lose, but that was different than being included.

He would hear anyone's complaints and would rule evenly in disputes among his men. He also made them much wealthier and was a visionary when it came to adopting new technologies. He found the correct people to "put meat on the bones" of his ideas. They came from all walks of life, but they had to leave their old lives behind and pledge to La Hermandad.

Many urged him to run for public office, but he wasn't a politician—compromise to him was failure. He didn't mind negotiations with a rival so long as the end result was more money for him. He seldom had to resort to violence or threats. While most in his position ruled by fear, he merely used his skills of persuasion. If force was required, there was always Cuda.

Nearing the end of the game, Cuervo checked his watch.

"I have to go. Tell Ramon I saw his goal and I'm very proud of him. I'll see him at dinner tonight. Thank you again, Donte. You are a good friend."

"It's I who thanks you, El Cuervo."

Chapter Twenty-Nine
Cabo San Lucas, Baja California Sur, Mexico

The sidewalks bustled as Chase strolled into the Green Parrot Club just a block east of the marina on Lázaro Cárdenas Road. Three cruise ships had invaded before noon and hundreds of tourists had stormed the beaches.

The music from the live band boomed into the street luring the party-ready crowd. It was only seven p.m., but the club was already shoulder-to-shoulder. The men in their T-shirts, shorts, and flip-flops looked like they had just left the beach, while the women in their halter tops and short skirts were ready for a night on the town.

Chase found an empty stool at the bar and surveyed the scene, his nose immediately assaulted by the smog of tobacco, marijuana, stale beer, and cheap cologne.

The elevated bandstand stood opposite the bar, separated by a large circular dance floor, and row upon row of small round tables in constant rearrangement to accommodate the ever-changing multitude. Banks of lights suspended from the ceiling pulsed to the music. As homage to the seventies, a huge disco ball hung from the ceiling and reflected the beams of laser lights onto the frenzied dance floor crowd. Two large backlit aquaria stood on either side of the bandstand, a rainbow of tropical fish swimming in total disregard for the chaos surrounding them.

"What'll ya have?" shouted one of the battalion of bartenders manning the fifty-foot long bar.

"Gimme a Pacifico for now." Chase handed the man a twenty-dollar bill. "But keep 'em coming."

Chase selected the Green Parrot because of his limited wardrobe. He looked like the typical turista, but he wasn't there for the drinks and entertainment—he had a goal. He needed money and had one source of income, but he couldn't get caught—he was holding too much. Like at the San Quintin beach, he ditched most of his goods in the motel room, but he also stashed a few envelopes in other places.

He spied a couple of guys eyeing the action on the dance floor and settling in for a long night.

Chase grabbed his beer and walked over to the small table.

Sidling up to the pair, Chase asked, "Mind if I sit here?"

"No, it's just us, so far," a twentysomething in a University of Oregon T-shirt said with an expectant laugh.

Chase set his beer on the table and settled into a chair. "You from one of the cruise ships?"

"No, we flew down. We're meeting some friends."

Chase pointed to the Oregon T-shirt with his bottle. "You a Duck?"

"Was. Now I'm paying off the four years of fun."

His taller, blond-haired friend in the Corona tank top and jeans chuckled. "You know you could have worked a little during school. What about you?"

"Here fishing with some friends. Heading for La Paz tomorrow for some yellowtail," Chase said.

"Tail...sounds good to me." The three men shared a laugh.

Chase leaned in closer. "Look, I've got some pretty sweet blow with me. I need to get some cash for the trip tomorrow and a flight back home. You interested?"

The two looked at each other and smiled. "This is too easy. You gotta be a narc or something," Corona said.

"Me? Do I look Mexican? Do I sound Mexican?" Chase said, arching his eyebrows in surprise.

"No, but what about DEA?" Duck asked.

Chase half-rose from his chair. "OK, I'm outta here."

"Wait. If you're a cop, you have to tell us if we ask, right?" Duck asked.

"Then I'm not a cop."

"How much?" Corona asked.

Chase slowly lowered himself back into his chair. In a moment of panic, he realized he didn't have a clue about the street value of coke. He drew a deep breath and cast a furtive gaze to his left, then right. "Look, I need money in a hurry, so I can deal. This stuff's good, but I'll take fifteen hundred for an ounce." He waited for a reaction on the men's faces.

"Man, I've only bought grams. That's more than we can do," Corona said. "Plus, we don't have that much cash on us."

"I thought you had friends? This is uncut, pure. You could sell it yourself and make some bucks."

"I don't know..." Corona said.

With false bravado, Chase began to rise again. "Screw it. I'm wasting my time."

"Hold on now...give us a second."

Chase turned toward the door as the two men conspired.

"We need a little sample before we buy," Duck said.

"Fair. Tell you what. Take this into the bathroom and try it out. If you like it, meet me on the sidewalk by the marina." Chase slipped a small folded piece of paper the size of a matchbook to Duck under the table. "After fifteen minutes, I'm bolting."

Unsuccessful in containing their enthusiasm and buzz, Duck and Corona were out of the bar in ten minutes.

"It's okay, but fifteen hundred is a little steep," Duck said, trying to suppress his guilty laugh.

"This ain't a bazaar. I have no patience for negotiations. Pay or walk."

"Okay, okay, we had to try." Duck reached into his front pocket and began counting out hundred-dollar bills. "What about the stuff?"

"It's hidden. I'm not getting caught holding that much."

"Where?"

"You stay with me, Blondie," Chase said and pointed at Corona. "You walk over to the trashcan by the bench. There's a McDonald's cup with a cover and a straw at the side of the trash. Pull it out and look inside. You'll find an envelope with slightly more than an ounce—I want

117

happy customers. Test it, taste it, and wave to me when you're done. Me and Mr. Oregon here can then part ways and you guys can start the party. Don't be too obvious with all these people around, okay? You won't like the Mexican prison system. If you get caught, you don't know me."

As soon as Chase saw the wave, he turned to Duck and said, "Be good, I'm gone," and left.

Chase sold three more ounces by the end of the evening, each at a different club. He had enough money, for now, and didn't want to press his luck. He never thought he'd be pushing drugs, but he didn't have any alternatives. This was the hand he was dealt, but at least he was playing with house money. He'd head for La Paz in the morning without leaving any tracks.

* * *

After a few hours at their hotel room and carousing a few more clubs, Duck and Corona had made it back to the Green Parrot in search of companionship.

The place was even more crowded than before, if that was possible, and overflowing onto the sidewalk.

They elbowed their way to the bar.

"What can I get you guys?" a bartender asked.

Duck looked up to see the massive hunk of humanity looming over him. The bartender had to be six-foot-six. He had short-cropped marine-style hair, but with long sideburns and a moustache worthy of Poncho Villa. His huge biceps and pecs strained the seams of the tropical shirt in testament that all drugs, even steroids, were available and abundant in this town.

Unable to contain his euphoria, Duck giggled. "Give me a beer and something with an umbrella for him."

"Wow, you guys been eating donuts? And what's with your eyes?"

"Whaddya mean?"

"You got powder on your nose, and I know you didn't get it here. Where'd it come from?"

"Piss off. Get our drinks," Corona said.

Unknown to the boys and to most tourists in Mexico, La Hermandad and the other cartels were heavily invested in the entertainment business. Like the tuna industry, it was the perfect place to launder money. But it was also a very successful profit center. Substantial money was made on the liquor, but even more on the coke, weed, ecstasy, and meth available in the clubs. Even if the organization did not own a particular club, it sold the owner the booze, had the exclusive franchise for drug sales, and, of course, the protection tribute. And one thing the cartels could not tolerate was competition within their territories. It was a concession to free enterprise that was not tolerated.

So, when Bruno, the hulking bartender, saw the coked-out tourists in his bar, but knew he hadn't sold them the snort, he was very concerned and became highly territorial.

Bruno looked down the bar to a couple of guys nursing their longnecks. He gave them a slight nod and, within seconds, the men dragged the boys out the side entrance and into an alley.

The first bouncer grabbed Duck by the neck and pushed him hard against the concrete-block wall of the club. He rummaged through Duck's pockets but found nothing. He turned and stared at Corona and said in heavily accented English, "Empty your pockets."

Corona pulled the small envelope from his back pocket, which was immediately snatched by the second bouncer. He opened the envelope, fingered the powder and asked, "Where'd you get this?"

Duck saw his friend's courage evaporating in a major buzzkill and answered for him.

"From...we bought it from some tourist," Duck said, his voice trembling.

"Where?"

"Here, a couple of hours ago."

"What'd he look like?"

"A gringo. Tall, brown hair, Hawaiian shirt...I didn't—?"

"Is he still here?"

"No. He sold it to us by the marina, then split."

"We discourage drugs in our club. I'll take this. But if you need more, you ask Bruno at the bar, understand?"

"Yes."

The bouncers walked back into the club.

It was more than enough excitement for Duck. He headed back to the room, where the rest of their stash would soothe his wounded pride.

Chapter Thirty
La Paz, Baja California Sur, Mexico

Chase walked through a neighborhood he would normally avoid. He and the other tuna fishermen had docked in La Paz on occasion and he knew the safe spots, and this wasn't one of them. But the taxi driver at the bus station gave him the address and just dropped him off after another thrill ride on the Mexican bus system from Cabo. But not before providing another juicy tidbit of intelligence—coke was going for two grand a gram. Duck and Corona made out like bandits.

Chase checked the address scribbled on the slip of paper for a second time. The numbers matched.

He knocked. After several seconds, the door opened partway and a short man of about sixty-five answered. "Sí?"

"Señor Cabrera?"

"Sí."

"Do you speak English?"

"Poquito—a little."

"I was told you could help me arrange for some papers to go to the States."

Cabrera raised his thick wire-rimmed eyeglasses and squinted hard giving Chase the once-over. "Aren't you American?"

"Canadian, but I need US papers. Can you help?"

"For what purpose?"

"Why do you need to know?"

There was a hint of impatience in Cabrera's sigh. "So, I can get you the right papers. Something good enough for Mexico is not good for the States."

"I can't use my own passport. My ex-wife left with the kids and went back to her home in Texas. She got a restraining order and I can't get past the border. I tried to get papers in Ontario but was told I'd have better luck in Mexico. So, here I am. I just want to see my kids for a couple of hours, that's all."

Chase saw the suspicion in the older man's glare before he finally unlatched the chain and let Chase into the living room, which doubled as his photo studio.

A 35mm camera mounted on a large tripod was in the center of the room and aimed toward a scenic backdrop screen depicting a Pacific Ocean overlook. Photo floodlights flanked the tripod.

"Come this way." Cabrera signaled him to sit at the kitchen table and took a seat next to him. "What do you need?"

"Passport and driver's license would be great, and maybe a social security card. You know this better than I do, what do you think?"

"Those will get you by, all right. But I would suggest a couple of 'confidence' papers for your wallet. Things that add authenticity."

"Like what?"

"A credit card or two. A college alumni ID, a voter card, maybe a membership card to Costco."

"You can do all of those?"

"And more, it just depends on how much you want to spend."

"I've got two thousand dollars."

"We can work with that. Let's get some photographs."

* * *

Chase lay low in his hotel room for the rest of the day, only leaving to hide the stash again and grab a meal. No more clubs for him for a while, unless he needed an infusion of cash. Cabrera said his "order" wouldn't be ready for a couple of days, so he bided his time.

* * *

"Man, it was pure, I mean one hundred percent, uncut. I have never seen anything that good in town," the first bouncer said.

Bruno, the bartender, dipped the tip of his wet index finger into the white powder and rubbed it against his upper gum. "Whoa," he said, flexing his neck backward in surprise. "Are you sure about the test? No lactose, no manitol, no cornstarch?"

"The tests don't lie. Man, it's like pharmaceutical shit."

"How much did they pay for it?"

The first bouncer scoffed. "That's the strange thing. They said they only paid fifteen hundred for an ounce. It could have been stepped on and sold for more than twenty thousand. Those guys were lucky their noses didn't fall off, or they didn't die from tachycardia."

"Who sold it to them?"

"They said some gringo down here on a fishing trip. They met him here at the Green Parrot."

"Some guy from the States comes down here to sell pure coke and at insane prices? That doesn't make sense. He could make much more up north, much more. And who would risk bringing it in here? While it's a unique idea, that makes even less sense. He must have bought it here and didn't have the time or experience to cut it. But who is going to sell him pure stuff and allow him to sell it in our town? Could be an inside job—maybe someone's skimming it from a supplier? You better check around the other clubs, see if anyone else has run into our independent contractor. Find this fisherman. I'm gonna make some calls."

* * *

Lee Wilton, Tulsa, Oklahoma. Chase held up his new driver's license to the ceiling light.

"He died about a year before you were born, so you can go to the courthouse and get a birth certificate. But the social security number has been used many times, so be careful, and don't try to use the passport to get back into the States. I can't duplicate the biometrics. It's safe to use while you are here—no one cares, so no one checks. But you'll have to sneak across the border. I know some people in Tijuana who can help you," Cabrera said.

"Thanks. If you could give me a number, I'll call when I get up there."

"I'm afraid there's a slight fee for the information."

"How much?"

"Let's say, five hundred. Of course, our friend up north will require some money to get you across."

Chase, or Lee, peeled off five more bills from his quickly thinning wad, as the photographer jotted down the coyote's telephone number.

"Ask for Rodrigo. Tell him Cabrera sent you. We have a long-standing relationship."

* * *

Chase was down to a couple of thousand dollars, but it was enough for him to move up from the "No-Tell" motels he'd frequented. The ones where the only identification required were a couple of pictures of Benjamin Franklin.

Some new clothes were in order too. Clothes for more upscale places—the ones with the NO SHIRT, NO SANDALS, NO ENTRY signs.

Chapter Thirty-One
Ensenada, Baja California, Mexico

Nico phoned as soon as he was informed.

"You're sure it's from the *Bella*?" Manny asked.

"That is what the Navy officers said. They called to confirm we were the owners of the skiff. They said two surfers from the States were scouting locations from the cliffs and saw the overturned vessel partially submerged at low tide."

"Why would they report an abandoned boat? The coastline is littered with them."

Nico snickered. "Oh, they were angry and wanted it moved. They complained the beach had a perfect shoal break, but the boat was directly in the way. They wanted someone to haul it off. No one took them too seriously, but an inspector was sent out a few days later. He was able to read some of the boat's name, *Bellita*, with binoculars. They knew of our report about the *Bella* and phoned immediately."

"Were they concerned?"

"No, it was more like they were puzzled. The wreckage was almost due east of the last reported position of the *Bella*."

"So?"

"If it broke loose from the seiner, it should have drifted with the current."

"And?"

"And the current is southeast. It should have drifted almost two hundred miles to the south, maybe even south of Cabo."

"Couldn't a strong wind have blown it shoreward?"

"Yes, maybe a hurricane or tropical storm, but nothing like that has occurred."

"What do you think?"

"Somebody drove it there."

With his new clothes and better accommodations, Chase was confident he blended in better. But now he was almost broke. He had to hit the clubs again. As much as he hated selling the coke, it was, for now at least, his only means of survival. He could try getting a job, but he'd need a work permit, and that would entail going to the US consulate office with a fake passport. He could work without papers—an illegal gringo, he laughed—but where? Maybe a marina, an auto repair shop, but he would not get enough money to hide deep.

Invoking the innate libertarian streak of all fishermen, he rationalized he was merely providing a product to individuals who would get it one way or another. In his small way, he was not enriching the cartels. And while it was technically illegal in Mexico, it was the growth industry, so everyone was doing it.

He worked a couple of the clubs in the evening with some moderate success. He stayed with his tried-and-true method of leaving the drugs out of the clubs other than a few samples now folded into tight aluminum foil packets less than a half-inch square. If busted, he would claim it was only for his personal use and he had bought it at some club in Cabo.

He sat at the bar at the Tequila Sunrise Club on La Paz's Avenue Álvaro Obregón. Alone, nursing a Tecate dark, he sized up the twentysomethings as they strolled in from the waterfront patio. A warm salty breeze drifted in from the bay, which except for the dim running lights of a few distant boats, was a dark void.

He'd thought about sitting on the patio, but it was too open, and the strings of overhead lights didn't afford much concealment. Instead, he skulked in a dark corner.

He eyed a couple of potential candidates. The guys had downed a few rounds and, from the increased volume, they were beginning to enjoy the evening.

With his hands sunk in his jean's pockets, he strode casually over and sat in a chair next to them. "You guys on vacation?"

"Yeah," one said. The other remained silent and Chase saw he was focused on a couple of girls together on the dance floor.

"Interested in some party favors?"

"What are you talking about?" asked the attentive one.

"I have a little coke I'm trying to get rid of before I have to return to the States. It's good stuff, and pretty cheap."

The girl-watcher turned suddenly to Chase. "We're here for the beer. We don't do drugs."

"Okay. Sorry. Didn't mean to bother you."

Chase walked back to the bar, ordered a fresh beer, and returned his focus to the incoming crowd.

"That's him," the girl-watcher said, pointing out Chase to the three bouncers.

The tallest bouncer, maybe an inch or two taller than Chase but easily one hundred pounds heavier, grabbed him by the arm, and pulled him off the stool. Chase tried to regain his balance when a second bouncer grabbed him by the other arm.

"You better come with us," the first bouncer said as they half-dragged, half-carried Chase to a door at the opposite end of the long bar.

The third bouncer opened the storage room door and Chase was thrown face first into the wall as the door slammed behind him.

Chase's arms were pinned behind his back and the left side of his face was flattened against the concrete wall by the huge hands of one of the bouncers. Chase struggled, but the man just pressed harder.

"Where is it?" the third bouncer asked as he rifled through Chase's pockets grabbing his wallet.

"Where is what? What are you guys looking for?

"This," the third bouncer said, fingering the aluminum foil packet in front of Chase's eyes. "Where'd you get it?"

"It's not mine."

"Look, we're not the police. We're not going to arrest you, but we don't want any hoppers poaching in our club. Are we clear? Now, where'd you get it and who sold it to you?" He began going through

Lee's wallet, checking out his driver's license and credit cards, and leafing through the two hundred and fifty in cash.

As he had done in Cabo after each transaction, Chase would return to the hotel, hide the cash in another baseboard niche in the closet, and grab a new plastic bag. Without much cash or coke, he wouldn't be mistaken as a dealer, that was the plan at least.

Chase remained silent.

"Mr. Wilton, you're a long way from Oklahoma and without many friends right now. Again, where and who?" This time, he punctuated his question with a swift punch to Chase's right kidney.

The searing pain ripped through Chase's body. His knees buckled. He would have collapsed if not propped by the other bouncers. He tried to talk but only gasped as his diaphragm quivered in spasm.

The third bouncer walked to the other side of Chase and was about to unleash another punch when Chase, in a barely audible voice, said, "Okay, I'll tell you. Let go and let me sit."

The third bouncer grabbed a chair and set it behind Chase. The other two loosened their grips and Chase slumped into the chair.

Chase bent over his knees straining for breath and in a halting voice said, "I bought it from some dealer in Cabo a few days ago."

"From who?" the third bouncer said as he placed a bit of the powder on his tongue. "This is some good shit."

"Just a guy from a bar. Is it good? I sell it, I don't use it."

"How much more you got?"

"Why? You wanna buy some?"

"Tell you what. We can do a trade. How about this...you give me what you got, and you can live."

"Look, I've got maybe five grams, that's all. You can have it, just let me go."

"Where is it?"

"Along the waterfront. I'll take you there."

"No. I have a better plan. I'll go get it and when I return maybe, just maybe, we'll let you go."

Chase was in no bargaining position. He only hoped letting him go was the path of least resistance for these guys.

"Okay. It's in a crushed Pemex soft drink cup in a trash can down the street," Chase said, trying to recall the precise number of trashcans he had counted. "It's the third one down. It's under a palm tree across from a bench."

After about five minutes, one of bouncers returned. He pulled a plastic bag from his pocket and laid it on the table.

"That's it?"

"Yup. All of it."

"I'm gonna let you go but listen up. Don't ever, I mean ever, try to sell any drugs in any club in this town. And you better be gone by tomorrow." He opened the door and nodded to the other bouncers to release Chase. "Go."

Chase sprinted from the storeroom and the club.

"Ernesto, follow him."

* * *

Chase returned to his motel room and dropped on the bed exhausted from the long night and the beating from the bouncers, but his mind was racing. That was too close. I've got to get out of here.

He had six thousand dollars along with his new passport stashed in the closet, which he figured would last him a few more weeks as he tried to sort things out. But he had to move. He had to find out about the *Bella*.

He had just drifted to sleep when the knock on the door awoke him.

"Señor Wilton, please open up. It's the policía."

"Just a second, I'm getting up."

He walked to the door and looked out the peephole at a police officer flanked by two other men with their backs to him.

Chase asked through the closed door, "What is it?"

"I need to ask you some questions about illicit drugs."

Chase began to sweat. How did the police know his name, how did they know where he was staying, and who told about the drugs?

He looked around the room for anything incriminating.

"Okay." He opened the door an inch, keeping the security chain latched.

In the next instant, the two men barged through, ripping the chain lock off the wall.

Chase recognized the two bouncers as they again grabbed him by his arms.

One bouncer looked over to the policeman. "Gracias, Tito, please close the door."

Tito complied and left.

The bouncers dragged Chase to the bed and forced him to sit. One bouncer watched Chase as the other began tearing the room apart.

Chase's anger was welling, but he knew he had little chance against the two men. He did what the old Navy shrink told him: breathe slow and deep—take control.

"I know what you're looking for, but you got it all at the club. I've got nothing more."

After he searched the drawers, the second bouncer began on Chase's bag. He threw everything onto the floor, checked for a false bottom, and patted the sides for any hidden panels. Chase saw the frustration on the bouncer's face as he threw the bag to the floor.

The bouncer went to the bathroom, where Chase's toiletries were spread out on the narrow counter. With a sweep of his arm, he knocked them all to the tile floor. He looked in the shower, in the toilet tank, under the sink, in the toilet rolls, and under the towels.

He went to the closet, where Chase's two new shirts hung on cheap wire hangers. He looked under the pillows on the top shelf, and in and around Chase's huaraches on the closet floor.

"I'm tellin' ya, you got it all at the club," Chase said, looking up at the bouncer holding him.

The second bouncer continued his search under the mattress and bed and behind the headboard. He took out a small screwdriver and unscrewed the light switch and electrical cover plates and searched behind the outlets. Finally, he unscrewed the register and vent. He used a small flashlight to illuminate the ducts and then, lying on his belly, reached as far as he could beyond the bends in the sheet metal duct.

He looked behind the two picture frames and ripped the brown cover paper to reveal only the back of the cheap artwork.

"Take off your clothes," the first bouncer ordered Chase.

"I told you the truth. You have it all. I got two hundred bucks to get home on, that's all."

"I'm just gonna make sure," the first bouncer said with a glare that sent a shiver up Chase's spine.

Chase removed the T-shirt and stood in only his underwear. "See. Nothing."

"Take those off and bend over."

"Ah, come on. Why would I hide it there? I didn't know you were coming."

"Take 'em off and spread 'em."

Chase complied.

"Get dressed and be out of here in the morning. Got it?"

"I'm gone."

* * *

The bouncers left the room and called the club.

"He's clean, Jefe. Nada."

"Claro. Get back here."

When they arrived back at the club, the third bouncer was still in the back room.

He examined the plastic bag for the third time. It had to be an amateur. The Ochos and Los Moros would not poach their territory—the price would be too high. Maybe in disputed territory like Mexicali, but not on La Península, no...Baja was theirs. Plus, the packaging was lame, just a plastic sandwich bag. The cartels prided themselves on their marketing and advertising. A gram or more came in small, business card-sized zip lock bags with a new logo every month or so. Anything less than a gram came in a paper "fold."

And the product was too pure. He didn't need a test kit to prove it—his tongue was the best gauge. He would report this.

* * *

"What did he look like?" Manny asked over his cell phone from the bunker.

"Just a gringo. Tall, over six feet, very tanned, light brown curly hair, around thirty. Just a typical tourist," the bouncer said.

"Where'd he get the stuff? A hopper? I wanna be sure nobody is moving in on us."

"I didn't find anymore. Maybe he brought it in from the States or maybe he smuggled his own supply from South America."

"That pure? Who'd sell him such refined stuff?"

"I don't know."

"You better follow him. Better yet, bring him to me for some questions, or maybe Cuda should have a few words with him."

* * *

Chase peeked out the window and as soon as the bouncers left the parking lot, he ran to the closet. He pried the baseboard free and reached in the wall for the rest of the coke, his money, and the tracker box. He put them all into his bag, bolted down the stairs, sliding his hands on the railings and skipping every other tread. He wasn't risking it again. He really was gone.

* * *

It was just over two hours when the bouncers returned without Officer Tito. They tiptoed up the stairs. The men positioned themselves on either side of the door. Counting with their fingers, on three both men rammed their shoulders into the door and burst into the empty room, shattering the lock and splintering the weak pine frame.

"Check the bathroom," bouncer two said.

He went to the closet and the saw the three-foot piece of wood molding laying on the floor and the neatly carved but empty niche in the drywall.

"Holy   shit,   that's   where   he   hid   it.   Vámonos!"

Chapter Thirty-Two
Near Tecate, Baja California, Mexico

One of the keys to the success of La Hermandad was its short management tree. The street informants, the halcones, and sicarios were only a few levels from the boss. As a consequence, news filtered upstream very fast. Manny sat at his desk as he digested the three disparate bits of information. He had a call to make.

"El Cuervo, I have something puzzling you should know about."

"Go ahead."

"It may be nothing, if so, I'm sorry to bother you—"

"You sound concerned, tell me."

"I had two reports in the last few days of renegade coke sales at our clubs."

"The Ochos?"

"No. In both cases it was a tourist, maybe the same guy, but the clubs were in different locations—one in Cabo and the other in La Paz."

"Did you get him?"

"They had him in La Paz but let him go when they only found a few grams."

"So, what's the problem? I hear the worry in your voice."

"El Cuervo, the coke was pure, uncut. Where would some gringo get hold of it? I don't think he knew what he had. He could have stepped on it more times and still had quality stuff."

"Has any been reported missing? Do we have a problem employee?"

"Here is the other thing. Nico had a visit from the Navy. One of our tuna skiffs was reported beached near San Quintin."

"Huh..."

"Yes. It was the *Bellita.*"

El Cuervo sat deep in thought, slowly stroking his moustache in slow twists, as his eyes focused on the ripples dancing across the pool.

"It was the *Bella* who helped recover the bales. All but two of them, El Cuervo."

"So, what do you think?"

"It's possible someone got off the *Bella* and drove the skiff to shore."

"And the coke?"

"The missing bales."

* * *

Manny was on the phone to Nico for the next hour after his report to El Cuervo. He had to find out who was selling the coke. If the man was from the *Bella*, then he had seen and knew too much.

"He was Anglo?" Nico asked.

"That's all the information we have."

"But you had him at one time?"

"Yes, but that was before we knew about the *Bella*."

"No one took a cell phone photograph?"

"No."

"Well, let me run through our records. If he was from the *Bella*, it could only be two or three guys. I'll send you the photos and you can have your men in La Paz check them," Nico said.

* * *

Nico was now gratified that the government required photographs and files of all personnel on Mexican-flag vessels.

He shuffled through the files arrayed on his desk. There were three Anglos on the crew: Tommy Beagle, Jimmy Lynch, and Chase Brenner. The others were either Hispanic from Mexico or other Central American countries, or Portuguese Americans.

Nico emailed their photographs, photocopies of their passports, and the crew's maritime papers to Manny.

* * *

"The bouncers from the club are sure the man they saw was Chase Brenner. He was the assistant engineer," Manny said.

134

Cuervo stared at the enlarged passport photo of Brenner that Manny sent him. "Do you have any idea where he could be?"

"No. It has been several days, and we know he had enough coke to sell, so money would not be a problem."

Cuervo paused. "He will need papers, credit cards, and identification to travel. He couldn't barter everything with drugs. Have our men check out the paper mills in the area. The forgers may know something. And check with our friends with the police. See if any tourists fitting his description have been robbed or lost their wallets. One more thing, what about his family?"

"He has a wife and two children in San Diego."

"Better keep a watch on them—see if he tries to contact them. If he has a passport, he may try to get home."

"I'm not so sure of that," Manny said. "He would know if he went home, the word would get out of what happened. More investigations would begin, and he would know that we could not have that. No, he is playing it smart—not involving anyone—but I can't figure out his plan. Maybe it's just to disappear."

Cuervo grinned. "We can help him with that."

Chapter Thirty-Three
Near Tecate, Baja California, Mexico

La Hermandad controlled its coca plantations, transportation and processing of the raw materials, packaging, and the wholesale distribution of the finished product. It jealously guarded its market and expected nothing less than a one hundred percent share. Competitors, particularly rival cartels, were never tolerated.

Along with this vertical integration, Cuervo dreamed often and fondly of a similar horizontal control of the market. But this would require taking over the Ochos and Los Moros, and he knew the battle would be bloody. So, he bided his time. La Hermandad controlled the territory from Baja to Mexicali with its golden corridor into the west coast of the US. The Ochos controlled Mexicali eastward, including Nogales and Juárez, and the Los Moros cartel claimed everything from Laredo and Matamoras eastward. While La Hermandad specialized in coke, with its huge profit margins and low volume, the other cartels were generalists and handled everything—marijuana, heroin, meth, pills, and people. This resource partitioning resulted in mutually assured profits, and greatly reduced risks.

Cuervo had made a fragile and uneasy truce with his rivals and did so only in the interest of La Hermandad, but he still had scores to settle and unresolved debts to collect, the very reason he sat at the head of La Hermandad.

It had begun twenty years earlier when the seventeen-year-old Fernando still lived on his family's small cattle ranch. It had been a good life, but it took all the efforts of his parents and his three brothers and sister just to scratch out a living the bleak desert landscape. They were, however, blessed with a very large extended family, all of whom regularly gathered at the ranch after mass every Sunday and for holidays. It was on the ranch where all the children, especially Fernando and his cousin, Tomás, learned to ride.

Fernando enjoyed the work and especially helping his father herd the cattle between pastures, but he was the third son and would have no chance in ever taking it over. He knew early in life his destiny lay elsewhere.

He did well enough in school, but knew he had little chance to attend college; even finishing high school would be a challenge. He persevered and became the first in his family with a high school degree. He excelled in his business classes and hoped to combine his experience on the ranch with his newfound interest in accounting and marketing—maybe a job with one of the huge agriculture companies that had sprung up since NAFTA relaxed trade between Mexico and the US.

But plans change.

* * *

On an early Sunday morning, Alberto, his oldest brother, had been out in the fields herding a few wayward cows when he encountered an old Ford flatbed truck with a canvas-covered bed stopped alongside a dusty dirt trail.

Alberto greeted the driver.

"Hello," the man said.

"Do you need any help?"

"No. The truck overheated from our long drive. I need the engine to cool before I fill the radiator."

"There's a spring with a cattle trough just down that draw." Alberto pointed east toward a small valley. "Have you got a bucket?"

"We have water in a jug but thank you. I just need to wait. I can't open the radiator cap yet."

"If you need help, our house is just over that rise. My father is an excellent mechanic. He has to be with our old equipment."

Just then, a shot rang out from behind the canvas canopy and Alberto fell dead twenty-five feet away.

The driver leaped from the cab and ran to Alberto's side. The veins in the driver's neck were bulging in anger. "Why did you shoot him, you idiot?"

"He was asking too many questions. He would alert the federales," the man with the rifle said, peeking from behind the canvas.

"No, he wasn't. He was just a boy and just trying to help us. Now the federales will be called for sure."

"Yeah, but we'll be gone. Now shut up and get this truck going. We have to drop this load."

The driver, kneeling beside Alberto's body, crossed himself and rose. He returned to the cab and turned the key partway. He saw the engine temperature gauge was in the green, twisted the key a little farther, and the engine sparked to life. He shifted into first and slowly steered the two-ton truck with its full load of marijuana to the north.

* * *

Tending the horses in the stable, Fernando had heard the distant echo of the rifle report but hadn't given it much thought. It was likely one of the neighbors dispatching a marauding coyote. No one worried until about two hours after Alberto failed to show for lunch.

"He's never late for a meal," their mother said with a foreboding look in her eyes. "Somebody go get him."

It was Fernando who found his brother's body curled on the ground. He collapsed next to Albert, drew his knees to his chest, and rocked back and forth. Tears streamed and anguish wracked his face. He could not let his mother see Alberto this way. He removed his own shirt and gently wrapped it around his brother's shattered head and neck. He looked skyward. "Why, God, why?"

He looked around for any reason his brother would have been killed. He found tread imprints from a large truck. And, perched low in a mesquite bush, shimmering black and green in the afternoon sun, a squawking raven stood sentry over Alberto.

In that moment, he swore to avenge his brother. It was a long and lonely ride back to the ranch house.

The family received little help from the police and even less from the federales. Everyone knew it was the Ochos. It wasn't their land, but it was their territory, and nobody challenged them, not even the other cartels.

He knew it wasn't wise, but it was a much younger, more passionate, and enraged Fernando who started the small guerrilla war on the Ochos—El Cuervo, The Raven, was born.

* * *

Days later, Cuervo returned to the spot where he'd found Alberto's body. Gone was the raven, but not the tracks. The dual tires on the left rear axle were still distinct and impressed deep into the dry clay soil. He misted the tracks by quickly whipping a wet bandanna only inches above the ground, repeating this until the ridges of the track were moist. He ripped a page from a spiral notebook from school and carefully laid it on the wet tire track. The moistened fine clay soil adhered to the paper, replicating the tread pattern. He repeated the process for the inside tire track. After the imprints had dried in the sun, he meticulously traced the tread in pencil to preserve it. For weeks he compared the pattern against every truck he encountered.

* * *

He finally found it outside a mercado where it was unloading produce. It was a perfect match.

As the truck left the market, Cuervo ran up from behind and jumped onto the rear bumper and clambered into the bed. He kept his head down and out of range of the rear mirrors.

The truck drove several miles before it turned onto a small private road leading to a large row of agricultural storage warehouses. Just as it stopped to park, Cuervo scrambled from the bed and slipped from view under the truck.

He lay quietly as the driver left the cab and walked into a small office.

From his vantage, Cuervo could see many trucks backed up to docks and off-loading crate upon crate of produce—lettuce, tomatoes, peppers, corn—collected from area farmers.

He rolled out from under the truck, dusted himself off, and walked toward the warehouses.

In the flurry of activity, he went unnoticed—just another of the dozens of young laborers unloading the trucks.

He saw one warehouse near the back of the property had no trucks and all the doors were closed. He walked around the back of the deserted building. Behind him was nothing but acres of cornfields as far as he could see. The back door was locked and all the windows blackened. He craned his neck toward the roof, where three large ventilation fans rotated slowly in the almost windless day. He shimmied up a rain gutter to the roof, lifted one of the fans, and peered down the shaft to the blackness below.

It would have been a hard twenty-foot drop to a wood floor were it not for the stacks of burlap-wrapped bales of marijuana that broke his fall.

He rolled off the ten-foot pile. His eyes adjusted slowly to the faint light filtering through the shaft. In front of him were three sixty-foot-long rows of bales, each at least fifteen feet wide, spanning the entire length of the warehouse.

He knew immediately what it was, but more importantly, he knew it was why his brother was killed.

Leaving the back door unlocked, he ran and hid in the tall cornstalks until nightfall.

* * *

He wasn't sure how much he'd need, so he crept to the guard's car parked next to the front office three times that night, siphoning off buckets of fuel with a rubber hose removed from the outside spigot.

In the warehouse, the dry rough pine floor absorbed the fluid almost as fast as he poured it, but he completed his circle around the bales.

Timing his exit to outrun the flames, he put a match to a pile of fuel-soaked rags at the far end of the bales. Cuervo watched from the doorway as the small flames consumed the fuel trail around the bales, growing ever larger as the wood floor and burlap added fuel. Smoke clouded his view as he ran from the warehouse, leaving the door open to draw more oxygen.

It had taken longer than he had expected, but after five minutes the thick, intoxicating smoke billowed from the roof vents and through the open door. Cuervo stood mesmerized as the yellow-red flames engulfed everything in their path.

Just before he escaped through the cover of corn, Cuervo, with the heel of his right boot, scrapped a large letter "A" in the dirt road leading to the burning building.

There will be more, he vowed.

* * *

It was common knowledge the Ochos were using the ranch roads in the deserted hill region to smuggle drugs into the US.

The ranchers complained, quietly, among themselves about having to repair downed fences and wrangling runaway cattle. But it was safer to mend fences than inform the federales. A few ranchers took advantage and made very lucrative accommodations.

The warehouse fire whetted Cuervo's revenge. He needed to hit again and figured the drug shipments would be most vulnerable because fewer men would be guarding them and shipments were through deserted areas. But he first had to determine the routes.

Cuervo and Tomás crisscrossed the backcountry on horseback and when they encountered a wide trail or road, Cuervo would grab a handful of dry cement mix from his saddlebag and spread a thin layer onto the roadbed. They would return on different days to see if the tracking dust had been disturbed.

Over the course of a month, they mapped the routes most used by the Ochos and, in another few weeks, they figured out the delivery schedules, but it took more time until Cuervo found exactly what he was looking for—his next target.

The rough road, nothing more than two tire ruts, rose gently to the crest of the hill and then descended steeply into a valley.

* * *

They dug for most of the day; their only companions on the hot dry day were a couple of wayward ground squirrels, an armadillo, and a kettle of expectant vultures.

When they were finished, Cuervo and Tomás, sopped with sweat and dirt, leaned on their shovels and admired their work—a six-by-six-foot trench dug at least four feet deep.

Cuervo toweled his forehead with a bandanna and tossed the pickax and shovel from the pit. He climbed out and extended his hand to assist his cousin.

"You did well, Tomás, but now you must leave."

"But I want to stay with you."

"No, it's too dangerous, and I'll have a better chance to escape if I'm alone. Take the same trail back, and I'll meet you at the ranch in the morning."

"What do I tell your family? You know how they worry since Alberto. How do I explain coming home alone?"

"Just tell them I'm after some of the herd that broke out—you went after some and I went after the others, and we were to meet back at the house."

"I don't know—"

"Believe me, It's better this way. Now, go."

Tomás packed the tools, mounted his horse, and rode off.

Cuervo waited.

* * *

A brown haze settled over the barren hills as dusk fell. Cuervo sat with his legs outstretched and his back against a cool granite boulder, his only respite in the scorching desert heat. The distant rumble of the diesel engine caught his attention. Headlights shot erratic beams into the dark sky with each rut encountered on the rugged road.

The truck wheezed and groaned under a heavy load.

Just as Cuervo hoped, the driver gunned the engine up the small hill to gain speed over the crest. In the dark, the headlight beams shot right over the trench and the driver had no warning until the front wheels and bumper crashed into the hole. The cab lurched forward and slammed into the front of the pit. The momentum from accelerating over the crest flipped the truck onto the driver's side. The unbelted occupants smashed hard against the dashboard and windshield.

The engine continued to whine, and the rear tires spun aimlessly until Cuervo reached in and switched off the ignition. The two men were slumped together across the seat, bloody, broken, and semiconscious. He grabbed the shotgun in the passenger's lap and was tempted to empty both barrels but refrained. Instead, he removed the gas filler cap on the driver's side and the fuel gushed onto the ground and under the truck.

Cuervo doused a rag in the spilled fuel and stuffed it into the filler pipe. He lit the soaked rag with a match. In a clear spot near the truck, he etched another "A" and ran for cover with no concern for the smugglers or the four tons of marijuana now consumed in flames.

He hoped the night would not hide the clouds of black smoke belching skyward.

* * *

Cuervo and Tomás kept the two-man onslaught against the Ochos with a series of hit-and-run forays. The last one involved shooting the tires and windshield of another two-ton truck. But the cartel adapted fast and chase cars now tailed each delivery truck.

Outnumbered and with the element of surprise gone, Cuervo knew it was time to retreat. But he wasn't done with the Ochos yet; he would just change tactics. He would hit them where they would feel it the most—in the pocket.

His guerrilla actions hadn't seemed like much—supplies were still getting through—but it damaged the Ochos more than they realized. Their vulnerabilities had been exposed and their buyers grew restless when the Ochos were not able to capture the culprits. More importantly, the disruption caught the attention of La Hermandad.

La Hermandad's market share expanded but made them immediately suspect by the Ochos—La Hermandad had the most to gain by the Ochos' troubles.

A high-level summit was convened. At the time, La Hermandad was a much smaller operation and its leader, Marquez Espinosa, wanted to keep it that way. He knew the larger the operation became, the less real control he could exert. His lieutenants, eager to advance, thought differently. Without expanding operations, they were stuck, and they knew without adequate manpower, their territory was vulnerable. Espinosa had grown fat and happy on the tributes from his men and was not about to risk a war with the Ochos. He was satisfied if his few tons of marijuana made it into San Diego every week.

Espinosa had been embarrassingly diffident during the meeting with the Ochos leader, Comandante Guerra, and his men cringed. Pegged La Onza—the cheetah—for his penchant for camouflage uniforms, Guerra was a forceful and intimidating presence. Trained as a commando in the Mexican Army, he specialized in psy-ops. He had even attended the infamous School for the Americas and had been able to apply his newly acquired skills during the Sandinista insurrection in Nicaragua. Espinosa was simply no match for La Onza.

Espinosa not only disavowed any knowledge of the attacks on the Ochos, but to the disdain of his own men pledged to assist the Ochos in locating the outlaws. Within a month, La Hermandad captured Cuervo and brought him to Espinosa's ranch. From there, things went awry. Espinosa's top lieutenant was disgusted by his boss' capitulation to Guerra and saw Cuervo's actions as an opportunity the organization should not only embrace, but exploit; they would never get a better chance.

A week later, at an isolated crossroad in the Sonoran Desert, instead of Cuervo, it was Espinosa's body delivered to Guerra's men.

"La Onza will not like this," Guerra's lieutenant said.

"There will be many more things your boss will not like," La Hermandad's new capo replied with confidence.

So began the two-year war, and the slow but steady rise of the young El Cuervo in the ranks of the brotherhood. All of Cuervo's dreams of a quiet life of a businessman had been shattered by the blast from a rifle. It had been the start of the blood feud with Guerra, for now Cuervo knew who was responsible for Alberto's death.

Chapter Thirty-Four
Near El Rosario, Baja California, Mexico

Chase suspected Pescadero Baja was involved—Garza has said as much to the crew—but he had to be sure before he could figure a way out. Maybe he could turn them in to the authorities; maybe he could negotiate a deal with the rest of the coke. He just knew he couldn't live like this for long—someone would eventually catch him—maybe the police, maybe the smugglers.

It had taken a lot of planning and this was his best chance to find out who killed his crewmates. He sat hidden among the dense and spindly manzanita and ceanothus shrubs carpeting the hillside in a blaze of pink and purple flowers. The sweet scent of sage mixed with the briny mist from the sea was a relief from the mildewed interior of the old truck he purchased the previous week—no questions asked—and slept in the past few nights. He'd parked the truck down the coast road a few thousand feet on a little used beach access trail. Even if someone spotted his truck, it could never be linked to him. There was no registration, no bill of sale, and stolen plates.

The trek up the slope was exhausting in the dry, hot scrub, but it was the vantage he needed. Now, all he had to do was wait, and hope they would take the bait. With the cheap binoculars he'd purchased, he scanned the beach where he planted the bricks of coke and the transmitter box.

It had only taken him a few minutes, a cheap soldering iron, and a new set of batteries to fix the transmitter a few days earlier as he waited in a cheap motel room on the main coast road to Ensenada. He soldered the broken lead to the circuit board and resoldered the battery connection. He had carefully reinserted all but the last new battery. If the device worked, he didn't want it sending a signal for more than a

145

second. When he inserted the last battery, a small red LED flashed. Confirmation. The batteries were removed before the next flash.

He returned to the cove near San Quintin, descended the cliff, and retrieved a few more buried bricks. Over the course of a day and a half, he worked his way down the coast road. At each of five stops, he walked to the water's edge, inserted the batteries into the transmitter, let it signal the satellite for a few minutes, and then removed the batteries again. This he repeated at each stop until he reached his present destination—the one meeting his needs.

* * *

In the bunker the day before, the satellite technician saw it first. The white light flashed on the large monitor. At first, he thought it was some anomaly, some phantom signal, but it remained on the screen for a few minutes. He noted its position after the signal disappeared. He thought it strange, but not enough to involve Manny, at least not yet.

When it happened a second time just four hours later and further south, Manny was alerted.

"What is it?"

"Better get down here," the technician said.

Manny, rubbing his chin, squinted over his reading glasses at the white dot for about a minute before it disappeared again. "What was that?"

"It's from one of the lost bales. This is the second signal I've had. It's drifting down the coast."

"But why is the signal in and out?"

"Maybe the antenna is caught on some debris and is only coming to the surface occasionally. Or maybe it's a bad connection. I don't know. We'll have to get it back before I can tell for sure."

"Or before anyone else finds it. Keep close watch if it shows up again. I'll send someone out to see if they can recover it." Manny's eyes were locked on the now ghost image on the monitor.

* * *

It took two more calls before Cuda, who was making sure the last shipment got safely to the tunnel in Tijuana, was in his car and heading south.

Manny texted him the coordinates and Cuda downloaded the positions into his handheld GPS unit. By the time he reached the isolated cove, he had four positions recorded. But now he had a fifth, and Manny said it had been steady for over an hour, unlike the other transmissions.

The road sliced through a narrow coastal terrace sweeping gently to the ocean. To the east, the terrace rose abruptly to the high coastal foothills. Cuda parked his car in a wide spot along the shoulder. The beach was just three hundred yards from the road, and less than a quarter mile between the north and south spits bordering the cove.

His GPS was accurate to only about fifty feet, so Cuda knew he'd have to search for the bale. He only hoped it wasn't beyond the surf line or, worse, submerged.

He followed the track on the GPS's LCD screen until he was on the exact position but saw nothing. He stopped, removed his black leather shoes and socks, and rolled his slacks to his knees. He twisted his feet a few inches into the cool wet sand. He first walked north, searching the beach for any signs of the bale. The sound of the crashing waves was interrupted by squawking gulls as they protested their temporary dislocation from favored roosts. He took in a deep breath. Like the cool sand, the salt breeze was a refreshing break from stale air of the confined car, but the crashing surf invoked bad memories of his queasy stomach on his last trip to sea.

The beach was cluttered with driftwood, rotting piles of kelp, flotsam, and trash. Cuda swatted away thick swarms of sand flies and gnats in his path. After about thirty paces, he turned and headed south. He carefully examined each structure, lifting logs and kelp, and kicking the sand.

Partially buried in the moist sand near the surf's edge was a thin coated wire. Cuda picked it up and began to follow its trace. He saw the two bricks, still wrapped in thick plastic, but separated from the bale.

Further still, he found another brick, then a fourth. Finally, he found the small black plastic box at the end of the wire.

He paced the beach for another thirty minutes but found nothing more. Retrieving his shoes and socks, he returned to his car. El Cuervo would not be happy most of the bale was gone. But, most important, he recovered the transmitter.

* * *

Chase watched as the big man slogged along the beach, strangely out of place in his dark dress trousers and white shirt. All he was missing was a tie and coat—not the clothes of a beachcomber. Chase laughed. But what caught his attention was the man's sharp triangular face, high prominent cheekbones, wide forehead, and pointed chin. His hair was jet black as were his almost continuous eyebrows. Even through his binoculars, Chase shivered at the man's cold, menacing glare. Was this the big man from the service boat? Was he the one responsible for the death of his crewmates? He couldn't be sure; he'd only seen a faint silhouette from the skiff.

The man took the bait and drove off. Chase took careful note of the man's green Toyota Corolla. He tried to read the license plate, but all he saw was the last three digits—7-2-1. It wouldn't be a difficult car to follow on the coast road.

Within five minutes after the man departed, Chase was halfway to his truck, and in another ten minutes, he was speeding north in pursuit of the Corolla.

He had sinking feeling he knew where he was heading.

Chapter Thirty-Five
Point Loma, San Diego, California, USA

What she hated most was waking. In sleep, she found respite; in dreams her life was perfect again as she relived happier times with Chase. But as the flaxen rays of sun filtered through the curtains, she stirred to consciousness and the sadness returned. She wanted nothing more than to pull the covers over her head and sleep, isolate herself from the whole world in her linen cocoon. But she couldn't; the kids needed her, and as brave as they pretended, she knew they were confused and their hurt profound.

Her feet barely touched the floor as she marched to the kids' room. In her best drill sergeant imitation, she shouted, "Okay you guys, you've had enough sleep and we have a busy day ahead of us."

"Oh, Mom," Kevin said in a groggy voice before pulling the Spider-Man sheet over his head in protest. "Can't I sleep just a little longer?"

"No way. You've got school. Hurry and get dressed. Whoever is first to the table gets to pick where we eat tonight."

Hearing that, Denise sprung from bed and double-timed it to the bathroom. It was her only chance for Taco Bell, which both Kevin and Maria tried to avoid. Denise was always outvoted, but now she had a fighting chance.

Denise beat Kevin by three minutes and was munching her Lucky Charms when her brother made it to the kitchen.

She bobbed her head from side to side as she walked her fingers tauntingly over the sides and top of the cereal box. "Let me think, where do I want to eat? McDonald's...no. Wendy's...no. Maybe Taco Bell."

"You mean Taco Hell," he said.

Maria chided her son. "Hey, that's enough of that language, young man. You lost fair and square. Maybe you'll get ready faster tomorrow."

Thirty minutes later, Maria was back at the house after dropping the kids off at school. She was already exhausted but hadn't done anything yet. The stress and loneliness were wearing her down. As much as friends and family tried, she could not get over Chase's death, nor did she want to. She couldn't live without him.

In her darkest moments, she thought the unthinkable. Maybe it was a mortal sin in the church's eye, but at least she would not be suffering in this life. Could eternal damnation be worse? A merciful God would reunite her with Chase. It would be easy—a warm bath, a sharp knife, a painless sleep.

But Denise and Kevin always broke the spell—she couldn't orphan them. She owed it to Chase. Just the thought of her children brought a smile to her face, however fleeting. It was just enough to get by, just enough to make it through another day. It had to get better.

Chapter Thirty-Six
Near Tecate, Baja California, Mexico

"Estrella, two iced teas, por favor," Serena shouted from the patio before returning her attention to her husband. "Fernando, we have discussed this a thousand times. Ramon must learn how to ride. I had been on a horse for two years and in jumping competitions when I was his age. My family was riding the plains of Seville two hundred years before coming to the New World. It's our tradition; It's his heritage." She stood with her hands perched against her hips.

Cuervo could but smile at his wife's insistence and marvel at her beauty even when angry, or maybe especially then. She had the proportions and symmetry that separated beautiful from stunning. Her high cheekbones, full ruby lips, and thin, delicate nose were set in a flawless oval tawny face. Her black eyebrows perfectly accented her glistening black-flecked emerald eyes. Her lustrous black hair—the result of at least one hundred brush strokes a day—cascaded in waves down her back. Thin and athletic at one hundred and ten pounds, she could easily be mistaken for a fashion model if not for her slight five-foot, two-inch frame, though most of her wardrobe was borne of the highest fashion houses.

Serena fidgeted her interlocked fingers and drew her eyebrows tight. "You know I have spoken with him about this, but he cares only about one thing—fútbol. I can't even get him to go see a movie. That boy would rather kick a ball than eat. It's Donte. He is a bad influence."

Cuervo issued a chiding laugh. "It's the other way around. Poor Donte does not stand a chance against the relentless Ramon."

"This is funny to you? How is he to develop into a gentleman without the proper training? I sometimes thank God my father cannot see this. He would be appalled. Fútbol is something we watch; It's not the game for our kind."

"Our kind? I played much fútbol, and I still like it. Am I not our kind?"

"You know what I mean. He needs a proper education, and I don't just mean school. I mean refinement, the social graces. He must someday be a man of great distinction to attract a proper wife." A tear trickled down her cheek.

Cuervo knew this was a fight he could never win. Even with the totality of La Hermandad to draw upon, he was as helpless to her onslaught as a spring lamb.

"I'll call Tomás. We can have Ramon stay on the ranch over the holiday. He will have the boy riding like a gaucho in a week. It would also do him some good to learn to care for our horses—cleaning the stalls is always a character builder. It keeps you close to nature, to your horse. I did as much as a child. Would that be satisfactory to you?"

"It's a start. Thank you."

Cuervo sighed as he saw her body relax.

Serena walked to the kitchen door and clapped her hands loudly. "Estrella, hurry with the tea." She turned to her husband and confided quietly, "That woman may be too old for this job."

Cuervo raised his eyebrows and changed the subject.

"Serena, it will be you who tells Ramon he can't play fútbol for a week. And please be sure I'm out of the house. I know he inherited his temper from your side." Cuervo smiled, lowering his head and peering from the top of his eyes.

"That should not be a problem because you are never home," Serena said, her lips pursed and her arms folded in defiance across her chest. "I never know where you are or what you do. You never involve me with your business or any of your colleagues except for that...that, what do you call him, Cuda, you send here. You know I'm smart, at least as smart as he is, and could be helpful if only you would let me."

"Serena," Cuervo said in calming tone, "you must know my business is dangerous. I must associate with people who would like to see me fail—some would like me dead. I have with great pains harbored you and Ramon from these realities. I hope I have provided for all your needs. You are never wanting for anything."

"I know, my darling," Serena said, stroking Cuervo's cheek, "I'm sorry. I just sometimes feel trapped. I feel worthless. I just want to do more. Go out in the evenings, travel, enjoy our wealth. All I ever do is shop, care for Ramon, and look after our home—the servants can do that—I...I want to be needed, to help you, that's all."

"You help me every day in ways you never know. It's my fault I do not tell you enough. For that, I truly apologize. What you do for me cannot be measured, but I promise you this, there will be a day when you will know much more of our enterprise. But for now, I ask you to understand that we must keep our lives private for our safety and the success of the business."

"You promise I'll be part of the business?"

"If that is what you really want."

Chapter Thirty-Seven
Ensenada, Baja California, Mexico

Chase caught up to the Corolla and tailed it from a safe distance. He was relieved when it merged onto Highway 1, since he would be less conspicuous with more vehicles.

With traffic and one stop, it took two and a half hours to drive the hundred and twenty miles to Ensenada.

Chase lost sight of the Corolla in Ensenada's congestion, but thought if his instincts were correct, the man might head to Pescadero Baja's headquarters on the harbor. He still had trouble processing his employer's treachery.

He parked within sight of the building. He did not see the Corolla in the parking lot but decided to keep watch for a while. Maybe the big man got caught in traffic.

It was three in the afternoon and would be another two, maybe three hours, before all the employees left for the day. Fortunately, there were only a couple of tuna seiners in port, and the crews would be staying on the boats except for a little R&R at the local bars. If he were lucky, maybe he could make a little midnight visit to the office—but not today. He had to reconnoiter and he had to stay hidden—he was a familiar face and known by many of the mechanics and office staff. He even saw his truck still parked in the lot.

* * *

The next morning Nico was already in the office and downing his second coffee when Cuda arrived at six thirty and tossed the daypack onto his desk.

"What's in this?" Nico asked.

"See for yourself."

154

Nico averted his eyes from Cuda and focused on the pack. He pulled out a couple of bricks, and then saw the black case. The smirk seemed out of place on Cuda's normally dour face.

"El Cuervo will be pleased you found this."

"I'll deliver it to him. You make sure the bricks make it north. Call Manny, let him know I'm coming to the ranch."

"Why?"

Cuda removed the cover on the transmitter. "That's why."

Nico stared at it intently and shot Cuda a quizzical look. "What's the problem?"

"Look at the wires. They have been repaired. See all the excess solder. This is not how these were originally constructed. I noticed it last night at the hotel."

"Maybe Manny or someone at the ranch repaired it. That would explain why it only worked part of the time."

"But why would the seals be broken? Manny needs to inspect it—to see if it's his work."

"And if it isn't?"

"Then who repaired it and why? My guess is that Brenner guy. We must find him."

"What about Jonny? What are we going to do with him? The other sub is due to off-load in a couple of days, so we have at least one more experienced skipper now."

"I'll have a little talk with him. His old crew told me some interesting things about good old Captain Jonny."

Nico shot Cuda an uncomprehending look. "About what?"

"Benji thought Jonny sunk his sub intentionally."

"That's crazy. Why?"

"I don't know, but I intend to find out. Is there a quiet place to keep him overnight? I don't want him going anywhere."

"We have some rooms down below. But don't do anything until after the workers leave for the evening."

Chapter Thirty-Eight
Ensenada, Baja California, Mexico

Jonny paced like a caged cheetah between steel bunks in the cramped crew's quarters at Baja Pescadero's headquarters. He wasn't surprised that Joaquin and Benji hadn't returned—he expected as much knowing Cuda's reputation. But now he was concerned about his own neck. First, Nico was restricting his activities, having him move out of the motel to live in the crew's bunkroom. Then there was the delay in getting him new papers, a routine task. Nico was evasive, never offering a straight answer. Jonny always figured that the company needed him, but now he wasn't so sure, and unless he got a new boat soon, his entire plan was out the window, maybe worse.

Chapter Thirty-Nine
Ensenada, Baja California, Mexico

Chase waited until everyone had left—all but Nico, whom he knew was the one who always locked up.

The building was an old structure from the 1930s. It was shaped like a giant Quonset hut with two-story concrete-block walls topped with an arched metal roof. It had a pair of forty-foot-tall steel doors on the far end facing the harbor. Large vessels were hauled into the open bay on the steel rails from the launch ramp. The bay also housed the repair shops, machine shops, and warehouses for Pescadero Baja's fleet. The building's smaller second floor extended about a quarter of the distance of the first floor and housed the administrative offices and a narrow balcony overlooking the work bay.

Chase hadn't been into Nico's office, but had been in the adjacent office with the clerks who helped him with his income statements for his US taxes. It was something Chase always dreaded—it was complicated working for a foreign corporation in a foreign country while still living in the US. And, of course, both the US and Mexican governments sparred over his earnings.

Chase knew about the small alcove under the staircase near the front entrance, and this is where he hid in the shadows of the dark and almost deserted building.

The worn wooden steps creaked over Chase's head as Nico descended in a slow and deliberate pace. When he reached the bottom, Chase heard Nico switch off the second-floor lights. The thick wooden front door closed, and Nico's keys clinked as he locked the deadbolt from the outside.

Chase realized his predicament. He hadn't had time to check for any alarms. If the building had motion detectors, he was dead meat. If the windows and doors were wired, he'd set them off getting out. To be captured by Pescadero Baja now carried the death penalty.

What the hell, he thought. How are they going to explain this lone survivor of the lost tuna boat, unless the police are in on it, too?

He took first tentative steps from the shadows, stopped, and waited. No alarm. He took a few more steps. Except for his excited breathing, it was silent. He let out an audible sigh and made his way up the stairwell. Just enough light penetrated the windows for him to negotiate his way into Nico's office.

The office was crammed—a large desk, several chairs, a couple of tables, and three walls lined end-to-end with file cabinets. Document storage boxes were stacked haphazardly atop the file cabinets.

He sunk into Nico's chair and surveyed the room. He didn't know what to look for, or where to begin. Maybe there was something in the files on the *Bella*. He figured there must be recent entries with all the investigations, insurance claims, and family inquiries. He focused on the storage boxes and began to read Nico's neatly printed labels from top to bottom. Although written in Spanish, it only took three minutes to find the box labeled *Bella* Inquiry.

He removed the cover. It contained a series of neatly organized files—personal, la póliza de seguros, investigación, archivos de mantenimiento, comunicación por radio. He didn't know what he expected to find but assumed they would have scrubbed any incriminating evidence.

His conversational Spanish was much better than his reading skills, but he understood most of the papers except for the legal language in the insurance files. He gleaned just enough to realize the proceeds from the life and accident policies had been promptly paid to the crew's survivors, including Maria. The faster they were paid, the less likely the families would dig deeper. Chase was sure the company didn't want any deep dives by private investigators or lawyers.

He perused the personnel files. Each crewman's file contained a copy of his application, job history, pay records, copies of licenses and passports, and family contacts.

A small two-by-three-inch color photograph was stapled into the inside front cover of each file folder.

He grabbed Gus's record and stared at his photograph. A deep loneliness and loss enveloped him. A single tear was dispatched with the swipe of his hand. How he missed the pugnacious, crusty old guy. Only a few knew what a warm heart had pounded under his crass exterior. He remembered the sheer joy in Gus's eyes when he played with Kevin and Denise, and the kids could see right through the gruff veneer to the marshmallow below. Chase removed the photo and placed it in his wallet.

He promised he'd someday tell the kids it was Uncle Gus who saved daddy's life. But he imagined the conversation with Gus: "You old fart. You'll do anything for a little attention. I didn't need your help. I could have figured it out."

"Not so fast, Navy boy. You don't have the sense God gave a squid to survive. Without me, you'd have jumped from the skiff and would have been mincemeat. You're just lucky I took pity on your sorry ass. And it wasn't for you, dammit—you ain't worth the skin you fill. I did it for Kevin and Denise—they need a dad, and you better take care of them."

It was too much for Chase.

He checked his own folder—Brenner, Charles A. There were copies of insurance papers, cancelled checks, releases signed by Maria, but something was missing—his photograph. He replaced the file, covered the box, and returned it to the stack.

There had to be something. He switched on Nico's computer and after a few seconds the monitor glowed to life. He scrolled through the introductory boot-up screens to the log-on page. Chase tried a few passwords, but nothing worked. He switched it off.

He looked at Nico's desk pad calendar and noted the arrival and departure dates for a few tuna boats, notations about ordering provisions, scheduled loading at the fuel dock, and some unreferenced telephone numbers. He shuffled through the papers from the wire in-and-out baskets. Most were invoices from suppliers ready for payment.

A computer printout for a hotel reservation at the Grande Vista Hotel caught his attention. It was dated about a week ago, but the reservation was for a full two-week period, including today.

He had been correct—not much to find. Maybe the big guy knows something, he thought. But now he had a real challenge—how to get out.

He walked down the stairs and through the hallway leading to the open bay. Both side doors were secured with deadbolt locks with no way to unlock without the key. He walked to the rear of the bay to the sliding steel doors to the harbor. They were chained from the inside. Chase figured both the lock and chain would be easy to cut with a grinder, but he didn't want anyone knowing he had been snooping around.

The rows of windows on both sides of the building were the ventilator type, hinged at the top to open outward. Chase jumped onto a workbench and unlatched a window. It was about a ten-foot drop to the concrete below.

Suddenly, he froze. He heard something. There it was again, very faint, like a wounded animal. He opened the window full and stuck his head out but heard nothing. He stepped down from the bench. It was coming from the front of the building, but he had been there just a few minutes before. He walked slow and strained to isolate the sound. It grew louder as he neared the front entrance. There were a series of doors on either side of the hallway between the front door and the open bay. They were labeled in Spanish—engine parts, ship's gear, food supplies, and electronics.

Chase stood in the middle of the hall. He heard it again; it was coming from the left side. He pressed his ear against each door and finally found the source.

"Why are you doing this?" Chase heard from a trembling voice.

"I asked the questions, you just answer," Chase heard in reply, followed by a loud slap and then a long plaintive moan.

"I think you scuttled the boat on purpose and I want to know why."

"What are you talking about? I saved the shipment; the boat was sinking."

Chase heard another sharp blow and a muffled groan.

"I'll get the truth from you one way or the other. Now why did you sabotage the boat?"

"You're crazy. I didn't—"

* * *

The fist landed with a dull thud on his ribs. Jonny gasped for air and wanted to scream, anyone would, but he knew better. His stepdaddy taught him the longer he screamed, the harder the beating. And in school, he was the target of all the bullies. He never stood a chance against them. They beat him because he was small, because he was poor, and because he looked different. When he wasn't in a fight, they taunted him without mercy—the little black boy in the white neighborhood. But Jonny learned to suck it up, to stay quiet, and not give them the satisfaction of knowing his pain.

"You see, Jonny, I became friends with your crewman, Benji—it really was so terrible that we lost him at sea after the recovery. We had long talks together on the service boat. He seemed to think you sunk the boat intentionally."

"Why would he say something so stupid? I would never—"

Jonny took another blow and issued a long, low grunt.

"Let us not speak ill of the dead, Jonny. Seems our friend Benji watched as you opened the ballast tanks while you thought he was sleeping. He couldn't figure out why you'd mess with the tanks while recharging."

"Look, Cuda, I don't know what Benji saw, but he was wrong. Tell ya what, I have a plan that will make us both rich. More money than you'll ever get with La Hermandad."

"Yeah, Jonny. You're gonna make me rich. Maybe I think you're just stalling. Tell you what, I'm gonna start breaking your tiny little fingers. Maybe I'll get some answers that way."

* * *

Chase knew someone was being beaten but didn't know what to do. He went over to the workbench and looked for a weapon. The workers had locked their tools in the crib and all he found was a two-foot-long piece of lumber on the bench used to prop a window open.

He picked up the board and returned to the storage room door. He had no idea who was being beaten, why, or by whom. He wasn't sure if he should get involved or even if he should care. He had nothing to gain by interfering. But he also couldn't just stand around and ignore it. He thought of Gus—he didn't have to do what he did, but he did, and I'm alive. But Gus was my friend, and I don't know who is behind the door.

Chase knew in his heart it didn't matter—something else compelled him.

He quietly twisted the doorknob. It was unlocked. Whoever was administering the beating wasn't too worried about anyone bothering him.

Chase opened the door just a crack to see if anyone noticed. After a few seconds, he opened it a little further—still nothing. Finally, he opened it enough to get his head through to see.

Seated in a fold-up chair facing him was the pained grimace of a small black man with his arms tied behind his back and his ankles tied to the legs of the chair. From the cold light of the overhead fluorescent fixture, Chase could see the man's dark face was smeared with blood and his eyes were bruised and swollen.

A very large man with his back to Chase towered over the restrained victim. With his fully extended right arm, he punched the helpless man with such force the sound reverberated in the confined storage room. The small man's head recoiled, and a spray of blood spattered the wall.

"Make me rich, what a laugh. You know what's even funnier? Captain Jonny with a plan," the big man said.

Chase had seen enough. The little man couldn't survive much more.

"Now, why did you sink it?"

"Benji is wrong," the little man stuttered. "I...I—"

Another punch, this time from the left hand, and the little man's head fell backward, limp.

A fiery rage boiled over Chase and he threw open the door. In a single motion, he leapt across the floor and slammed the wooden club with all the power he could muster into the big man's right temple. He lifted the club again as the big man's knees buckled and struck him a second time, a direct hit on his left jaw. Then a third. The man turned toward the source of the assault.

As he looked straight into Chase's eyes, Chase saw an instant of recognition register on the man's face before his eyes rolled back and he slumped unconscious to the floor.

At that moment, Chase also recognized him—it was the big man from the beach, the man he'd lost in traffic just a few days before, the man he wanted to question.

Chase dropped the club and stepped over the hulk obstructing half the room to the dazed man slumped in the chair. A trickle of blood flowed down the man's cheek and he reeked of stale sweat and fresh fear.

Chase placed a hand on the man's shoulder. "Are you okay? Can you talk?"

The man shook his head violently to regain his senses. "We've got to get out of here. He'll kill us both."

"He'll be out for a while," Chase said, untying the man's ankles and then his hands. "Can you walk?"

"I don't know." He tried to rise from the chair but teetered and Chase steadied him.

"Stand here for a minute and get your balance. I need to tie up your friend. Here, hold this on your eye." Chase passed him a handkerchief.

"He's no friend of mine," the little man said as he kicked the unconscious hulk in the gut with all the strength he had left.

"Who is he?"

"They call him Cuda. He works for my boss."

"Nico?" Chase asked as he searched the pockets of the downed man. He grabbed a cell phone and a wallet, both of which he placed in his own pocket.

"You know Nico? No. He works for Nico's boss. He's their enforcer."

"Why was he beating you?"

"He thinks I know something. Get me out of here. He has other men around."

"Who are you?" Chase asked, propping the man as they headed out the door.

"Everyone calls me Jonny. You?"

"Lee."

"I haven't seen you before. How do you know Nico?"

"I used to work here—it's a long story."

Chase led Jonny to the window he had opened earlier.

He boosted Jonny up on the workbench and through the opening. He held him until he was out of the window, then let him go. Jonny winced from the four-foot drop.

Chase then lowered himself until he was fully extended and dropped to the pavement.

Chase held Jonny's right arm to support him as they half-ran, half-limped to his truck.

"How'd you find me in there?" Jonny asked as they left the harbor.

"I was looking for something and I heard you, barely heard you. Why didn't you scream?"

"My stepdaddy, the third one, beat the emotion right out of me. I reckon I learned to suffer in silence."

"I guess so. Who's this Cuda?"

Jonny's chest heaved as he struggled to catch his breath. "I can't tell you. Just forget you ever saw me or the warehouse or they'll come after you, too."

"If I'm gonna die, I'd kind of like to know why. This wouldn't have anything to do with a cocaine shipment, would it?"

164

Jonny turned to Chase, his eyes wide. "How'd you know about that?"

"I saw the Cuda guy on the beach picking up some bricks that had floated to shore."

"Who exactly are you? The police?"

"No. I just need to find out who Cuda is and who he works for."

"Why?"

"Later; first, I need to know right now how you are involved in this."

* * *

Once they were a safe distance from the wharf, Chase parked and pulled Cuda's phone from his pocket. He scrolled through the phone's call log but didn't recognize any of the numbers.

He tossed the phone to Jonny. "Recognize any of these?"

Chase pulled the wallet out. Not much was there, just a couple of credit cards, a driver's license, about five hundred dollars in cash, and a hotel key card.

He eyed the card. It was the hotel on the reservation confirmation he'd found in Nico's office.

"I got a pretty good idea where this Cuda guy is staying. We'd better get over there fast before someone starts looking for him," Chase said.

"I know some of these numbers."

"Write them down before I pull the battery—I don't want them tracking the phone."

* * *

Chase had the keycard, but not the room number, and the front desk wouldn't give it out.

They pulled into the parking lot of the Grande Vista. It was easy walking distance to Pescadero Baja. As he approached the front entrance, he spied Cuda's car, the one he'd tailed from the coast road. It had the same green color and the same last three digits on the license plate.

Chase strolled into the large open lobby. It was a statement in glass. Floor-to-ceiling windows surrounded the lobby on three sides and afforded an almost two hundred and seventy-degree panorama of the beach and marina area. The long front desk was a two-inch thick slab of glass atop a translucent glass brick base illuminated in pale sea mist green lights. In the far corner near the entrance to the bar and restaurant stood a large glass sculpture almost reaching the ceiling. A wall of water cascaded down the sculpture into a blue pond filled with orange, gold, red, and white koi swimming unperturbed by the plunging waterfall. For a moment, Chase also felt like the koi—trapped, but in a larger tank.

He walked with purpose to the bar, nodding to the clerk as he passed the front desk. Next to the bar's entrance was a hallway leading to a bank of elevators.

He took a stool at the bar. Only a quarter full, most of the patrons were nursing drinks and waiting for dinner seating. Even with the sparse crowd, it was a couple of minutes before the bartender approached.

"Can I help you, sir?" the bartender asked, muddling a sprig of mint at the bottom of a cocktail glass.

Chase grabbed a handful of peanuts from a glass bowl on the bar. "Just a Tecate for now, thanks. I'm waiting for a friend. How late is dinner served?" He tossed a few nuts into his mouth.

"Until midnight. Can I get you a table or would you like to see the bar menu?"

Chase crunched on the nuts. "No. Not yet. Just the beer for now, thanks."

In contrast to the light and airy lobby, the bar was designed as a subterranean grotto. The walls and ceiling were sculpted to appear as a cave with nooks, crannies, and even a few faux stalactites suspended from the ceiling. The paint was granite gray with black-and-white marbling. The casual lighting over the bar subtly highlighted the rows of multihued exotic liquors on the shelves. The rock-shaped sconces on the walls cast a dim wash over the walls and a warm glow from the aquarium shimmered through the bar. The booths were steel gray leather with smoked glass tabletops. This was a place to not be seen if you chose—shadows and anonymity.

Chase waited ten minutes before he waved for the bartender.

"My friend is late. Would you mind calling him?"

"What is his room number?"

"I don't think he told me. His name is Aleta, Enrique Aleta."

The bartender called the front desk and asked the clerk to call Mr. Aleta's room. After about a minute, the bartender cupped the mouthpiece and said there was no answer in the room.

"Damn. I'll bet he's in the shower. Could I have a message delivered to his room?"

"Certainly," the bartender said, passing a notepad and pen to Chase.

Chase wrote out his message. The bartender phoned the front desk.

In a few seconds, a bellman was at the bar. Chase handed him the message along with a ten-dollar bill. "Could you slip this under Mr. Aleta's door? I'll wait for him in the restaurant."

"Yes, sir. Thank you."

* * *

The bellman walked to the elevators and stepped into the first arriving car, along with Jonny, who had entered the hotel ten minutes after Chase.

Jonny moved to the rear of the elevator and watched as the bellman pressed the fourth-floor button.

The bellman turned to Jonny. "What happened to you, sir?" He frowned inquisitively at the battered man.

"I was in a little traffic accident," Jonny said. He had rinsed the blood from his face in the hotel's bathroom off the lobby, but he couldn't hide the bruising and swollen lips.

"I'm so sorry for you. What floor, sir?" the bellman asked.

"Thank you. I'm fine, but you should see the car. Number four, please."

When they arrived on the floor, the bellman held the door for Jonny, who turned immediately to his right. He figured he had a fifty-fifty chance. He walked a few steps and then turned, patting his pockets in search for a nonexistent keycard. This went unnoticed by the bellman, who had turned left.

Jonny watched the bellman as he walked down the hallway.

The bellman stopped in front of a door, gently knocked, and waited. When no one answered, he stooped down and slipped the note under the door.

From the distance, Jonny could not tell the exact room number, but he had enough landmarks—potted plants and a wall mirror—to find the room.

He turned again and headed to the stairwell at the end of the opposite hallway. He walked down the four flights to the lobby and into the restaurant where Chase was seated and waiting.

"Did you get it?"

"Yes. It's on the fourth floor, south hallway. It's the sixth or seventh door on the right. It's just past a large potted plant."

"No room number?"

"No. The bellman was there. But it'sone of two, and the card will only work in one."

"Okay. You stay here and order dinner. I'll be back in fifteen minutes."

* * *

The keycard worked in the second lock. Chase entered the room and pocketed the note on the floor.

An empty suitcase was open on the luggage rack. Chase patted the bottom and sides for any compartments. He opened the drawers to the dresser. Cuda had neatly stacked his clothes in the three drawers. In the closet, Chase found two of pairs of black trousers, some short-sleeved white dress shirts, a light windbreaker, and a pair of black leather shoes. A small safe with digital keypad was bolted to the shelf above the clothes. He tried the handle; it was locked. He entered the room number on the keypad, then 1-2-3-4, then 0-0-0-0. Nothing.

He checked the small desk, the bedside tables, and the bathroom.

It was then Chase realized he had found no car keys in Cuda's pockets when he searched him, nor any in the room.

He looked again toward the safe. His car, Chase thought.

Back in the restaurant, Jonny was halfway through a thick rib eye he should have ordered raw and applied directly to his swollen face. He looked up when Chase returned. "Anything?"

"No. We need to check his car. Finish your steak and let's get out of here."

"What's the hurry? I'm enjoying myself for the first time in days."

"It won't be so pleasant if the big guy heads back here. From the looks of what I saw, he was none too happy with you, and I only made it worse."

Jonny hesitated for a couple of seconds, grabbed a couple of fries, and rose from the table. "You got any cash?"

Chase laid a twenty on the table and they left the hotel.

* * *

Chase walked around the green sedan. Both doors were locked. He scanned the parking area for any security cameras or people. The lot was deserted. With one swift blow of a tire iron, the driver's window shattered. He reached in and unlocked the door.

He handed the tire iron to Jonny. "Pry the trunk."

Chase rifled through the glove box, the visors, and under the front and rear seats. The inside was clean.

Jonny's search was more fruitful. "Whew, would you look at that!"

Under the spare tire and a damp and sandy beach towel was a small arsenal—a sawed-off double-barrel shotgun, an AR-15 rifle with three full magazines, three handguns of assorted calibers, a combat knife, and a satellite phone. There was something else Chase recognized immediately—the transmitter he had set as bait, along with another larger black box with a series of switches, a digital readout screen, and two telescoping antennas.

"Know what this is?" Chase asked, handing the box to Jonny.

"I've seen those transmitters before but not the black one. You know?"

"Maybe. Let's get this stuff out of here."

"You want both of these phones?" Jonny asked.

"No. Ditch the cell but keep the sat phone." Chase handed the cell phone to Jonny along with the SIM card and battery. Jonny reinserted both. He walked around the car and stashed it in the glove box.

Jonny said. "I got his cell number just in case."

Chase pulled his truck up to Cuda's car and Jonny loaded it.

Once they were done, Chase hit the gas. His rear wheels fishtailed from the parking lot into the evening traffic.

* * *

"Maybe it's time you told me a little more. Otherwise, I might have to drop you off back at the warehouse," Chase said.

Jonny turned his attention from the side mirror to Chase. "I work for Cuda's boss, El Cuervo."

"El Cuervo?"

"Yeah, he's La Hermandad's capo...boss. He run's the Baja cartel."

"No shit, the cartel?"

"A cartel, there are others. Cuda is El Cuervo's chief sicario, his enforcer, and now he's after us both."

Chapter Forty
Ensenada, Baja California, Mexico

"You're certain it was him?" Nico asked

"Yes, dammit," Cuda shouted back, rubbing his temples and fighting the lingering fog and splitting headache from the concussion. In fact, his whole body ached from the night on the cold concrete floor. Sitting in Nico's office and downing his third cup of coffee, he was in no mood for Nico's insolent challenges. "It was him and he's heading north."

"Is he trying to get back to the States, to his family?"

Cuda was contemplating why the man would come to the office when the realization hit him as hard as the blast to his skull last night. "He knows Pescadero Baja sank the tuna boat."

"How could he know?"

"He has been tracking me. He was the one who repaired the transmitter. He planted it and the coke along the beach. He sent the transmissions. He did it to follow me here. And now he has Jonny. If they go to the police or DEA, we're dead. We're going to need help. I need to call El Cuervo. Get me to the hotel."

* * *

Cuda stormed into the lobby, ignoring the obsequious greetings of the hotel's staff, and headed for the elevator, leaving Nico to catch up. It was only then he remembered his missing wallet and keycard.

He returned to the front desk and asked for a new key. He impatiently explained he had lost his wallet the previous night.

"I'm going to have to see some identification, sir," the clerk said.

"I just told you, I lost my wallet. Look, I'm Enrique Aleta. I have stayed here many times. Look it up on your computer. You have a record of my car in the parking lot. It's a green Toyota, license number 22-EXI-721."

171

The clerk entered a few keystrokes. "What was your room number?"

"Four-two-seven, and it's still my room. I have it until the end of the week."

Satisfied, the clerk said, "I'm so sorry for the inconvenience, sir. But we're very concerned about the security of our guests."

He swiped a blank card through the encoder and handed it to Cuda. "Would you like a second card?"

Before the clerk finished the sentence, Cuda snatched the card from his hand and sprinted for the elevator.

"I hope you find your wallet, sir."

* * *

He knew instantly the room had been searched, someone other than the maid. The clothes in the drawers were in disarray and his suitcase had been moved. He went to the safe and entered the street number for Pescadero Baja's office. The lock disengaged. Cuda opened the door and looked inside. His car keys, passport, and pocket notebook were undisturbed.

He ran from the room with Nico in close pursuit. When he saw the car's broken window, bile singed his throat. He knew he'd been robbed even before he opened the trunk. He lifted the spare tire and blanket. His knees buckled for the second time in twenty-four hours.

* * *

"So, Lee, you gotta plan?" Jonny asked, setting a match to the cigarette dangling from his lips.

Chase gripped the steering wheel white-knuckle hard as he weaved through the unfamiliar traffic. He turned and caught Jonny's gaze. "Not a clue. I've been living day to day. I wasn't even sure until yesterday about Pescadero Baja. You mind opening the window?"

Jonny rolled his head back. "Great, just great. Our lives are on the line and you're worried about secondhand smoke? Just get me out of town, would ya."

"Hey, a little gratitude. You'd be dead if I hadn't found you, and because I did, those guys know I'm alive. Maybe it's your turn for a

172

little planning. You know much more about these guys than I do." Chase waved the smoke from his face with his right hand. "Besides, it's a bad habit."

"Look, this is my last addiction, okay? Man, I tried the gum, the patches, even one of those vapy things, but there ain't nothin' like the draw. But I tell ya, I just need a little money to disappear. I still have family in the Caribbean—in places where few questions are asked and even fewer answers are given."

"Like where?"

"Haiti. I'd fit in real good, see." Jonny placed his cocoa-brown left arm tight against Chase's tanned, but much lighter, right arm. "My grandma was from there—a mulâtresse."

"Huh?"

"Mulatto, and that ain't the half of it. My granddaddy was born in New Orleans and he claimed he was part Choctaw and part Cajun. My mama would say I was 'Caribbean gumbo—a little dis, a little dat.'"

Chase laughed. "You must tick a lot of boxes on the census form."

"Never seen one."

"What did you mean back there when you said everyone calls you Jonny?"

"My name's Isosceles Beauregard LeBeau."

"Huh?"

"Yeah, I know. It was my mama. She kinda named us kids by whatever hit her at the time. I guess my head looked like a triangle when I was born.

"It's original. I'll give your mama that, but I'm gonna stick with Jonny."

"It ain't so bad. I got a sister named Pyracantha and a brother called Welder. What about you, you have a family? If so, you better just forget about 'em."

"I have a wife and two kids, but I haven't contacted anyone." Chase's voice broke, the emotions were starting to catch up. "What do you mean, forget about them?"

"They're much better off without you. That way they'll stay alive as long as you disappear."

"You mean run and hide the rest of my life?"

"If you don't, it will be a short life. These guys will kill anyone in their way. They don't want anybody to know about their operation. They sent Cuda to recover the shipment I lost. And because of that, my crew is dead, and I would be, too, if it weren't for you. Haiti don't look that bad right now."

* * *

Chase drove as far east as they could go. Jonny tried to stay awake, but the fatigue and the beating took their toll. He stared trancelike as the broken highway stripes merged as one in the thin beams of the headlights. Finally, his eyes succumbed.

Jonny felt a nudge on his shoulder.

"Hey, you want something to eat?"

His lids responded slowly. He looked around. Chase had pulled into a small gas station surrounded by agricultural lands. The musty air of wet crops rushed through the open door. The single light fixture over the pump buzzed with a haze of insects. "Where are we?"

"The middle of nowhere," Chase said. "Almost out of gas. You want something or not?"

Jonny shook his head to revive. "Ya, sure." He looked out the window as Chase walked away.

Jonny devoured candy bars and chips and slurped his bottle of Coke as Chase proceeded east.

"I need to know what I'm up against. Tell me about this cartel. What should I do?" Chase asked.

Jonny figured they'd be parting company soon because this guy would probably get them both caught. And besides, he had nothing to hide. *La Hermandad screwed up his plan. I should have killed Benji and Joaquin myself.* He told Chase everything he knew about La Hermandad and the smuggling operation.

"Submarines! You gotta be kidding me. You built actual subs, and they worked?"

Jonny smiled and shrugged. "I'm here, ain't I? They thought about old military surplus subs at first."

"For real? Could they afford to buy something like that?"

"Hell yes. Whole fleets of 'em, if they wanted. But they wouldn't work—no need to dive to five hundred feet and to stay under for a month. And you'd need twenty-five men to drive it, men who would need clothes, food, and money. All this would take up too much space that could be used much better.

"This guy who worked for the boss, Manny, told me what he wanted. He figured they couldn't see you from the air if you're deep enough. And you can fool sonar if you are small and made of the right stuff—something that absorbs the signals and doesn't reflect them."

"But how'd they get you?"

"I was running drugs for them. I had a shrimper and was doin' a pretty good business. I would pick up cargos in Venezuela and drop 'em off in southern Louisiana. But the narcs were on to us and started inspections. The Coast Guard even brought a big-ass mean German Shepherd one time, but he couldn't find shit. I'd hid the coke under a one-inch steel deck plate. But, still, everyone was getting nervous. So, this guy Nico, he's the guy who worked for Manny—"

"Nico...from Pescadero Baja, are you sure?"

"Yup, same guy. Anyway, he came by and asked if I could help them build a submarine."

Chase craned his neck closer to Jonny. "For real?"

"Yeah, I couldn't believe it either. He was kinda sketchy on what he wanted, like a range of fifteen hundred nautical miles, able to submerge deep enough and long enough to avoid detection. Oh, and enough space to carry five to ten tons of cargo. I told him I was no marine engineer, but he said the boss had 'confidence' in my skills. What he really meant was I'd better get it right."

"How the hell did you do it?" Chase asked.

"I did a lot of reading. I worked night and day. Fortunately, they supplied me with plenty of stimulants. I researched the best marine engines for the weight-to-power ratio, a small tractor diesel would be best. I knew the engine exhaust was a tricky problem because I had to cool the gases before they were vented; otherwise, satellites can see you with infrared detectors. I also had to get a steady stream of fresh air in for the crew and engine."

"You couldn't run the engine underwater unless you had a long snorkel, right?"

"Yeah, the tiny diesel engine would drive the boat on the surface and also power two electrical generators that charged a bank of batteries. The subs run on batteries when underwater, but they only last about twelve hours. So, the plan was to surface at night to power up the diesel and recharge the batteries. Just before dawn, we'd submerge again until the batteries were nearly dead."

"What did you use for the hull, aluminum?"

"No. I didn't use hardly any metal at all, especially above the waterline—only fiberglass and composites. Better to hide from sonar and radar. My first try was butt ugly, like two fiberglass fishing boats glued together, but at least it was watertight. I used it to test the different systems."

"I don't know much about subs, but I do know you need to sink and surface. How'd you do that?"

"I had no problem figuring how to flood the ballast tanks to submerge. I just had to use the correct valves to control the flow into the tanks. I had more of a problem in purging the tanks. They had to evacuate quickly and evenly, or I could flip the whole boat and make a wrong-way trip to the bottom."

"What'd you use?"

"Same system as the big boys—compressed air. It was crude, but it worked. I used a small contractor's compressor, like for an air wrench or nail gun. I connected two compressors to a manifold and the four ballast tanks. I had to fiddle with the valves to fine-tune ascents and descents, but they worked like a charm. Like I said, I'm still here."

They drove silently for several minutes. Jonny shifted in his seat. "I still don't get why you're here. What's the deal?"

"I worked on one of Pescadero Baja's tuna boats, the *Bella*. A few weeks ago, we were sent up the coast to help recover a bunch of cocaine. We got most of the cargo back, but the guys they sent out to recover it blew up my boat and killed all my friends, all the crew, just like what happened to your crew."

Jonny froze as a cold chill gripped his spine. He sat dazed, unable to draw a breath. His heart raced, each pulse pounding his brain. He eyes were fixed in an idle stare through the windshield as the fields passed in a brown blur. He was dripping with sweat and his hands were quivering.

"You okay?" Chase asked.

Jonny couldn't talk. His mind was in turmoil, the first real emotion he'd felt in years. It was his fault—he killed all those men. He knew it and wanted to scream, claw his way out of the car. A breath finally came. He shook himself back, his sorrow deep, his shame profound.

"I...I...I had no idea they blew up the boat. Nico and Cuda said nothing. They're fuckin' ruthless—they'll kill anybody in their way; they don't want nobody talking."

Jonny regained his composure. "Why the hell did you go back to Pescadero Baja? You should have taken whatever money you had and run off to Borneo; somewhere where they would never find you."

Chase explained his escape, his ditching of the skiff, his escapades in Cabo and La Paz, and his baiting of Cuda. "I had to be sure it was them. I wanted to know why. I thought if I could prove who did it, I could give them back their drugs and transmitter and negotiate with them to leave my family and me alone. If that didn't work, I'd go to the Feds; maybe get into witness protection."

"You can't believe that. You're too smart. Think about it—after you witnessed the murder of an entire tuna boat and knew the details of their smuggling operation, do you think they're gonna just let you walk merrily away? How could anyone explain your sudden appearance? What do you say happened if the police questioned you? Besides, they don't negotiate, they dictate. You are a pebble in their shoe. The drugs you have are nothing. They want the transmitters back, but to them if their secret gets out, they will just find a new way. Look at me, I designed their damn subs and drove 'em, and Cuda was going to kill me. I was disposable, nothing more than a mechanic they would use and throw away.

"The only way you can hurt them, really hurt them, is to connect them to the tuna boat. Even the Mexican government can't hide that. You're lucky you didn't contact your family because, if you had, you'd be dead, they'd be dead, and any other relatives they could track down would be dead. You know what? I'd be dead, too. They need to shut you up and also send a message—a message everyone will understand. I only hope they haven't figured out who you are yet; if they have, I wouldn't buy any season tickets to the opera. These guys never forget a grudge and settle them all."

"Wha...What should I do?"

"First, we'd better keep driving and find someplace to hide. Too many people saw us. It won't be long until they figure out who you are. They have pictures of everyone. They'll just start flooding the whole area with money until they find out what they need. You know what, I'd get your family to somewhere safe. If they figure who you are, they're gonna use them as bait to get you."

Jonny saw the panic in Chase's eyes.

"Can you warn your wife, can she get away to somewhere safe?"

"Yeah, but how do I tell her? How do I explain why I didn't contact her earlier?"

"I don't know, but you better figure something out and you better do it damn fast."

"I guess I'll just have to call her. I can't risk crossing the border. If I get caught, it will be all over the news."

"Hell, man, as soon as they figure out who you are, she'll be watched. They may be on to her now. If they suspected anyone survived from the tuna boat, they would check out everyone, maybe even bug their houses."

"How about her phone?" Chase asked.

"Just look at the stuff in Cuda's trunk. They know technology. I wouldn't put anything past them. If it can be bought, they'll buy it. If they need an expert, they'll buy him, too."

Chase's body stiffened at Jonny words, then, in an instant, he relaxed, and his face broke into a half smirk. "I know what to do."

"I'm glad someone does." Jonny pillowed his head on his shoulder and fell to sleep in the bouncing truck.

Chapter Forty-One
Point Loma, San Diego, California, USA

The box arrived at the house just after three in the afternoon. In the past weeks, she'd received many packages from family and friends trying to buoy her spirits.

Yech, she thought, looking at the box of caramels, her least favorite candy. She opened the envelope and read the note:

Dear CeCe,

I know it's very difficult for you but remember the good times you and Chase had. Like the weekend you spent in Barstow you always told us about. Cherish those memories.

Enjoy the candy. I hope we can down some Heinekens together soon and talk about the fun days. Come see us at the office when you can.

Lake Murray Realty

Maria dropped the note, her heart fluttered, and she slumped back in the sofa.

CeCe, no one called her CeCe but Chase. No one ever heard her pet name nor knew what it meant. It was their secret.

Barstow, Barstow... That was on the trip back from Las Vegas where I had the caramel candy and pulled off a crown. I was in misery for a day. Chase and I joked it was the worst vacation we ever had, but who else knew?

Heinekens. When Chase returned from sea, Maria always met him with a six-pack. It was a secret little ceremony. Her folks would watch the kids, and she and Chase would have at least one night alone.

She sat dazed. No one else, not her mother, not Marcy—her best friend—knew these things. Only two people in the whole world would know, and one was dead, wasn't he?

She read it through a second time, a third, and a fourth. It can't be true, she told herself, praying it was. Tears were welling, but they were tears of hope this time.

Something in the tone of the letter confused her.

If it's Chase, he's telling me something—something no one else could know. It was why they had the secrets—their personal code. But why mention Barstow and the candy? Why not something more pleasant? We have such good memories. No, he is warning me!

This had to stay secret. No one could know he was alive, and no one could know she knew.

He sent the candy for a reason. He couldn't call, and he couldn't write or email. Why?

Maria knew she had to get rid of the note. She put it in the fireplace along with the wrapping paper and address label and lit them.

As she watched the papers blacken and curl, she remembered the Lake Murray Realty reference. She hadn't worked there in ten years. It didn't make sense to commute to La Mesa after they purchased the house in Point Loma. It was too far out, particularly with the kids in school. So, Maria had started working in a local office.

She picked up the phone and was about to dial the number to her old office but stopped. Instead, she dialed her mother's number.

"Hi, Mom. I have to head out for a couple of hours. Can you pick up the kids at school and take them back to your house?"

"Sure, honey. I'm glad to see you're getting out for a change."

"I am, too, Mom. Thanks a million."

Maria hung up and grabbed her keys.

* * *

"Hi, Tom."

"Hi, Maria. What a surprise. I haven't seen you in years." Tom stood and walked over to his former colleague. He embraced her and, as usual, she stiffened. His hugs were always a bit too tight and a little too long.

"Yeah, we were all so sorry to hear about the accident. Chase was sure a great guy. I'll never forget those cookouts when he got back from sea—all the grilled tuna, yellowtail, and mahi-mahi. What a feast."

"Thanks, Tom, I appreciate your concern. Say, I think an old client was trying to contact me. Did someone leave a message in the last few days?"

"I haven't heard, but let's check Linda's desk," Tom said, stretching his neck to peer over the top of the cubicle to see if the receptionist was nearby. "She may be at lunch, but she usually brings it back. Say, you still in the business?"

"Yes, well, sort of part-time with the kids and all."

They walked to the receptionist's desk at the front entrance of Lake Murray Realty. Behind the counter, Linda still maintained a little message center. It was a bit dated now with email, voice mail, and the other trappings of the 21st century, but the individually labeled mail slots still had some utility.

Tom laughed as he pulled a single pink telephone message slip from a box labeled To Do. "I didn't know they still printed these. Looks like she was going to call you."

He handed the slip to her. Her first name was penciled in, followed by a short message: "Have client moving to San Diego. Wants referral. Please call 011-646-555-525-055. Stan Waverly."

"Thanks, can I take this?"

"Sure, but if your client is looking in this area, have him give me a call."

"I will, Tom, and thanks. Please tell everyone I said hello."

"Will do and, again, so sorry about your loss. Please keep in touch."

Maria studied the note. Waverly was the name of the street where they had their first apartment. Stan was the obnoxious neighbor who kept them up at night playing his REO Speedwagon albums at full volume.

But the phone number was curious. It was not local; in fact, it had the international call code for Mexico.

There's a reason for this secrecy, and she'd better not use her cell phone. She needed something anonymous.

She'd passed a strip mall just before the realty office and saw a Target store.

She looked around before she pulled out, and even drove around the block twice to see if she was being followed.

This secrecy is making you a little paranoid, Maria girl.

She sat in the parking lot for a few minutes, then walked into the store and grabbed a cart. She inspected the housewares while secretly eyeing those entering.

After a few minutes she proceeded to the women's clothing department and picked up a couple of sweatshirts, went to the electronics department and got a prepaid cell phone, worked her way to the cosmetics and placed a few more items in the cart, and finally to the grocery section, where she loaded up on the cereals and canned soups for the kids. At every stop she lingered a few seconds, scoping out the shoppers.

After loading the bags into the car, she drove west to Point Loma. She entered the driveway to California-Pacifica College, a small religious school on the bluffs overlooking the ocean. The campus provided parking for the many surfers who accessed the waves just below the school's property. It was a good neighbor policy the community appreciated.

The parking lot was nearly deserted when Maria arrived. Backlit by the sun, the flat calm sea appeared like quicksilver. In the distance, a few optimistic amateurs were sitting upright on their boards laughing and joking, probably hoping against all odds the next set would be more productive.

She parked in a space far from any other vehicles under the canopy of a tall blue eucalyptus. She could see any approaching vehicle from her left and right windows, and anyone from the east through her rearview mirror.

Her nervous system was a jitter—excited, but a little scared. Gripping the cell phone's plastic packaging was difficult with her sweating hands. She rubbed them dry on her jeans. Who the hell designs these things, she thought as she finally freed the plastic-entombed phone.

She turned the phone on and immediately had good reception and at least one-half battery charge. Her hands shaking, she fumbled the phone, trying to dial the number from the pink telephone slip she'd memorized before discarding it in the trash at the Target store.

She closed her eyes and held her breath. "Please, please...," she whispered.

One ring, two rings, three rings.

"Hello."

She recognized him instantly and her world stopped. Her lips quivered into a smile and in a voice wracked with emotion barely managed she asked, "Chase, is... is it really you? I...I can't believe it!"

The weeks of pain and loneliness finally caught up, and Chase could barely choke out the words through a torrent of tears. "Yes, CeCe. I'm so sorry I couldn't call you before now."

Maria could hear his voice waver as he asked, "Are you in a secure place?"

"Yes, and the phone is a disposable. I'm ...I'm ..."

They drew a collective breath.

"Good girl. You understood the note. I know you have a million questions and I can't wait to hold you again and explain everything. But we don't have time. For your safety, I can't tell you too much, but the sinking of the *Bella* is not what I'm sure everybody has been led to believe. We're dealing with a criminal organization and if they know I'm alive; you and the kids are in danger."

"Do they know you are alive?"

"I'm guessing they do, so I need you to leave right away. Get the kids and get out of town. Tell nobody where you are going. Nobody. Not family, not friends."

"Where should I go?"

"I don't want to know, understand? If I don't know where you are, I can't tell anyone. Take a cab to the airport and get on a jet to anywhere. Do you have ready cash?"

"Yes, I still have the money from the refinancing and also your life insurance. It's in the bank."

"Go to any branch right now and make the withdrawal. Use cash for all your transactions, no credit cards. Leave no paper trail."

"What do I tell the kids?"

"Maybe tell them you are going to visit an old friend of mine who wants to meet them. You'll have to improvise."

"What do I tell our parents?"

"Call them after you are safe. I'll try to figure out things on this end. After this call, get rid of the phone. Take out the battery and SIM card. Destroy them. But remember the number you called. Once you get to a safe place, get a new phone and call, okay?"

"Can't you just go to the police? They will protect us."

"It's not like that. These guys are worse than the Mafia. They never forget. We have to figure another way out. Just do this now. It'll give me time to work something out."

"Are you involved? Did you do anything wrong?"

"No, honey. I was just in the wrong place at the wrong time and many friends—innocent guys—were murdered. I just got very, very lucky. I had a guardian angel named Gus."

"I love you, Chase. If there's a sliver of a chance to be with you again, I'll do it."

"Be safe and be very careful. Tell no one. I love you, too. More than you'll ever know, CeCe."

Maria just stared at the ocean through the windshield and a curtain of tears. The conflicting emotions left her numb; she was frightened but elated. Her head was spinning with all the new information, and she tried hard to process it—to try to make some sense of it—but it was not going to happen in her present state.

Just do what Chase said. Simple steps.

* * *

"That's a lot of cash. Are you sure you don't want me to get you a money order or cashier's check?" the teller asked, a concerned frown wrinkling her face.

"I wish I could. But the only advantage I have over the other bidders on the house is an immediate cash offer. It gives me leverage in negotiations. You'd be surprised how motivating a bundle of cash can be." Maria said.

To allay the suspicion of the teller and bank officer, she left five thousand in the account—more than enough to keep it open. She had opted for mostly twenty, fifty, and hundred-dollar bills.

She drove to her mother's house to pick up the kids. Her smile was forced, but she got through it. She knew her parents were used to her erratic behavior; they knew the emotional roller coaster she'd been on. But they were always supportive, and sometimes that meant saying nothing.

"I didn't want to tell Grandma yet, but we need to get home to pack for a little trip. There is a friend of your dad's we're going to visit," Maria said as they drove from her parent's house.

"When are we going?" Denise asked.

"Tonight, it will be fun. We're going to take a cab and then a jet."

"What about school, Mom?"

"It's okay. I have checked with your principal, and she thinks this will be a very educational trip."

"How about my game tomorrow?" Kevin asked.

"Don't worry. It's all right if you miss one. It's a long season and you will get plenty of games. But you better bring your glove so we can play catch. Now, as soon as we get home, I want you to start packing. No TV and no games. We have to leave in about three hours. Can you do that for me?"

Chapter Forty-Two
Point Loma, San Diego, California, USA

Cuda's call to El Cuervo ignited a firestorm. Photos of Chase and Jonny were blanketed over all of La Hermandad's territory—bars, boats, and businesses, and most importantly, his halcones—the street army.

The names and addresses of all of Chase's family were obtained from Pescadero Baja's files. Teams of Cuda's men were dispatched from the Tijuana tunnel, and the surveillance of the houses began.

Nothing unexpected was observed. When there were no reports of Chase or Jonny, a change in tactics was ordered.

* * *

When Maria returned home from her parent's house, her threat alert was high, but she could never have been ready for what happened. As soon as she opened the door, all she remembered was a terrible jolt surging through her body. She was still in shock when she lifted her head to see both Kevin and Denise sitting on the living room floor against the sofa with their hands and feet tied and their mouths gagged with duct tape. Tears were streaming down their eyes and Maria could hear Kevin's muffled whimpers.

She tried to sit up, but her hands were bound behind her back. She tried to yell to the kids, but her mouth, too, was taped.

She was still woozy, unsure of what had happened, when a tall, skinny man walked into her field of vision. She lifted her head a few inches, enough to see the plastic wand in his hand. She'd seen them before in the movies, but never in real life, and never had been shocked by one.

She tried to clear her head when she heard, "Get 'em in the van. Bring her purse and phone."

A second man entered her view. He and the tall man lifted each of the kids into their arms and walked from the room. Denise valiantly struggled and kicked but was like a feather in the man's arms.

Finally, the third man behind her lifted Maria by her arms. Her legs were free, but he held her tightly, and her equilibrium was suspect.

He led her to the garage and through the gaping sliding door of a white panel van. She was shoved to the floor, alongside the kids, and covered with a blanket.

The door slammed shut, and Maria heard the man tell the driver and a third man to head to the warehouse.

The garage door opened and the van backed out. The men drove with caution to avert attention.

* * *

It was a smooth ride; they were only jostled for the last few minutes after they turned onto a bumpy road. Maria guessed they drove about thirty minutes, but she was uncomfortable. She couldn't shift her weight off her right arm and it tingled. She was frantic about the kids. She wanted desperately to comfort them. They had no idea what was happening and she knew they were frightened. So much had happened to them. When they lost their father, their whole world collapsed—and now this. It wasn't fair, but Maria knew she was helpless. She thought about how long it would be until they were missed—less than a day, knowing her Mom. Chase wouldn't know for several days and only because he didn't receive a follow-up call.

* * *

The first man sat in the passenger seat, the contents of Maria's purse strewn on his lap. He picked up her phone and scrolled through the call list. He was looking for international calls but found none.

It was just dusk when they arrived at the dilapidated warehouse in the middle of nowhere. A tall chain link fence topped with barbed wire surrounded the building and its parking and storage areas. Tall weeds and spindles of grass snaked up through the cracks in the spalling pavement. The place looked deserted, just a few vehicles around the concrete-block building.

The first man led Maria through a steel door into the warehouse. Another had Denise and Kevin. The lighting was stark, just the cold glare of fluorescent fixtures suspended from the ceiling thirty feet above. The warehouse was empty; there was no hint of its previous use.

They walked toward the rear, and about ten feet from the cinder block wall they stopped. One of the men moved a large desk to reveal a trapdoor in the concrete floor. He lifted the door, grabbed a long extension cord from inside the opening, and plugged it into the wall. A yellow glow shown from the black hole. The top rungs of a ladder protruded from the hole. One man descended. The first man pushed Maria to the ladder and turned to help her down. The children followed, and then the tall man.

Once they were all down, the first man took the lead and said, "Follow me."

* * *

A rush of cool air greeted Maria at the bottom of the ladder. She peered down the tunnel and could not understand where she was. Was it a sewer or maybe a mine? Kevin's tiny fingers trembled in Maria's hand. She placed her other arm around Denise's shoulders and pulled her close. Fear showed in her children's eyes and all Maria could do was squeeze tighter.

After ten minutes of walking, they encountered a black line on the floor and walls. Hand-painted on opposite sides of the line were crude renditions of the American and Mexican flags.

The first man turned to face Maria and the kids. "Welcome to Mexico."

Chapter Forty-Three
Near Tijuana, Baja California, Mexico

Chase and Jonny circled back to the coast and holed up for a couple of days in a small hotel outside of Tijuana. Chase considered calling the coyote that the forger, Cabrera, had given him to get him across the border, but Jonny nixed the idea.

"If they see you in San Diego, they will know you contacted your wife. The only thing keeping your family alive is them believing you're dead."

Chase knew Jonny was correct.

"What can we do to get these guys off—"

"Shhh," Jonny said. "Did you hear that?"

"No, what?"

"Is your phone ringing?"

Chase reached into his pocket and pulled out his cell phone. He looked at the screen and shook his head. "Not mine."

Jonny walked over to the closet. "It's coming from in there," he said, pointing to the bag they had taken from Cuda's trunk.

"It's the satellite phone," Chase said. "You ever use one of these?"

"Yeah, we use them at sea," Jonny said, picking it up and pressing the "Talk" button. "Hello."

"Ahh, I thought I had lost my phone, but it seems someone has found it."

There was no mistaking Cuda's voice.

"Is this Mr. Brenner?"

"No."

"Jonny! Is that you? I was correct. I figured it was you who broke into my car. I'll add it to our list of unfinished business, my friend."

Jonny held the phone at an angle so Chase could listen. "No, I had an offer for you, but you wouldn't even listen. You just wanted to beat the shit out of me. I think our business is done," Jonny said.

"We will have to see about that, won't we? Could you put Mr. Brenner on? It was him at the warehouse?"

"Brenner? I don't know who you're talking about."

"Maybe he's using the name Lee Wilton."

An expression of confusion washed over Jonny's face as he caught Chase's gaze. "I haven't seen him since the night you tried to kill me. He went his way and I went mine."

"That's too bad. There is someone here who would like to speak to him. Here, just a moment. Let me lower this handkerchief."

"Chase is that you? Are you there?" Maria asked.

Chase heard the desperation in Maria's voice and grabbed the phone from Jonny's hand.

"Maria, I'm here," he shouted in panic. "Don't worry, I'll come for you. I'll—"

Cuda interrupted. "Hello, Chase. I just wanted to let you know your family is with me and they are doing just fine. You are lucky I found them when I did. They were about to leave on a trip, and you would have missed this opportunity to talk."

Chase's face distorted in anger. "I swear if you hurt them, I'll come after you and your entire operation. I have kept quiet and talked to no one—not the DEA, not the federales, no one. And I plan on keeping it that way, but you have to let my family go, or else I'll—"

"Relax, Chase, we have the elements of a mutually beneficial bargain. I think we can arrange a swap. I'll let your family go in exchange for a meeting with you and my good friend Jonny. I have been talking to your wife and she has convinced me she knows nothing about our little enterprise. She only knows that by some miracle you survived the tragic accident on the *Bella*."

"When do you want to meet? I'll be there."

"I have some other business in the next couple of days, but I promise to call you very soon. So please keep track of this phone. It's our only link." Cuda hung up.

"They have my family. I have to get them. You know where they'd take them?" Chase was manic; he reeked of fear. He brought this on. He should never have gone to the Pescadero Baja warehouse. In fact, he should never have survived. What good has it done? He put his entire family in danger.

"Who the hell is Brenner?" Jonny asked.

"That's my real name, Chase Brenner. I was trying to hide and got a fake ID in La Paz. Some bouncers caught me selling in their club."

"No way we can meet with Cuda. We do, and everyone is dead. No, we have to figure something out," Jonny said. "Let me see the phone, Mr. Brenner."

Chase handed it to him and Jonny wrote down the number Cuda had called from; it was the same cell phone they left in his car. He opened the back of the sat phone and removed the battery. He looked around for a small backup battery but found none.

"Why'd you do that?"

"These phones send a signal directly to a satellite, and the satellite knows exactly where the calls come from and go to. They can track us here. We know his number if we have to call him."

"What should we do now? Maybe it's time to call the police? They have my family."

"No. The police can't find them, or maybe don't want to find them. La Hermandad has deep roots. You talked about trading the coke and transmitter you had for your safe passage. That is nothing to them, especially now. But maybe we can find something they do value, a bigger bargaining chip."

"Like what?"

"Well, exactly what kind of business do you think Cuda has in the next few days?"

Chapter Forty-Four
Ensenada, Baja California, Mexico

Chase and Jonny were hidden at the marina when they saw the men from Pescadero Baja arrive, just as Jonny had predicted. Cuda had telegraphed it. Jonny and Chase waited at the marina for the next nights, hoping the men would use the same boats as on Jonny's previous transports.

Jonny thought with all of La Hermandad's planning, it was a flaw in their procedure to depart from the same marina each time. But it was to his benefit this time.

On all his previous trips, the speedboats would collect the cargo and off-load on a beach. Three or four different beaches were surveilled on the night of the shipment, in case too much activity was observed at one or another. It also assured the boat drivers would not try to hijack a load.

After the bales were off-loaded, the boats returned to the marina. Jonny knew where to find them; what he did not know was the rendezvous point with the sub, but Chase offered a suggestion.

Three men walked onto the dock and headed for the slips. When they removed the canvas cover off the first boat, Jonny sat up and leveled the AR-15 from Cuda's trunk at the men. They were startled, first by the surprise of someone under the tarp and then by seeing Jonny, who they recognized from other drops.

One man went for a handgun in his waistband.

"I wouldn't do that," he heard from behind.

The three men turned to see Chase behind them, holding a very large handgun glistening under the dock's halogen lamps.

"We meet again," Jonny said as he reached around the man's waist and removed the handgun. "Falco, right?"

Falco stared back with derision.

Within ten minutes, the men were tied up and lying under the tarp of the first boat being driven from the harbor by Chase.

Jonny followed in the second boat, towing the third. He figured if anyone were meeting the men after they dropped off the shipment, they would be curious as to why one boat remained behind. He pulled out Cuda's sat phone, inserted the battery, made a quick call, left a short message, and hung up.

They motored for about thirty minutes until the lights in Ensenada were just a distant shimmer on the dark horizon. Chase cut his engine and Jonny pulled up alongside. Chase stood and walked to the back of the boat and pulled the cover from the three men. He ripped the duct tape from their lips and ordered them to sit.

He held a single bright orange flotation vest in his left hand and the stainless-steel Smith and Wesson .44 in his right.

He looked over to Jonny and asked glibly, "What's your guess, twenty miles to shore?"

Jonny drew on a half-burned cigarette and blew plumes of smoke from his nostrils. "Yeah. Adjusting for the currents, we were going about forty knots for half an hour so, yeah, that's about right."

"How far can the average man swim before he is exhausted?"

"I read somewhere that Olympic swimmers do five miles a day in the pool. But could do another five if pushed. But that's in much warmer water. In the cold ocean, I'd cut it down a bit."

Chase rubbed his chin quizzically. "So, twenty miles would be difficult even for an Olympic swimmer? What about an amateur in cold water at night with sharks and barracudas circling?"

"I don't know," Jonny said, flicking the spent butt into the sea. "But a wild-assed guess would be seven miles before he was exhausted. And don't forget about hypothermia."

"What if the man had one of these?" Chase asked, dangling the flotation device around one finger in front of the men.

"Oh, it would easily triple it. You could rest for long periods and could use only your legs sometimes. It may even provide some insulation and keep you a little warmer."

"So, it's doable from here?"

"Maybe."

Chase turned from Jonny and faced the three men. Even with only the dim lights from the console, Jonny could see their eyes were wide with fear. None of them had moved much at all.

"As you see, I have one vest here," Chase said, raising it high over his head. "Now, all three of you are going overboard in just a few minutes. The question is: who will be wearing this?"

Chase fell silent.

"Oh, and just in case you think the stronger of you can rip it off a weaker guy, we'll be dumping you at different locations, and good luck finding the vest under these conditions. I've taken off the strobe," Chase said.

He turned back to Jonny and asked, "Could the vest keep all three of them afloat?"

"Nope, no way, not even two. It's a one-man device."

"Are chances better or not with clothes on?"

"That's a good question. On one hand, clothes hold in the heat better, even when they are wet. On the other hand, once they're wet, they add another ten pounds. I know the Navy instructs you to pull off your trousers, tie the legs together, and fill the pants with air, then tie off the waist with your belt to make a crude flotation device. That would be a benefit for the 'clothes on' option," Jonny explained.

"Okay. I don't want to make it too easy. Let's say they go over without clothes."

"Seems fair."

"Can you cover me from there?"

"Yeah, go ahead," Jonny said as he shouldered the AR-15 and aimed it toward the bound men.

Chase moved from man to man. He first removed their shoes and tossed them in the ocean. Then he unbuckled their belts and removed their trousers.

Chase stood and walked back to the console, picked up the vest again, and turned again to his captive audience.

"Here's the deal, the first of you who tells me the coordinates of the rendezvous point gets the vest, and a ten-minute start on your buddies."

They shouted at once.

"Sorry, I didn't understand. Falco, I think you were first," Chase said.

"No, I spoke first," the man in the middle said.

"No, it was me," the third man said.

"Hold on. I'm impressed by your enthusiasm. Go ahead." Chase pointed to Falco.

"It's programmed into the GPS."

"Which one?"

"All three, in case something happens."

"Jonny, check your GPS, would you?" Chase asked and turned back to the three men. "When are you supposed to arrive?"

"Zero-two-thirty."

"How far out from here?"

"Maybe thirty miles."

Chase studied his watch. "It doesn't give us much time."

"How are you supposed to signal them?" Jonny asked.

"Same as always. Four long, then two short flashes."

"I tell you what," Chase said in his best imitation of a game show host. "You are all winners tonight. Jonny, can you bring the other boat over here?"

Jonny put down the rifle and went to the stern of his boat. He untied the line to the boat in tow and brought it alongside Chase's boat. He held the third boat tight against the gunwale.

"OK, one at a time into the boat," Jonny said.

Each man rose, walked to the side, and half-fell into the third boat.

"I want you all on the bow," Chase said as he entered the stern. "Jonny, where's the battery?"

"There should be two under the console."

Chase lifted the small compartment and found the two marine batteries in their watertight plastic cases. He unstrapped them, disconnected the cables, and tossed both batteries into the ocean.

He took the handle of the Smith and Wesson and smashed the electronic array on the console. Finally, he pulled a knife from his pocket and cut a three-foot-long section of the rubber gas lines to the two motors. Satisfied with his mayhem, he stepped from the crippled vessel.

"This will come in handy. I have an extra," he said, tossing a collapsible oar into the boat. "You'll figure a way out of those ropes in a few hours. Until then, we'll tow you out just a little farther. At least you're now in a boat, and it sure beats swimming."

Jonny started his boat and checked its GPS also. He engaged the prop and slowly headed on a westerly course until the towline played out. Once it was taut, he pulled the throttle back full and the boat bucked forward.

Chase followed the two boats.

Jonny turned back and laughed as he saw the three men frantically trying to untie the ropes while buffeting like ragdolls in his wake.

* * *

It took three hours to reach the position indicated on the GPS. Their speed had increased since cutting loose the third boat after an hour. Jonny wanted to make sure he got the three men into the current so there was no chance of drifting back to Ensenada.

Jonny knew the routine well. All the meetings were at a position and at a certain time. The sub didn't even have a radio, which minimized any chance of alerting the authorities. All communication was by signal lights. The sub would remain partially submerged while the captain searched the horizon for the signal. Once he saw the correct sequence, he would signal with the reverse sequence and the boats would motor over and begin off-loading.

Jonny flashed the spotlight and waited. He looked down at the GPS screen. They were on station and only ten minutes late, well within the expected window. The subs were instructed to navigate to an alternate position if the transfer boats were more than two hours late, and to return the next night if more than four hours late. But this had only happened once.

He waited another five minutes and tried again. This time he saw a dim light in the distance. He counted—the sequence was correct. He shouted to Chase, "Stay beside me. You know what to do when we get there." They throttled up and sped toward the distant light.

Jonny anticipated the captain's first question. "Our third boat broke down about two miles back. I left the other crewmen to have enough space for the cargo. We'll motor back and tow them to shore," Jonny said.

"Pull alongside, and we'll start," the captain said.

"Load the other boat first. I'll come on board and help."

Jonny tied off and entered through the starboard hatch with the captain's help. He looked down the narrow tube with a perverse sense of pride. He saw the two crewmen wrestling with a bale from the top of a stack. Once on the deck, one pulled while the other pushed to move it to the hatch. After they passed where Jonny stood, he removed the .44 from the waistband he had swapped with Chase. He now had all men in front of him and he was between them and the explosive charges. They hadn't seen the gun until Jonny said, "I want you all to put your hands behind your head and move very slowly away from the hatch."

The captain stared intently at Jonny, his confused gaze evident even in the darkened hold.

"Do you know what you are doing? Do you know who we work for?" The captain's tone was menacing.

"Never mind that, just do as I say, and you may live until morning."

As they moved the few feet to the port side, Chase jumped through the hatch.

"Good job," he said to Jonny.

"Get them tied up."

Chase pulled the thick plastic cable ties from his pocket and selected the largest man first. He bound his hands behind his back and laid him face first on the deck. He repeated with the other two. He then tied their ankles together. He searched their pockets and found a couple of seaman knives and not much else. Once they were secured, he went over to the hatch and retrieved the AR-15 from his boat.

"Watch them while I go forward," Jonny said.

* * *

In his excitement, Chase paid little attention to the squalid conditions. But now the situation was controlled and he focused on his surroundings. The odor hit him first. It reeked of a damp musty locker room mingled with diesel fuel and mold. Without air conditioning, it was stifling. The sub's rudimentary ventilation system could not keep up with the humidity and moisture coated every surface. On the bulkheads, small droplets coalesced into trickles, leaving trails of black mold.

Chase smoothed his sweat-drenched hair, wiping the excess on his also-sopped shirt. He'd been in saunas that were cooler. What was the saying—he laughed to himself—it's not the heat, it's the humidity.

A few low-intensity LED bulbs provided dim lighting. He felt claustrophobic in the dark and cramped quarters. While Jonny and a couple of the crewmen could stand erect, Chase had to crouch to move around. He couldn't imagine what it was like being trapped underwater, but he soon would.

Chase looked forward. Jonny was at the helm.

"Oh great," Chase heard the frustration in Jonny's voice. "The port tank is a quarter full, and the starboard is even less. The batteries are fully charged, though."

"What do you want to do with these guys?" Chase asked.

"Get rid of them."

"Shoot them?"

"I don't care. Throw them over if you don't want to waste the ammo."

No way, Chase thought. He couldn't kill them; selling the drugs and his other transgression the past few weeks were hard enough on his conscience. But that was a matter of survival, this wasn't. Would he be any better than Garza or Cuda?

"What, you want me to do it?" Jonny asked.

"There must be a better way. These guys aren't innocent, but—"

"You got any ideas?"

"Put them in one of the boats. Let them try to make it back."

"Are you crazy? They would just outrun us and contact La Hermandad. This sub is slow."

"I can fix that," Chase said. "Give me a couple of minutes."

Chase exited the hatch into a speedboat.

He released the engine mount bracket and pivoted the drive shaft and propeller from the water. He grabbed a hammer from the toolbox and began beating on a propeller blade until it was bent and contorted backward of the other blades. He then hammered the edges of the other blades until they were dulled and flattened. He lowered the motor back in the water. He repeated it on the second motor.

He then grabbed the line to the second boat. He pulled it alongside and entered. He unscrewed the two mounting bolts, ripped the fuel lines from the motors, and disconnected the ignition system from the batteries. With all his strength, he lifted the motors one at a time the six inches needed to clear the transom and dropped them into the Pacific.

He returned to the first boat and released the line to the second. It slowly drifted away in the warm and clear Pacific night.

Chase shouted to Jonny, "Bring them out one at a time."

Jonny led the first man to the hatch. Chase steadied the man and helped him jump in. They repeated this for the other two crewmen.

Chase got back into the sub, still holding the line to the boat.

He grabbed his knife and tossed in onto the deck of the speedboat.

"Are you ready to go?" Chase asked Jonny. "Should I close the hatch?"

"Not yet. We need to air this stink hole out for a while."

* * *

Jonny walked back to the hatch next to Chase and climbed atop the sub. He crawled toward the bow and with a pair of pliers he cut the satellite communication antenna. He came back aboard and moved toward the helm. A half-inch-thick cable on the overhead bulkhead powered the transmitter. Jonny cut it too.

He turned to Chase. "This should get Manny's attention." He imagined the reaction at the bunker when the sub disappeared from the screen. He thought about deactivating the small transmitters on the bales, but they powered on automatically when in contact with water.

Jonny engaged the engine. "Yeah, let's go now. Secure the hatch."

Chase released his hold on the line and the small speedboat drifted off. He closed the hatch.

Jonny had a decision to make, and it was critical—north or south?

* * *

The submarine's captain watched as one of the crewmen crawled to the knife and rolled on top of it. It was awkward with his hands bound behind his back, but after a few minutes the crewman was able unfold the blade and cut the cable tie.

The crewman rubbed his wrists furiously to restore circulation and then freed the other two.

The captain went to the helm. The key was in the ignition. He turned it to the "ON" position and depressed the start button.

To his relief, the engine turned over instantly. He checked the gauges. Everything looked good, except the fuel supply, which only read half full. Hope it's enough, he thought.

He pushed the throttle forward and the boat started moving slowly.

"We have to get to shore fast. Hold on," the captain shouted over the roar of the engines.

As he accelerated, the engines began to shriek, and the hull shuddered violently. The turbulent prop wash sent a ten-foot geyser in the air. He pushed the throttle even further forward, but the boat screamed louder and lumbered slowly forward.

"Take the wheel," he said to the crewman standing beside him.

He went to the stern and saw the violent cavitation from the damaged propellers.

"Shut it down," he yelled.

It stopped instantly.

The captain lifted the motors to examine the drive train.

"Holy shit," he said as he saw the fruits of Chase's activities.

"What is it, Captain?"

"They destroyed the props."

"Can we get back?"

"I don't know. If they are too out of balance, we can snap the shaft."

"Can we fix it?"

"Not out here," he said, lowering the motor. "Start it up and go very slow."

The crewman did as instructed and the captain watched the prop wash increase.

As soon as he heard the motors begin to vibrate, he told the crewman to back it down.

"Keep it there," the captain said as he walked to the console. He looked at the tachometer and then the speed indicator—three knots.

It's gonna be a long night.

Chapter Forty-Five
Eastern Tropical Pacific off Tijuana Coast
31°51'36"N, 178°39'18"W

"I'm not sure how fast this sub is, but it has to be faster than a limping speedboat," Chase said. Jonny's laugh echoed when Chase had explained what he'd done.

"It's still dark and I'd like to start the diesel and stay on the surface, but we have a full battery charge. It's better to exhaust the batteries before running on the surface. If we motor when the batteries are full, we're wasting power," Jonny explained. When they did motor with diesel, they got the added benefit of the battery recharging. If they motored when the batteries were full, they were wasting power.

"Make's sense to me," Chase said, "but I'm not convinced this thing works."

"You'll find out in a minute because we're going down."

Jonny leveled the sub at twenty-five feet, which only took a couple of minutes in the gentle dive slope, and almost the exact duration Chase held his breath.

Jonny looked over at Chase, who was scanning up and down the sub's bulkhead. "What ya looking for?" he asked

"Leaks."

It was a smart cruising depth; they would be invisible from the sea or air and would not stress the boat. They could be detected by sonar, but because of its stealth design and acoustic insulation, would be dismissed as a small whale or big fish.

Jonny powered down all of the electronics. He didn't want anyone tracking fugitive emissions, and they were also a drain on the batteries. So, he navigated by dead reckoning, which was a challenge underwater. For the time being, as least for the next four hours, the compass would read east-southeast.

"You need me to do anything?" Chase asked. "I need to stay busy or I'll go crazy."

"You'll need a little lesson in operating this baby. Sit there." Jonny pointed to a single bale of coke positioned as a makeshift bench. In fact, the bales were improvised into sleeping berths, dining tables, and even compartment dividers. But all were very carefully placed for optimum weight distribution. It was the responsibility of one crewman, the loadmaster, to make sure all the bales were secured.

"This is the helm. It only controls the rudder—our position left and right. It has a very light touch, but it's also stable. Once you set it, it stays in place without too much drift. This handle here controls the sailplanes for pitch. You push it forward to dive and pull it back to rise. When you're at depth, bring it here to zero degrees on the inclinometer to maintain depth. Pretty simple, up and down, and left and right."

Jonny paused and drew a deep breath. "Now it gets a bit more complicated." He moved his left hand from the helm to two red plastic handles. "These two levers operate the port and starboard water ballast tanks. Even with a full load, the boat would just loll on the surface. She may submerge to half her height. We then open the vents in the ballast tanks to take on water. This increases our weight and allows us to submerge. But it can be tricky: too much water and we sink too fast, not enough water, and we don't sink fast enough. When we want to surface, we purge the tanks. It's these two controls here," he said, moving his left hand down to two blue handles. "This one for the left tank and this one for the right. They are mechanical in case we're down on power. You pull this back and it opens the air tanks to force the ballast water out through one-way valves in each tank. The farther you pull back, the faster air is released. But it's important to pull them back evenly so we don't roll too much and shift the cargo.

"Also, we need to make sure we balance the fuel in the two tanks. I like to switch tanks every two hours to keep trim." Jonny tapped two gauges. "This left gauge is for the port tank and the right one is for the starboard tank. This is the switch to change from one to the other.

"We have enough fixed ballast in the keel and with our batteries, so it won't roll all the way over if the tanks are out of balance, but it's difficult to control when you are at more than a ten-degree angle. Here, you take the controls, get the feel."

"I don't know," Chase said, rubbing his sweaty palms. "I'm an engine room geek. I fix 'em; I don't drive 'em."

"On a sub, everyone does everything. I can't drive twenty-four, seven."

"All right." Chase traded places with Jonny.

"First, try the rudder, it controls yaw. Keep an eye on the rudder angle indicator and see how she responds to left and right turns."

Chase slowly turned the wheel slightly to the right. It took a second for the gauge to respond, but it settled at five degrees. Chase reversed the wheel and the gauge slowly responded again, going ten degrees left. He corrected the course to zero as Jonny had set.

"Not bad, huh? She is pretty responsive, more so than some I've met." Jonny laughed. "Now let's play with the pitch. Move the plane control up one notch and watch your trim angle indicator."

Chase did. He pulled the stick back until he heard one click and it locked into place at five degrees. The depth gauge read twenty feet, fifteen feet, ten feet.

"OK, now level her out," Jonny said. "Put the stick back in position one."

Chase did, and the trim indicator returned to zero.

"Now, try a descent. Take her to forty feet, but don't go any deeper. We tested her to below fifty feet, but this is only a single hull, and I don't trust fiberglass with that much pressure."

Jonny saw Chase's face was taut in concentration, his eyes fixed on the depth gauge. He pushed the stick forward and felt the nose begin to lower. He pushed a little further and felt the pitch increase.

"Not too much or too fast," Jonny said.

Jonny recited the gauge readings. "Twenty, twenty-five, thirty, thirty-five, forty. Now, ease her to neutral and you'll settle at the correct depth. It's all a matter of touch, and you got to trust your instruments. The sailplanes also control the roll in the sub. If we start to tilt left or right more than about five degrees, vary the left and right plane controls to get us level."

"Can't we just set cruise control?" Chase asked.

"Wish we could, but I didn't design one. Maybe my next boat. While we're underwater, keep an eye on the carbon dioxide and oxygen gauges." Jonny pointed to two more gauges on the console. "If carbon dioxide gets to around six hundred parts per million, or the oxygen falls below twenty percent, let me know. We have to surface and get some clean air in here. If we can't come up, we'll have to use those oxygen tanks against the bulkhead. That will give us another couple of hours below."

Chase laughed. "Pretty impressive. You've built a very sophisticated boat, except for the missing cruise control."

"Since you're sitting there, why not take the first watch. Just keep it at thirty-five feet and on the hundred and thirty-degree heading on the gyrocompass. I'll take over in two hours. I've got some work to do aft."

"What's that?"

"I'm going to pull the batteries from all the transmitters on the bales. I don't want any chance La Hermandad can track us."

"Good idea."

* * *

It took Jonny about half an hour to disable the transmitters. He came forward to the helm with a handful of batteries and a grin on his face.

"Maybe I can squeeze another two hours of power out of these."

"Is there anything to eat back there?" Chase asked.

"I'll check but don't get your hopes up. It won't be much, and it won't be good."

Jonny returned a few minutes later with an opened can of tuna fish, a plastic fork, and a bottle of water.

"I was kinda hopin' for a hot meal."

"Fat chance. I can't even light up a smoke with all the shit in the air. Something's sure to explode." Jonny handed the can and fork to Chase. "There's only a case of water back there, so use it wisely. But looks like plenty of canned food—at least enough for two meals a day for a week. But it ain't steak and lobster."

"How long will it take to get to shore?"

"Well, if we did a straight haul back to Ensenada, it would be—how many hours did it take to the rendezvous point?"

"Four, five hours."

"About right, and we were traveling at forty knots, that's what, over two hundred nautical miles, maybe less because we were against the current. That's one hundred and eighty miles. This thing does, at best, eight knots, so maybe twenty-three hours, possibly a little less if we're not fighting the currents. But we need to go south a ways to find a deserted area. So, let's say another hundred and fifty miles, or nineteen hours. I guess a little short of two days, but that's if we have the fuel. I say we stay on this heading until we're close to the coast. Then we head south until we find something we like."

"It's fuel, not food, I should worry about?"

"Yup."

Chase was getting the feel for the boat. He would practice short dives, he would steer left and right, always returning to the heading. He now had a little control of his situation and was less fearful. He knew the sub worked. He knew he could surface in a few minutes if necessary.

Chase looked down at the controls; the sub was on course, at a steady speed, and at the correct depth. He turned to Jonny, who was slumped between two bales, and asked, "How'd you get into boats, anyhow?"

"I quit high school at fifteen to work on my uncle's shrimper on Barataria Bay...you know where that is...my favorite part of Louisiana...most of my kin are still there. Anyway, figured, hell, I could already read and write; mostly, though, it was to escape my stepdaddy. He used to whip me pretty good. He'd get drunk and call me a dirty half-breed and worse just because my real daddy was black. I don't know what my mama saw in him, her 'ragin' Cajun.' Probably just someone to buy the booze.

"Anyway, I learned all about diesels, booms, and nets and pretty much knew my uncle's whole boat after a couple of years." Jonny shifted to face Chase. "Know what I mean? I was bored, I needed something more, something bigger. So, my uncle told me to take the chief engineer test. I studied a little and took it, aced it, never'd done that in school. Then I took the marine pilot test, and passed it, too. But I had to work a few more years before the Coast Guard punched my ticket."

"Did you get a job as a boat captain?" Chase asked, casually glancing down at the controls.

"Not right off. I was about to get my own boat when the damn fishery collapsed. I had to start over. I got lucky, though. They needed an assistant engineer on a workboat ferrying man and supplies to the oilrigs. There were only five of us, but the skipper saw I could handle the engine room and the pilothouse, and just about everything in between. He had me at the helm most of the time, said he'd never seen anyone who could read the sloughs like me...what was it...yeah, I could 'divine the shallows.' I told him that's what I had to do to chase shrimp." Jonny laughed. "The skipper let the company know and, finally, I got my own work boat, but that's when I got into trouble."

"What, trouble with a boat?"

"Naw. I was makin' the company a bunch of money. They began callin' me 'Captain Jonny, the local legend' and I believed them...went right to my head. Started snorting a little coke, you know, just for fun, to relieve the stress. Loved it. Man, could I ever focus. Wasn't nothing I couldn't handle. And the thrill, wow, you can't describe it. You ever tried it?"

"Yeah, a little...in the Navy, but I was careful because they tested us. When I got out, I kinda stopped with the family and all. Couldn't afford it. Had to rely on beer."

"I couldn't stop, but the more I used, the less it worked." Jonny shook his head slowly. "I was chasing the dragon. It got bad. I thought I was doin' great, but I was the only one. The company paid for a few tries at rehab, but the hook was set. There I was, thirty-year-old Captain

Jonny, local legend, huh, no job, broke, and a two hundred-dollar-a-day habit."

"No shit," Chase said, turning to Jonny, who was fidgeting with a loose bolt on a cable. "But how the hell did you get involved with the cartel? Man, that's scary."

"It was my dealer. He knew my skills. I was pretty desperate...I needed money."

* * *

Jonny's mind wandered back to the meeting at the small café in the French Quarter.

He sat amused, watching the tourists as they sparred for the few shaded seats under the canopy.

He was halfway through his beignet when a tall mustached man in jeans and pressed white linen sport coat placed both his hands on the edge of the small weathered table and leaned across. "You Jonny?"

Jonny looked up but was distracted by his own image in the man's mirrored sunglasses.

"Yeah."

"Follow me," the distributor said, removing his sunglasses and placing them carefully into his breast pocket.

They climbed the flight of concrete stairs to the top of the levee holding back the Mississippi River from the fragile city below. The river was alive with pleasure boats, cruise ships, and strings of barges struggling upriver against the current.

The distributor walked slow and deliberate. His left hand clutched a white handkerchief he used to mop his sweating brow. It was midday and the temperature and humidity had already spiked.

"You smell it?" the distributor asked.

"What?"

"The aroma. It's everywhere...the fried food from a thousand restaurants mixed with the diesel from the river...it's N'Orleans."

Jonny looked squarely at him, but the man's eyes were flitting, observing everything and everybody.

They continued walking in an uncomfortable silence for another few minutes.

When the crowd thinned, the distributor stopped, turned, and stared hard and unblinking at Jonny. "I have a proposition."

Jonny's attention snapped back to Chase. "So, kinda like that movie, they made me an offer..."

* * *

"Jonny, Jonny, get up here fast," Chase yelled, struggling with the helm to control the trim, but the sub was in a steep, uncontrolled dive. "Something's wrong with the ballast tanks."

Jonny woke and sprang from his bed in the aft. He could barely maintain his balance on the steep deck and grabbed any handhold to stay on his feet. Just as he reached the helm, the sub rolled slightly to the port.

"What the hell happened?"

"I have no idea but look at the depth gauge."

The sub was approaching forty-five feet and descending fast.

Jonny wrested the wheel from Chase and turned the rudder hard to port. "Pull up hard on the planes and try to slow her down."

Chase pulled back hard on the port and starboard planes, straining to maintain them in position against the drag of the sea.

Jonny looked at the trim angle gauge. "It's slowing. It must be the port ballast tank. The vent is wide open and filling fast." Jonny stepped back from the console. "Keep her here until I tell you." He grabbed the ballast control lever. The lever looked like an emergency brake handle in an automobile. Moving it forward opened the ballast vent and pulling it back closed the vent. Jonny pulled it back, but it was free, no resistance. Jonny was living the emergency he'd faked weeks ago.

He saw a small nut and bolt connecting the cable to the handle were missing, and the cable, under tension, had sprung forward and opened the vent. "We got us a broken sub."

The panic was overwhelming Chase. He tried for deep breaths, but it felt like a two-ton weight was crushing his chest. "We're almost at fifty feet. What do I do?"

"We gotta pump air into the tank fast to evacuate the water. Turn the port tank air supply wide open."

Chase did as told and heard a loud whoosh. "Okay, it's open."

"Good. Keep her as steady as you can. I need to fish for the cable."

"Hurry, we're at fifty-five feet."

Jonny began unstrapping and moving bales to access the cable raceway in the bilge. "How's the trim look?" he asked.

"We're still in a dive but it's slowing, sixty feet now." Meanwhile, air was hissing at high pressure through the ballast vent, but just barely displacing the seawater flooding the tank. The entire electrical system was at full voltage as the air pumps struggled to keep up.

Jonny chased the cable raceway until he found the broken cable. He could not pull hard enough with his hands to close the vent.

"Chase, can you see the toolbox? I need the vise grips."

Chase jumped from the helm and tore through the toolbox.

"Got it."

"Bring 'em and the toolbox."

Chase did, and Jonny clamped the vise grips tight on the cable. "Okay, we need to pull this as hard as we can to close the vent."

Chase sat behind Jonny and reached around and put both his hands under Jonny's hands.

"On the count of three, pull," Jonny said. They both pulled as hard as they could but could not get enough purchase. "We need more leverage."

Jonny grabbed a small crowbar and looped the cable around it several times and locked the steel cable to the crowbar with the vise grips. Improvising a lever, he wedged the crowbar against a hull cross brace.

The sub was now at sixty-six feet, three full atmospheres of pressure. Over forty-four pounds per square inch of outside water pressure was squeezing against the sub's thin fiberglass shell and only its internal pressure was holding against a disastrous implosion. Jonny knew they had seconds. The boat was not designed for these stresses, and the hull was grinding and groaning trying to equalize against the opposing forces.

"Okay, now let's pull together," Jonny said.

Slowly the crowbar moved backward, first a few inches and finally flat against the deck, just enough to close the vent.

"Go back to the helm and bring her up to twenty feet slowly, very slowly. I want to give her time to adjust," Jonny said. "I'll have to jerry-rig a more permanent cable repair."

* * *

Chase did as directed and the sub ascended to twenty feet. He looked down at his shirt. It was sopping wet, as were his jeans. There was no water leak; he was sweating profusely from the stress and fear. His heart was still pounding, as he took deep calming breaths. He looked back down on Jonny, who was happily whistling an unrecognizable tune while splicing together sections of cable. The man was the epitome of cool, no fear, not even a bead of sweat.

Jonny came over and placed his hand on Chase's shoulder. "That cable's always been trouble, but you did good. I'll take over."

Relieved, Chase slid from the pilot's seat, limp from fear.

* * *

Jonny inspected all the gauges, particularly the gyro; Chase was spot-on.

Then he checked the batteries. They were down to less than a half-charge, and Jonny knew they only had a few hours until dawn.

"I'm going to bring her up. We need to recharge," he said.

The sea had a slight chop, but not more than a foot. Still, they just bobbed in place for a few seconds.

Jonny popped the hatch to look out. He was refreshed by the cool breeze and fresh air.

"Hand me the scope," he told Chase.

Jonny scanned the sea with night vision scope but saw nothing.

He reached into his pocket and pulled out Cuda's sat phone. He inserted the battery and dialed. He waited silently for a few seconds and hung up. He removed the battery again. He took a few heavy drags from the cigarette he'd dangled from his lips for the past hour. "'Bout time."

Jonny shouted to Chase, "Open the aft hatches and let's get some air flowin' in here."

Jonny started the engine and the annoying drone of the diesel replaced the quiet of the gentle electric whir.

* * *

Chase found a bale bed. It had been a full thirty-two hours since he had slept. The first night, he couldn't stop thinking about Maria and the kids. The second night was ocean-bound. But now a fatigue overtook him and, within minutes, he was in a deep sleep.

"Chase, Chase, get up." A voice called but it was distant and not anything like Maria's voice.

"Chase, come on. We gotta dive." He heard that one better. It was not a dream and now he was awake.

Chase shook his head to clear the fog, then rubbed his eyes, bringing Jonny into focus. "What is it?"

"I need you to close the rear hatch and check the cable to the port ballast vent. We're all charged and it's getting too light. We can't stay on the surface."

Chase rose slowly, loosened the cramps in his arms and legs from the unforgiving bed, and made his way aft.

After he dogged the hatch, he walked toward the helm, stretching as best he could. "How long have I been out?"

"Well, you missed sunrise, and it's now 6 a.m. I'd say three hours."

"I needed it."

"Don't we all."

"Hey, I gotta piss. Where's the head?"

"See those buckets over there? Whatever you got to do, do it in there, but you are responsible for throwing our own stuff overboard. Make sure you put the lid back on. It gets pretty rank in here without ventilation."

"What about showers?"

"Use a different bucket and a washcloth. It goes over the side, too."

"Just like in the old days," Chase said.

"Naw, in the old days they hung their asses over the deck."

Chapter Forty-Six
Near Tijuana, Baja California, Mexico

Cuda, Martinez—the distributor—and their men waited at the cove. It was well past dawn, but not a hint of the speedboats on the horizon.

"Did they go somewhere else?" Martinez asked.

"No, this is the place," Cuda said.

"Can't you call them? Do they have a radio?"

Cuda didn't answer; the situation was bad and getting worse. This was the second time La Hermandad's delivery was late, and Martinez was livid. El Cuervo had sent Cuda after the last shipment was lost, and Martinez was only appeased when Cuda recovered most of the cargo, but it was many days late. The distributor didn't warehouse the product—it was too dangerous. He got it through the tunnel and to his network and onto the street. He was the quintessential middleman, but with the most lucrative cut considering the level of risk he assumed and the amount of effort he exerted.

It was his clients, the street-level retailers, who took the product, cut it to the desired concentration, and sold it. The dealers in Beverly Hills might cut the product three times, while those in the tougher neighborhoods cut it five or six times. It all depended on what the clientele could pay.

But Cuda was about to lose all the goodwill El Cuervo cultivated with Martinez, whom he never liked anyway. He was arrogant, demanding, and had an annoying habit of talking out of the side of his mouth while he tongued a large cigar. It was as though he were too important to even consider removing the cigar to talk clearly.

"I'm afraid your organization is becoming unreliable, and that is something my clients don't like." Martinez spat a brown wad to the pavement. "Without the goods, we have no business."

Cuda smiled and nodded. "I understand. This is a difficult situation I have put you in, and I'm sorry." This was the attitude El Cuervo had told him to use in dealing with disgruntled clients. He was told to apologize, seek forgiveness, and promise to improve. All were lofty ideals, but behind his insincere smile, Cuda seethed. The man in front of him was threatening him, El Cuervo, and La Hermandad; he was considering another cartel, and that could only end badly for someone.

Cuda's cell phone rang. He read the screen; Caller ID unavailable. He put the phone to his ear. "Hello," he said, but there was no response. He hung up.

"Any news?" Martinez asked.

"Nothing yet."

"I can't wait around much longer. People will start using the cove."

"You go on ahead. I'll wait. Take my car and leave the van. We will deliver the load to you. And for all your troubles, you deserve a little discount," Cuda said.

It was the smart thing; it's what El Cuervo would want.

"Maybe It's time for me to talk to the Ochos," Martinez said.

Cuda knew of the man's violent reputation in controlling the drug trade in the back alleys of Tijuana. But he'd had all he could take.

Cuda grabbed the man by the hair on the back of his head and jerked it down hard. With the fingers of his left hand, Cuda jammed the cigar down the man's throat, blocking his trachea.

Gasping for air, the distributor fell backward, writhing on the ground, frantically clutching at his throat to dislodge the burning cigar.

His men were about to draw their weapons, but Cuda's men were faster. It was a true Mexican standoff. No one moved, no one dared. All were frozen except the gasping figure on the ground. It took three minutes before his last twitch, and another three until the brain, starved of oxygen, sent its last signal to the man's heart.

Cuda turned slowly to the distributor's crew. "Who's the new boss?"

A younger man, maybe thirty-five, stepped forward.

"Should we wait a little longer for the boats?" Cuda asked.

The man nodded in agreement.

The boats never arrived. Cuda made new arrangements with the new boss, and each left the beach. As a final tribute, the dead distributor was unceremoniously dumped into the back of the van. His body would never be found, nor would he be spoken of again.

Cuda informed El Cuervo of Martinez's sudden death. But El Cuervo always told him no one in this business was indispensable. A deal would be made with the new boss to continue the relationship, and if not him, then his replacement. La Hermandad's product would get over the border one way or the other.

Cuda knew El Cuervo would not be so understanding that another shipment failed to get through, and this time without a trace of the submarine or the speedboats. They should have returned hours ago.

As he pondered the missing sub, Cuda thought that this just might be the chance they were waiting for.

Chapter Forty-Seven

Eastern Tropical Pacific Near Vicente Guerrero, Baja California, Mexico

30°44'37"N, 116°02'44"W

"By the time we get back to shore, they'll know something went wrong. The shipment should have arrived almost two days ago," Jonny said.

Chase shrugged. "But they won't know it was us."

"Someone will figure it out, but now we have that bargaining chip."

Jonny had studied the charts of central Baja. Like any pilot, he wanted alternate sites where he could safely ditch in an emergency. He had a few specific criteria: it had to be isolated; it had to be deep enough to hide the sub, but not too deep to recover the bales; it had to be swimming distance to the beach; and no dangerous surf. The problem was these were the same conditions attracting tourists.

Jonny had a site; he'd flagged it months ago, but for a different plan.

It was night and Jonny peered through the top hatch. There were no lights from the beach. They'd run the diesel for the past two hours and the tanks were empty. Jonny didn't want any oil slick from a breach in the hull telegraphing the location of the sub.

"Motor in a little closer," Jonny said, looking down the hatch to Chase at the helm.

After a few minutes, Jonny slid down to the helm. "Go open the port hatch and get the raft out," he told Chase.

Chase tossed the canister into the water and pulled the release halyard. The raft opened and inflated. He pulled it alongside the sub.

"Get in and stay in the area. I'll swim to you."

Chase did as he was instructed.

Jonny ran down and opened the starboard hatch, then returned to the helm. It was a risky plan, but he stayed calm.

He maneuvered the sub to the position he wanted. The seabed was soft sand and only forty feet deep—an easy depth for salvage divers. Jonny cut all power, disconnected the batteries to avoid any shorts in the electrical system, and disarmed the explosive charges. He made sure all the bales and other equipment were stowed and lashed tight so not to float to the surface before returning to the helm and flooding the ballast tanks. The seawater rushed through the vents and into the tanks in a loud surge.

The sub descended slowly and evenly as he had designed it. Jonny stood on the pilot's chair and lifted himself halfway out of the top hatch. Any second now.

Suddenly, the bow lifted three feet as the ocean flooded the stern of the sub through the two open rear hatches.

Jonny pulled himself through the hatch and jumped into the ocean. He shuddered at the shock of the cold water and began swimming the hundred feet to the raft.

Chase struggled to get the tired and shivering Jonny aboard. The flimsy raft provided little stability and nothing to brace against. Finally, exhausted, Jonny flopped in like a dazed mackerel.

Both watched as the sub began to level out as the seawater rushed forward, flooding the bow compartment. In seconds, only the top hatch cover, protruding like a shark's dorsal fin, was visible until the sea flooded that portal, too. Then she was gone—a few bubbles of displaced air and then nothing, just calm.

"You got the sat phone?"

"Yeah, but I ditched the cell phones like you said. I hope you remember the position," Chase said.

"Yeah, me too. G-g-get paddling, will ya."

Chapter Forty-Eight
Nido del Cuervo Ranch

Aside from an earthy blend of manure and wet hay that permeated the stable, the caretaker Tomás' room was comfortable. It was in a corner of the stable and had windows on two walls. The finished pine floor was covered with a large rug. A dark-stained wainscoting dressed the lower wall and the plastered walls and ceiling were painted in a light adobe tone. A slow rotating ceiling fan cooled the room, while weathered brass fixtures provided light. A small bed and bedside table were positioned in the outside corner, and a dresser and a heavy upholstered chair were opposite the door. There was even a small bathroom with a toilet and sink through a doorway next to the chair.

It was just what he needed to catch some needed sleep once the horses were settled for the night.

But the thick door provided the security for the room's present function as a cell. A luxurious jail, but confinement nonetheless, and Tomás had moved to the house.

Maria and the kids were relieved when they arrived at the ranch. After leaving the tunnel, they were herded into a horse trailer and driven for what seemed over two hours. The people at the ranch were much nicer to them. They were fed well, could hose off in one of the empty stalls, and even allowed to walk around the stable. Maria had no fantasy about escaping. She had no idea where she was and could only see a vast expanse of mountains and woodlands beyond the stable. And she saw the guards. They usually patrolled near the barn across from the corral, but one guard—the heavy one with the bushy red beard of a Viking and Wayfarer sunglasses—seemed out of place and he lurked closer than the others. The big man in the black suit said he was negotiating with her husband. She would have to put all her trust in Chase. He had never let her down. It was her job to keep the kids safe.

She noticed that Tomás, took a liking to Kevin. He said Kevin reminded him of his nephew. He even let Kevin walk with the big black horse around the paddock. Maria was frightened when the man lifted Kevin onto the stallion's back, but she could not show fear—Kevin would sense it. Instead, Kevin giggled in delight, and could not wait for his next chance. Denise, ever the worrier, stayed behind gritting her teeth because Kevin got the ride and she didn't. But when Tomás finally asked her, she declined.

It made Maria smile. Maybe there was a chance.

Chapter Forty-Nine
Colonia Vicente Guerrero, Baja California, Mexico

Jonny's research had paid off. If it weren't for the new moon, their beaching would have been darker and a little drier. But the spring tide was enough to create the six-foot wave that flipped the raft. Although only fifteen feet from dry land, Chase swam furiously until he looked around and saw Jonny's head in the four-foot surf. He was wading toward the beach.

"Keep going, you're almost there." Jonny shook his head and stifled a laugh.

The both sat on the dry sand, luxuriating in its warmth, and looked seaward.

"You think you can find it again?" Chase asked.

"We have a lot riding on it. We better get walking. We need to find somewhere to hold out for the next few days."

"Do you know where we are?"

"I think so. There should be a little colony to the south, but we need to get to the road."

They made it to the highway and started walking.

Traffic was light during the predawn hours, and the two men didn't attract much attention—just a couple of vagabonds, something the residents of Baja knew well.

"What's in the village? Has it got a hotel?" Chase asked.

"No, it's just a few of the beach houses, and most are owned by people from the States who come down for vacations. They're usually empty in the off-season."

"If someone is there, won't they be suspicious?"

"Maybe, but some are rented out, and others are timeshares. Plus, I don't plan on staying long. Just to rest and dry out. We've gotta keep moving."

* * *

"You must have done this before," Chase said as he watched how easily Jonny jimmied the latch on the rear window of the small cottage.

"Once or twice. Here, give me a lift."

Chase bent his right leg to create a stair step for Jonny, who used it to boost himself over the sill and onto the hard tile floor of the cottage's single bedroom. He unlocked the back door and greeted the waiting Chase.

Sealed from the outside air and baking in the Pacific sun, the interior of the cottage was hot and stale. Jonny circled the living room, opening windows. He rousted a banded gecko that escaped across the ceiling in defiance of gravity.

The cottage was spare. The floors were linoleum, the sofa and chairs vinyl, and the tables a faux-wood plastic. It was perfect for the beach: waterproof, sand-proof, and sun-proof.

"Couch or bed?" Jonny asked.

"Couch. You did the hard work."

* * *

Chase awoke to full daylight around noon. He looked around but saw no signs of Jonny. The damp clothes Jonny had draped over kitchen chairs were gone.

Ha, he deserted me already. Chase rose from the couch and stretched. The five hours were the best sleep he'd had in days. He was revived, alert, but ravenous.

He walked to the bathroom and relieved himself. He saw the shower and some towels. He went for it. Unfortunately, the water heater was off, so the shower was short and bracing.

The clothes were now dry, but stiff from the salt and sand, and carried a faint aroma of diesel and seawater. They would have to do.

He walked to the kitchen and looked in the refrigerator, it was empty and warm. He checked the cabinets, but there was no food. He decided to wait a few minutes for Jonny before heading out to find something to eat.

* * *

Unlike the snoring Chase, Jonny had barely slept. The bed was comfortable, maybe too much so, but his head was spinning. He knew they were in big trouble and it was only a matter of time before La Hermandad found them. He had to do something first, something unexpected, something bold.

Around ten a.m., he could take it no more and rose. Chase was snoring loudly on the couch, but he tiptoed through the cabin anyway in search of food. Frustrated, he decided to head for the mercado down the road. He would rustle up a good Louisiana breakfast for them.

Jonny grabbed some eggs, some hot chorizo, fresh baked pan, cheese, peanut butter, some orange juice, hot sauce, a couple packs of smokes, and some candy bars.

He handed the clerk a twenty-dollar bill and got his change in pesos. *I will need them.*

He thanked the clerk and left.

* * *

As the door clicked shut, the clerk pulled the flyer from under the counter, well hidden from any patron. There were two photographs and descriptions: a tall Anglo with sandy brown hair and a short, skinny black man. Cuda's men had distributed hundreds of flyers after Jonny and Chase escaped. The clerk inspected the photographs. They were grainy, but there was no mistaking who he had just seen.

He dialed the number—he could use the two thousand dollars.

* * *

"I see you have awakened, sleeping beauty," Jonny said, walking to the kitchen and setting down the bag. He was sweating from the long walk and now hungry, even though he devoured two candy bars on the way back.

"And here I thought you left me," Chase joked.

"Naw, just went to get us some food. Sorry I didn't leave you a note. Did you miss me?" Jonny went to a cabinet and pulled out a frying pan. He turned on one of the stove's burners, but nothing happened, not even the hiss of escaping gas. He walked around to the back near the window he'd tumbled through in the early morning. On the side of the house was a large torpedo-shaped tank. He found the valve and opened it, hoping some gas remained. Just a few minutes, that's all I need.

By the time breakfast was finished, the water tank had heated up, and Jonny was the happy recipient of a long, hot shower. Jonny laughed when he saw the dismayed looked on Chase's face. "That's the price of impatience," he said as steam rolled out from the bathroom.

Showered and dressed, Jonny told Chase, "You're safe here for a day or two, but I got to head out."

"You really *are* deserting me?" Chase said with a serious expression. "Shouldn't we stay together?"

"No, I can go faster alone. I can blend in better and know the area," Jonny said, not wanting Chase to know the real reason. If they were caught, Chase would do and say anything to save his family. He'd give it all up, and Jonny would lose his leverage. He needed Chase as a diversion—to keep Cuda's men occupied here while he tended to his plan up north. Even if Cuda caught Chase, he wasn't likely to kill him, at least not right way—they'd try to use him to find the lost sub. And having Chase leave after a couple of days would give Jonny the time and cover he needed.

"What do I do here? What if someone sees me?"

"Keep low. If anyone asks, you have rented the cottage for a week. A couple from Burbank named Beaton own it—it says so on the emergency contact sheet on the wall. Just drop that name, no one is going to call them."

Jonny handed Chase a slip of paper. "In four days, I want to meet you at this location. Take the bus but stay out of sight." Jonny reached into his pants pocket for a wad of bills that he handed to Chase. "Here's some cash. Buses comes down the road every thirty minutes or so. Just raise your arm and the driver will pull over. I'll take the sat phone and try to make a deal with them for the sub."

"I don't know." Chased looked down in apprehension at his hands, one holding the note, the other the money.

"Look, you saved me, give me a chance to do the same."

Chapter Fifty
Colonia Vicente Guerrero, Baja California, Mexico

Cuda was on the road within minutes. It was the only hit they had gotten. The flyers had been distributed widely, but no calls had come in until the morning. It was curious, Cuda thought, we get the information only after the shipment went missing. He had a feeling, and it was a bad one.

It was nearing six p.m. when he finally arrived at the mercado near El Rosario.

The clerk explained he had only seen the black man. No one was with him.

Cuda glared at the clerk through black eyes. "What was he driving?"

"I didn't see anything. Maybe he took the bus." The clerk swallowed hard.

"What bus goes by at that time?"

"The north bus from Guerrero Negro."

"What did he buy?"

"Just a few things: eggs, bread, sausage. He mumbled something about a good breakfast. I didn't pay much attention—I was just looking at his face."

"Where are places to stay to the south of here?"

"There are only a few hotels, but there are several rentals near the beach. The tourists come in spring after the rainy season."

"Here." Cuda slapped an envelope into the man's hand.

"This is only a thousand," the man said and was sorry the instant he made the comment.

"You'll get the rest when we catch them, or if you see them again. My cell number is on the envelope." Cuda slammed the screen door on the way out.

* * *

The clerk exhaled deep and took a new breath. He'd be satisfied not getting any money if it meant not having to deal with the big man again.

Cuda had that effect.

Chapter Fifty-One
Near El Rosario, Baja California, Mexico

Jonny got on the bus just outside El Rosario. In Ensenada, he took the bus on Federal Highway 5 to Mexicali. It wasn't hard to blend in. He looked like any other campesino on the bus waiting to queue up in Mexicali for a dash across the border to Calexico, followed by a serious game of hide-and-seek with the Border Patrol through the agricultural fields of Imperial County. The only difference was the money in his pocket and his US citizenship.

If he was caught in some roundup, he figured he would be locked up a few nights until they confirmed his identity. For once, he was thankful he'd been fingerprinted and in the FBI's Integrated Automated Fingerprint Identification System, which was required for all vessel masters. He was developing a cover story if he was caught on why he didn't just go to the embassy to get a new passport rather than risk an illegal crossing. Unfortunately, the story needed work.

His biggest worry was whether La Hermandad had a source in the Immigration Office who was on the alert for him. He couldn't imagine a worst surprise than have Cuda or Nico waiting as he was released from custody.

But the crossing and deserting Chase would be a desperation move. He still had a few other options.

* * *

Jonny knew La Hermandad well. He knew they'd be in close pursuit and had to do something to divert their attention.

On the bus to Ensenada, Jonny made a call. He noticed the bus driver glancing at him in the rearview mirror.

"I have been trying to reach you," Cuda said.

Jonny could hear the loathing in the man's tone. "The battery was dead, and we've been busy. I hope the family is well."

"They are well and living in the lap of luxury. You know how El Cuervo cares about families. If it were me, you'd be sent a photograph of a severed finger every day until you turned yourself in. But I'm not the jefe."

"You've got a little problem. Where would you send it? Where would we see it?" Jonny goaded.

Cuda didn't answer.

"And this is precisely why El Cuervo is in charge and you are just a goon taking orders." Jonny sensed Cuda's rage and pressed on. "But we could change that. I keep telling you, I have a plan. It would not be that difficult with what you know and what I know. We wouldn't have to work for anyone else."

"Maybe I like working for El Cuervo."

"And maybe I'm talking to the wrong man. Maybe Nico would be interested."

"What are you talking about?"

"I happen to know exactly where a hundred fifty million dollars-worth of coke is buried. It seems one of El Cuervo's subs landed at the wrong port. Weren't you supposed to pick up a shipment a few days ago? Wasn't it the second shipment lost in a month? It must be difficult satisfying your clients. El Cuervo must be very concerned about your management skills." Jonny smiled at the taunt.

"Speak to me a little more clearly. What are you saying?"

"I'm saying I know where you can get a whole lot of money. Enough money to break out on your own, maybe even take over La Hermandad."

"What would you get out of it?"

"I'd be your partner running the shipping, but you'd be the capo because you know the whole business and you got the muscle. Think about it, you could live in the manner of El Cuervo. But you'd have to get rid of him and his lieutenants."

"I have a better plan. Why don't I find you and start pulling out your toenails until you tell me where the coke is? Then I'll start on your hands until you tell me where Chase Brenner is. If that doesn't work, I'll just have to show Brenner what we're doing to his children. He will talk. He'll give you up in a second to save those kids. I just need to send him one video, that's all."

"You could be right. But, again, you have a couple of problems—I have the phone and the number. He doesn't know your number and you can't call him. And, personally, what do I care what happens to his family? I've already cut him loose. He's on his own, I'm the one you want now. And good luck if you find him. He has no idea where the shipment is hidden. Besides, if you kill him and his family, I'll have a hundred million ways to overcome my guilt. You need to think this through a little better, warm up to the idea. It's a big step for you. I have to go, but you'll be hearing from me." Jonny hung up and a sinister smile crossed his face. He'd pushed all the right buttons.

He looked at the driver and noticed he still had him in the rearview mirror.

Jonny placed the sat phone under his seat and wedged it tight between the seat leg and the side of the bus, so it wouldn't slip when the driver hit the brakes. This time, the batteries stayed in.

Now, Jonny had a big decision. Chase could never find the coke, and Jonny could easily disappear.

He'd done it before.

Chapter Fifty-Two
Colonia Vicente Guerrero, Baja California, Mexico

By midnight, Cuda had four men scouring the area. He told them to first check out the comings and goings at the hotels and motels, passing out cash with the flyers.

They would then drive to the small towns, particularly the tourist enclaves, to look for signs people were living in the cottages. They talked to bus drivers at different stops along the highway. Cuda needed to recover the shipment, and the only way he was going to get it was catching Brenner and Jonny. But Jonny had the advantage—the only communication link. There was no way to contact Brenner except through Jonny. What good would it do to threaten the hostages when nobody knew?

He had to find Brenner, but first he had a call to make.

Cuda fumbled for his cell, unable to contain his excitement. He dialed the number from memory. After the call he would delete all traces.

"Hello," she answered in a soft, hesitant tone.

"Can you talk now?"

"Yes, but make it fast," she said.

"I had a call. It was from one of El Cuervo's men—the one who hijacked the shipment."

"Go on."

"He has an offer. He wants to make a deal to return the cargo."

"And?"

"He thinks he and I could take over La Hermandad. Me with my knowledge of distribution, he with his expertise in transportation."

"Very enterprising of your new friend. El Cuervo won't go easy. He has many loyal men."

"It will be up to us. I know who we can trust. I know who can be turned and who can be bought. It will be bloody, but we have the advantage. It's what you've dreamed about for years, you know it."

"What did you tell the man?"

"I told him he was crazy, and I would kill him as soon as I found him."

"Good. So, he has no idea you'd be disloyal to El Cuervo?"

"Not a clue. He is desperate for a deal because we have hostages."

"How did you end the call?"

"He said to call back if I reconsider."

"How much is he holding?"

"At least a hundred and fifty million street."

"This could work. What would we do with our new partner?"

"We both know three is a troublesome number."

"Indeed, it is." She sighed before hanging up.

Chapter Fifty-Three
Ensenada, Baja California, Mexico

Nico was worried. He would have Manny check it out.

The call came from the Tijuana bus station the day before. The dispatcher said a bus driver handed him a telephone lost by a passenger. The driver had not noticed it until he finished his route and he was cleaning the bus for the return trip to Guerrero Negro.

The dispatcher found the number of Pescadero Baja in the directory and called to see if someone lost the phone.

Nico told the dispatcher a phone had recently been stolen from one of the company's employees.

Earlier in the morning, Nico had driven the seventy miles north to the Tijuana bus station and retrieved the phone. He asked the dispatcher for the contact information of the bus driver, so he could send him a reward.

When he returned to Ensenada, Nico called the driver. "I want to thank you for finding our company's phone. We would like to send you a little gift to express our gratitude."

"That won't be necessary, but thank you," the driver said.

"No, we're grateful and want to do it. Could I ask you a few questions?"

"Certainly."

"Well, the phone was stolen, so we're trying to identify who took it. Do you remember who was using it or who was sitting near where you found the phone?"

"I believe it was a man in the third row. He was making calls, but I could not hear what he was saying."

"Can you describe him? Would you recognize him if you saw him again?"

"Yes, I think so. He was a black man, maybe thirty, thirty-five. I noticed he was short and very thin, a laborer, with worn shirt and pants. A very expensive phone for such a man."

"Did you remember where he got off?"

"I'm sure it was Ensenada. I didn't see where he went when he left the bus."

"Did he get off on the road?"

"No, he went all the way to the terminal."

Nico hung up and made a note to send the driver fifty dollars—it was money well spent.

* * *

The sat phone was the model used by all of El Cuervo's men. He plugged it into the charger and began checking the directories.

His face tightened in concern. They were pretty sure it was Jonny and Chase who had broken into Cuda's car and stolen the phone.

Only a few calls were logged since it went missing. Using the satellite phone tracking system La Hermandad used to keep tabs on its crews, Nico found calls originating from three locations: one from the marina where the speedboats were launched, one from out at sea, and a recent call from Ensenada. All were outgoing calls.

He cross-referenced the dates and times. The first was the night the shipment was to be delivered; the call at sea was the next evening; and the Ensenada call was just two days ago.

Then he checked the metadata. There was only one number, and Nico recognized it immediately. He wrote down the geographical coordinates of the incoming call. He entered the first set of coordinates into his computer and a map of Ensenada with a bright red star near the Grande Vista Hotel appeared. He entered the second set, and the star moved to the parking lot of Pescadero Baja. The third set, the different number, was on the south side of Ensenada near the highway.

* * *

Cuda was the one-man Nico did not want to cross—it could be deadly. On top of that, he was El Cuervo's most valuable asset. But he couldn't make sense of it. He dialed the bunker.

"It's very confusing. Why would his sat phone be at the marina after he said he lost it? Who had it at sea?" Manny asked.

"Maybe it means Jonny and Brenner stole the shipment. They broke into Cuda's car, they stole the boats, and they hijacked the sub," Nico said.

"Yes, but we knew that."

"But why are they calling Cuda?"

"Why?"

"Could they be working with Cuda? Think about it. Jonny and Brenner just happen to overpower Cuda? Maybe. Cuda just happens to recover the shipment Jonny scuttled. He also finds the missing bales when the broken transmitter was fixed. And when he returns, he only brings back a couple of bricks when we know at least seventy-two went missing. Brenner is selling the stuff in Cabo and La Paz, and a week later an entire sub is lost." Nico paused to let it sink in. "And who are the only guys who know the sub's arrival time, where the speedboats depart, and how to drive the sub?"

"Explain why Jonny would bring the sat phone back. Wouldn't it make more sense to keep it, even destroy it?" Manny asked.

"I don't know, but there can only be three possibilities. First, Jonny is setting Cuda up to get back at him, revenge for something, maybe for blaming him for scuttling his boat. Second, Jonny is trying to expose Cuda to El Cuervo. Or third, they are working together, and Jonny just lost the phone. Or maybe a fourth reason: it's all just a coincidence."

"What's in it for Jonny by snitching on Cuda?"

"Jonny figures if he can prove to El Cuervo that Cuda is working on his own, maybe he will be given another chance, that La Hermandad would not pursue him," Nico said.

"Maybe, but why not just call?"

"Would you believe him? No, we'd need proof, and this is why he left the phone. But if he just lost the phone, maybe they are working together. You going to take this to El Cuervo?" Nico asked.

"Yeah, unless you want to do it."

Chapter Fifty-Four
Near Tecate, Baja California, Mexico

"This is a serious allegation. Do you realize what he would do to you if he knew what you have just told me?"

Manny tried to still his trembling hands. "El Cuervo, this is not something I bring to you lightly. But if my suspicions are correct, if I had waited to tell you when I had more proof, I might too late. If I'm wrong, I beg your mercy."

Cuervo sat at his desk lightly rubbing together the thumb and forefinger of both hands. "Have you spoken of this with anyone?"

"Yes, I talked to Nico. It was he who told me about the phone."

"This puts me in a very difficult situation. I have Cuda involved in very delicate operations with the network and in trying to get our product to our customers. It's Cuda I dispatch to do the things that must be done. He has always been a trusted associate," Cuervo said, but he had to admit, silently to himself, that the situation was curious. The seeds of doubt had been sown, and he could take no chances. No one, not even Cuda, was beyond reproach with the amount of money and power at stake.

"We need to increase your security, El Cuervo."

Cuervo nodded in approval. "Let's just watch him a little closer." Cuervo knew, all too well, it was through deception and treachery that he arose to power.

He knew, too, that kings fell and most often to princes.

Chapter Fifty-Five
Mexicali, Baja California, Mexico

The Ochos had always coveted La Hermandad's territory. It never made sense they would relinquish the Baja peninsula, particularly with its direct access to San Diego and on to San Francisco and north to Vancouver. The Ochos' territory had more risks because of the distance to the coast. It was great for smuggling people, but hard for drugs—too vulnerable to detection from the sky. Los Moros cartel was even farther away, but it had Dallas and San Antonio, the ports of Houston and New Orleans, and everything east.

That sliver of a peninsula made a huge difference, and it was a sweet plum for a takeover. What puzzled Comandante Guerra was how La Hermandad got the product from Colombia. As a former military commander with close connections to the Policía Federal, his network of informers was wide. He even planted a few in La Hermandad, but they were never more than mules.

When Guerra got the phone call, he was intrigued. A street dealer in Mexicali had contacted his supplier, who passed it on to one of Guerra's lieutenants. It was information of such potential value no one dared not deliver the message.

The contact gave only a cell phone number and the fact that he knew the entire La Hermandad transport network. Guerra thought it was a bluff—too good to be true, maybe even a trap. But one doesn't ascend to his position playing it safe. He wasn't reckless but embraced risk. He had no problem making the call; it couldn't be traced. At worst, it was a waste of time; at best, who knew?

He waited a day, not wanting to seem too interested.

He placed a half-burned cigar in the ashtray and dialed the number.

"Hello," the stranger answered.

Guerra scratched at his three-day stubble. "My men tell me the information you have is maybe useful to me."

"Yes."

"How?"

"I have been having problems with La Hermandad. I think the leadership is failing."

Guerra picked up the cigar and took a long draw. "Why would I want to upset my good relationship with El Cuervo?"

"I can give you five hundred million reasons, maybe two billion."

The cigar clenched tight between his teeth, Guerra flared his eyebrows. "I'm listening."

"I know the operation from Colombia to San Diego. I know when, where, and who," the stranger paused, "and I'm sure you know why."

"What is it you want?"

"I'll get to that, but first, I must prove to you I'm who I say."

"How is that?"

"Is this phone secure?"

"Yes."

"Okay, write down these coordinates. Send two or three men. Take the path down to the cove. On the south end, have them look for a series of lines etched into the rock. Have them dig there. Once you are satisfied with what they bring back, call me," the stranger said and hung up.

Guerra sat and contemplated the possibilities. If I can get back at El Cuervo, I must try. A coup is always better than a war.

His memory went back to his first meeting with La Hermandad's new capo. He remembered asking himself how this "El Cuervo" rose so quickly to power. They never met before, yet Guerra could see the hate burning in the younger man's eyes. The question that eluded him was why?

"We finally meet," Guerra said with a hint of disdain in having to deal with the upstart. But behind his attitude, there was a grudging respect. This was the man who was responsible for Espinosa's demise, and had outlasted two predecessors.

Cuervo looked like he wanted to leap across the table and strangle Guerra, but both knew he would have been shot in a second, even with Cuda over his right shoulder. Instead, Cuervo calmly reached his hand across the table to shake. A wry smile crossed his lips.

"I have waited many years for this day," Cuervo said.

"I understand your men call you El Cuervo. What is your real name?"

"El Cuervo is good enough for my men, and it will have to do for you, Comandante Guerra."

"So be it. I was just hoping for a less formal relationship. After all, we now have much in common. So much of your new territory was once mine. And we share the same burdens of leadership."

Cuervo pushed an envelope across the desk.

Guerra stroked his gray beard and cast a steeled glare toward his rival. He felt El Cuervo was taunting him to accept it. He took a silent deep breath and reached for the envelope. He opened it and removed a sheet of writing paper. Guerra stared at the sheet but was confused. Had he seen it before? What did it mean? He placed the paper on the table. It had but a single letter, handwritten in pencil: "A."

Guerra looked to El Cuervo, confused.

Cuervo, his face taut with anger, stared back. "I, too, have lost much."

Chapter Fifty-Six
Mexicali, Baja California, Mexico

The call came.

"It was a fine treasure my men uncovered. But I still don't know how they get it to the States."

"Let's just say by boat," the stranger said.

"That is impossible. I have contacts at every port, in Customs, in all the police departments, Navy, everywhere, yet none of these bricks have been found."

"It's a special boat—a very special boat—and I have it. I have one more piece of information for you. El Cuervo's chief enforcer, the man they call Cuda, is looking to get out. I can arrange a meeting with him in Mexicali."

Guerra remembered the man; he was hard to forget. It had been at the first meeting with La Hermandad's new capo, El Cuervo, ten years before. He had been his bodyguard.

"So, what is it you want?"

Chapter Fifty-Seven
Mexicali, Baja California, Mexico

Cuda sat alone, drinking his coffee and second-guessing his presence in this dusty café outside Mexicali.

He hadn't wanted to think about Jonny's idea. He was sure it was just a ruse to keep him off guard—to give Jonny and Brenner more chances to hide, but he still had the hostages. Then the second call had come—one he never expected to happen, and now he couldn't help but think about it, nor could his partner.

Jonny wanted him to meet in Mexicali, which was a curious choice. His men were miles away searching the coast near El Rosario. It wasn't neutral territory, but La Hermandad and the Ochos existed more or less peacefully. It was at the farther reaches of El Cuervo's influence, and Jonny said Cuda would not be known here.

Cuda thought about it. What did he have to lose? He was still in pursuit of these men, but if what Jonny had to say was—well, he could listen.

The meet was scheduled for ten in the morning, but it wasn't fifteen minutes later when a haggard taxi driver, no doubt suffering the effects of sixteen hours behind the wheel, entered the cantina.

The six patrons watched as the driver immediately approached the big man seated alone.

"Señor Aleta?"

"Sí."

The driver handed a small bag to Cuda and turned to leave.

"Wait. Who gave this to you?" Cuda asked.

"A man in town, he told me to deliver it to you."

"When was this?"

The driver shifted anxiously and looked at his watch, "Maybe fifteen minutes ago."

"What did he look like?"

"A small black man with a ball cap. He was wearing jeans and a T-shirt."

"Where was he? Was he alone?"

"At the bus station, and I didn't see anyone else. Can I go?"

Cuda said nothing; he just turned his attention to the bag. He opened it and looked inside—a plastic-wrapped brick of coke, a transmitter, and a short note.

I have many more, and they are all yours. Will call with more details.

What the hell. Why come all the way here to this hole-in-the-wall for this? He could have given me this in Ensenada.

Seething with anger, he rose to leave. The little shit Jonny had played him. I should have killed him when he returned to Ensenada.

* * *

As Cuda left the café, two men sitting at a back table exited shortly after and tailed him loosely.

All these comings and goings were observed from across the road.

Chapter Fifty-Eight
Ensenada, Baja California, Mexico

In their last few conversations, Cuda had sensed the distance in El Cuervo's voice. He was relying more on Manny and Nico while Cuda was consigned to the heavy lifting. El Cuervo seemed ready to blame him for the problems with the shipments, and Jonny's escape, but it made no sense. It was not his responsibility. He believed others were undermining him, scapegoating him for their own failures. While he hated to admit it, it was a blow to his ego, and he felt his influence waning. He was becoming but another disposable functionary.

When Jonny's offer came, Cuda was open to options, although his distrust of the little man made him hesitate. He conceded the timing was perfect. It was not as if Cuda hadn't thought about him and his partner running La Hermandad. He knew they could do as well as El Cuervo, maybe better, because they were not fearful of confronting the Ochos; they had no problem raising the level of violence to get things done.

Access to an entire shipment was the leverage they would need. He had spoken to the dealers; he knew they were distressed. It would not take much for them to abandon La Hermandad—it was just business. Without supplies, they had no income. What Cuda had to avoid was the dealers going elsewhere. The Ochos knew supplies were tight along the coast and were circling—there was blood in the water. Cuda had to act fast; he had to act decisively.

It was time.

Chapter Fifty-Nine
Nido del Cuervo Ranch

Maria felt a nudge, a warm hand on her shoulder—just enough to break her dream and awaken her. The room was dark, but against the dim light from the open door she could make out his silhouette as he turned toward the light. She saw he had one finger pressed to his lips, the other hand pointed to her children beside her on the bed. He gestured her toward the door and whispered, "Tomás needs to see you."

Maria was confused; she had only seen the bearded man from a distance, and never in the stable. She looked to her right. The kids were asleep, Denise with arms and legs straddling half the bed, while poor Kevin was curled in a ball between them, ceding all territory to his sister. She rubbed her eyes. The man beckoned her forward again and she slipped from the bed and followed him from the room.

Once into the stable area, he closed the door gently and locked it. He again placed his finger to his lips and said in a hushed tone, "We don't want to wake the children."

Maria looked around. The gallery was empty. She fixed a suspicious glare at the man. He motioned toward the stable doors, past El Diablo's stall, and a good forty feet before Maria asked, "Where's Tomás?"

"He'll be here shortly."

Maria was not ready for it, too tired or too trusting, but her guard was down. In an instant, the man's right arm was around her chest and his left hand covering her face, muffling any scream. She tried to resist but was only kicking air as he lifted her off the ground. She was no match against the two-hundred-pound assailant as he mauled her into an empty stall.

With a leg sweep, she fell hard on her back to the straw-covered floor and he was immediately astride of her with her arms locked against her sides by his knees. The fall knocked the wind from her lungs and she gasped to scream. But he covered her mouth again once more as he bent over and whispered in her ear, "You can make this

243

easy or hard. It's up to you, but you got two kids in the room, and I'll bet they'd still like to have their mother alive when I'm done."

Sweat was pouring down his ruddy, bearded face and dripping onto Maria. There was a dullness in his brown eyes, a crazed smile on his lips, and whiskey on his breath.

He rose and slowly moved his right hand from her mouth to her neck and began to squeeze. His left hand slid under her shirt until her left breast was cupped into his hand. He issued a deep, primitive moan.

Maria couldn't speak as he tightened his grip slowly and steady. Her eyes bulged in fear and concern for her children. All she could manage was a frantic nod.

He released his hand and his body relaxed, but his full weight was still on Maria's belly.

She groaned. "Please, you are too heavy."

When he lifted onto his knees, Maria took a deep breath, the first full one in a minute. She was trapped and had no choice. She couldn't fight this man, and if she did, she had no idea what he'd do to her children. It seemed so inevitable, yet why had nothing happened until now? There were plenty of opportunities in the house, in the van, in the tunnel, and in the stable, but she had not been mistreated. In fact, Tomás had been kind. Why this, why now, she thought. No, something is not right about this man. What if he kills me? What will happen to Denise and Kevin? Her only chance was to escape, to get help. If someone rescued her, she'd know she wasn't wrong. If they ignored her, she and the children were in deep trouble. Gaining her wind finally, she said, "Okay, please don't hurt me, I won't fight you. Let me get undressed."

Maria still had on the jeans and blouse she'd worn on the day they were kidnapped. They had no change of clothes and she felt safer sleeping dressed. She managed to at least wash her and the kids' underwear in the sink.

The man rolled off her and began unsnapping the faux pearl buttons on his faded western shirt.

Maria knelt on her knees. "No, me first." Her eyes caught his and she cocked her head provocatively.

The man stood transfixed as Maria unbuttoned and removed her blouse. She then unbuttoned her jeans and slowly unzipped them. With both hands on her waist she lowered her jeans, writhing her hips. She kicked the jeans across the floor. She then slowly sat again on her knees, reached around and unclipped her bra and tossed it aside, revealing her supple breasts. She was embarrassed but didn't dare show it. She shook her head and her long auburn hair cascaded over her shoulders.

The man was aroused; Maria's little show had worked as planned.

"Now, you," she said in a voice low and sultry. "But first those boots."

He was breathing heavy now, his face contorted in expectation. He lifted one pant leg and removed his boot and then the other. He unbuckled his belt and unzipped his pants and rolled them to his ankles.

As he lifted one foot to remove a leg of his pants, Maria jumped, shoved the off-balance man to the floor, and bolted toward the stall door.

He was big and he was quick. He could not stand with his ankles bound by the pants, but he leapt for Maria as she got to the threshold. He grabbed her left ankle and she fell to her knees. With all her strength she crawled past the doorway and into the main aisle. She kicked hard and jerked free of his handhold. The man was still flailing blindly for her when she rose, grabbed the bottom half of the stable door, and slammed it into the man's left arm, which had been holding her ankle.

Maria was in panic and heard only two things: the crunching of the bones and a ghastly scream that awoke even those sleeping in the ranch house.

Maria spied a steel hoof pick hung by a nail on the wall next to the tack room door. She grabbed it and slammed the three-inch steel hook through the man's broken hand and into the wood floor. She heard another wail before she, too, screamed, and ran for the children.

The key was still in the door. She unlocked it and slammed the door hard behind her. She turned on the light to look for something, anything, to block the door.

"Mom, what's the matter? Why are you naked?" Denise asked, awakened by the screams and commotion.

"Everything is okay, honey. Can you please help me push this?"

Denise got out of bed and helped shoulder the bureau to the door.

Maria grabbed a blanket to cover herself and sat with her back against the bureau and both legs wedged tight against the bed frame. "Here, sit next to me and help me hold this."

Denise sat, but her legs couldn't reach the bed.

Maria's breathing was frantic. Her heart was racing and her face twisted as she strained against the bureau.

"Are you alright, Mom?" Denise asked, sobbing quietly, fear welling in her eyes.

"Don't worry, hon. It'll be all right,.

Maria heard a knock and Tomás's sorrowful voice, "Señora, please open the door."

Maria knew if anyone at the ranch would save her, it would be Tomás. Draped in the blanket, she pushed the bureau aside and opened the door.

Tomás stood at the threshold, his arms extended and cradling Maria's clothes. His head bowed in contrition, he handed her the blouse and jeans.

"I'm very sorry. This will never happen again." He then closed and locked the door.

Chapter Sixty
Colonia Vicente Guerrero, Baja California, Mexico

Chase sensed it the moment he walked into the mercado. It was the clerk's eyes—how they widened ever so much in surprise, maybe even recognition, but Chase had never been there before.

He'd paced the cottage for a day since Jonny left. All he did was worry. He had no idea what was happening to Maria and the kids. He had no way to contact them. Worst of all, he had to rely on Jonny, a complete stranger, a drug smuggler, a man with a sordid past and questionable present.

He was more helpless and isolated than when he was stuck in the net skiff. There, at least, he was busy staying alive, and knowing his family was safe. He'd taken out the photograph several times. He drew comfort from it, but it brought with it tears—the pain of remembering.

He may have endured another day cooped up, but he was low on food. It was all the excuse he needed.

He strolled through the market casually, putting items in his handbasket. Peering over the few rows of shelving, the suspicious eyes of the clerk followed him to the counter, where he paid with cash. He smiled at the clerk, who returned it unconvincingly, and left the market.

Chase walked out of sight of the front window for a few seconds, turned, and reversed course. He looked in. The clerk had his back to the window and a telephone in his hand. The clerk turned slowly. His face froze when he saw Chase looking back.

It was all Chase needed to know. It was time to leave and fast.

* * *

This plan sucks, Chase thought as he distanced himself from the market. I've got no car, I can't contact Jonny, but I'm supposed to meet him. What if he just played me for the coke?

So far, his paranoia had paid off and he had eluded capture, but how long would his luck hold? He knew the clerk was calling about him. Just like when he entered the building, the clerk's eyes gave him away.

If Cuda had alerted the mercados, he would also cover transportation, which would mean no buses or taxis. But he had to get north.

Chase walked about a mile, staying near but off the main road. At the approach of any vehicle, he dashed for cover. His ears were attuned to the distant rumble of traffic, now a real threat.

He saw it from across the road; it was fueling at the Pemex station. The driver was oblivious to his approach, seemingly more concerned about the spinning dials on the pump.

Chase sprinted across the road as the man entered the gas station to pay. On the highway side of the truck, he was blocked from the view inside of the station. He grabbed an old wooden rail on the stake bed truck, placed his right foot on the right rear tire, and vaulted silently onto the mound of melons.

He lodged himself against the bottom rail and moved a few melons from underneath to lie flat on the truck's bed. He piled some melons over his legs and body and prayed the load wouldn't shift during transit. Never before had he appreciated the weight and hardness of melons.

The ride was hard and bumpy. The shocks on the truck were old and the steel and wood bed unforgiving. *At least I'm heading north.*

Chase regretted he hadn't pressed Jonny for more information. Whatever it was, he hadn't shared much. Jonny's strategy seemed to just keep moving. Once he caught up with Jonny, they would have a talk. But he had no idea where the melon truck was going, or how much longer it'd take to get to Tecate, or even if Jonny would be there.

* * *

Cuda's men responded quickly to the second phone call from the market. The clerk was sure the gringo was heading north, but Cuda's men were not taking any chances—two men headed south and the other two combed the area to the north.

The clerk said the man was on foot, so he could not have gone more than two to three miles since he left the market.

Cuda's men checked the scheduled bus routes but none had left in either direction since the call had come in. They figured he was looking for a ride, maybe hitchhiking or paying for a ride, so he'd be a passenger.

The north team surveilled every vehicle it passed. They looked first from the back to see if they saw more than one silhouette, and then they passed the vehicle for a closer look of the occupants.

The covered trucks and semi-rigs were troublesome, but the men figured it unlikely a driver would allow someone in the trailer or bed, particularly if there was room in the cab.

The slow-moving farm truck loaded with melons hugged the slow right lane. The men saw nothing from the rear and passed.

"Look," the man in the passenger seat yelled.

"What?" the driver asked.

"Slow down. Let it pass us."

The driver tapped the brakes.

"See. There. Look through the bottom rail. Something blue."

"What is it?"

"I don't know, pull him over."

* * *

"Damn," Chase said. From a small gap between the stakes, he could see the car pass slowly, brake, pull even with the truck, and speed ahead. He knew he had to get out.

He uncovered himself and climbed over the back rail. The car was in front of the truck and out of his view. He looked behind and there was no traffic close. He waited until the truck slowed and stepped from the rail and fell to the pavement.

The truck and car proceeded a few more hundred feet, by which time Chase had rolled undetected into a shallow roadside ditch. It was the worst place in the world to try to hide. Agricultural fields surrounded the area, some of which had already been harvested or left fallow with nothing but bare soil. Behind him was a tomato field with low cover. It would be easy for any pursuer to look down the rows and spot him. But it was all he had.

He crawled on hands and knees in the ditch until he reached the tomato field. The plants, about five feet high and tied to wood and wire trellises, drooped under the weight of the large fruits. Chase crawled into the four-foot space between two rows. He ran as fast as he could in a semi-crouch.

* * *

The men from the car inspected the truck's cargo and found nothing.

The driver looked around. "Go check that field."

The passenger ran along the shoulder, peering down each row. At the far end of one field, he spotted a man running. He signaled the driver, who jammed the car into reverse, sped backward down the highway, shifted into drive, and accelerated to clear the roadside ditch. The car bounced violently as it bottomed out on the crest of the ditch. It had just enough momentum to make the distance, but the rear wheels were spinning furiously and spitting a dense plume of dirt trying to grip the loose soil. One wheel finally contacted solid ground and the car lurched forward in a zigzag path while the second rear wheel still spun uselessly. The driver got his best foothold using the tomato row with its wooden stakes and plant stalks for traction. He slammed the accelerator to the floor and the car left a trail of crushed plants, broken stakes, and tangled wire. The driver didn't dare stop to pick up his passenger for fear he would bog down in the deep, loose soil. He just kept driving, skidding and sliding as each rear wheel alternately found something solid to grab.

* * *

From a full sprint, Chase turned and saw the car approaching. He looked around but there was no place to hide—no trees, no buildings, and no ditches.

He spotted a tractor and tank in an adjacent field. If I can start it, he thought, maybe I can outrun them in the dirt.

Chase clambered into the tractor's cab. There was no key in the ignition. He had no time to hot-wire the diesel engine. He looked back.

The car was bogged down. Its rear wheels had sunk halfway to the rims. There was nothing but the piercing revving of the car's engine and the whine of the spinning wheels as they burrowed deeper. Farther back, Chase saw the passenger bent over, his hands on his hips, looking winded as he limped to catch up to the car.

Chase jumped from the cab and looked at the tank. Large "Peligro—Pesticidas" warning stickers were plastered over the plastic tank. Attached to the trailer frame near the hitch tongue was a small compressor and gasoline motor to pressurize the tank. Chase yanked on the motor's pull-cord starter. The motor growled but didn't start. He looked up. The driver was running toward him, the second man trailing a few yards behind.

Chase found the primer and pumped it a few times. He pulled the cord again. The motor wheezed to life, and Chase heard the hiss as the compressor started.

The men were only two hundred yards away. Chase knew he had less than a minute before they got to the tractor, and only seconds when he would be within range of their weapons.

He looked at the pressure gauge. It crept to the green charged zone. A few more seconds passed. Chase studied the sprayer assembly. One large hose led from the tank to a mixing manifold and then into a series of eight small-diameter hoses feeding the sprayer heads. Each time the diameter of the tubing decreased, its pressure increased.

Chase knelt behind the rear of the tank next to the sprayer on the side away from the approaching men. He pulled one of the small hoses from its plastic coupling. He immediately kinked the end of the hose and only a small stream of the fluid was sprayed. He was only going to get one chance.

The men gasped and wheezed as they approached the tank. Chase, crouched tight behind the tank, was sure they would split soon to surround him, but he just needed them together for a few more feet.

The men slowed when they were twenty feet from the tank. They craned their necks in search of him.

It's now or never. He raised his arm, aimed, and released his hold of the kinked hose. A long, straight, and powerful stream of fluid jetted from the hose and doused the faces of the two men, now just fifteen feet away.

Writhing in pain and clawing at their faces as the chemicals seared their skin, both men tumbled to the ground. Chase grabbed the single revolver from one man and heaved it out of reach. He rolled the man onto his side, unbuckled his belt, and pulled it from his pants. The man punched blindly but Chase was able to cinch the belt around the man's neck and high around his arms behind his back until he had complete control. He did the same with the second man. Chase got them both to their feet and, holding the belts like reins, walked them side-by-side to an irrigation ditch, grabbing the gun on the way.

One at a time, he dunked their heads into the shallow stagnant water. He ripped the first man's shirt and used the torn rag to wipe his face and eyes. He rolled him onto his back with his arms pinned under his body, then tended to the second man. The men were panicked and Chase needed them calm; he needed information.

He rummaged through their pockets, pulling out everything, but the prizes were their phones. Now Chase would know their contacts. He tore through their wallets, grabbing cash, credit cards, identification, and anything the men could use to get help.

"Where's Cuda?"

Neither responded.

"Where's Cuda?"

Again, silence.

"You know what was in that tank? No, huh? Well, it's a very toxic pesticide," Chase said. "It not only kills bugs, but people too. It's very easy to counteract with the right drugs, but you must take them within a couple of hours. Otherwise, your liver will start to fail and brain damage will follow."

Chase waited a few more seconds, letting his last words penetrate.

"I could maybe pull over a car from the highway to get you to a hospital, but I need something from you first—just a little information. Now, where's Cuda?"

Both men lay motionless and squinting hard, hypersensitive to the sunlight from the chemicals.

Chase bent down over the first man and grabbed him around the throat. "I don't mind leaving you here to die. It's up to you. Now tell me, where is Cuda?"

"Fuck you," was the last thing Chase heard before his limbic brain wrestled control and his rage burned blast-furnace white.

* * *

Chase slowly came back to consciousness, as if from a deep sleep, a surreal nightmare. He was on his knees, his head braced in the palm of his hands and he was shaking uncontrollably. His chest was heaving, he couldn't catch his breath, and he had no idea where he was. He lowered his hands. A pair of eyes were locked on him in a frozen stare. He shook his head, blinked hard to clear, and looked again. The face was vacant, distorted, and bloody. He looked down. His own hands were covered with blood. He tried to stand, but couldn't muster the strength, and simply rolled on his side. His head was a thick fog... he remembered a tractor, two men...

"Please no, señor. Don't kill me."

Chase jerked reflexively to see a second man lying on the ground behind him. His hands bound, the man's eyes were strained wide at the terror he'd just witnessed.

Chase rose and walked unsteadily backward from the two men. His shoulders slumped and his arms were limp, as if all the energy had been purged from his body. Nothing made any sense...all the blood, the dead man...

The man whimpered. "I'll tell you all about Cuda."

"Huh?" Chase said, confused.

"He said he was going north. Nothing else. Just that we had to find you."

"Who else is looking for me?"

253

"Four of us, two teams. The others are checking to the south."

His mind's puzzle was reassembling the pieces, but his memory was still in fragments. Cuda, yeah, he is after me. Jonny. Gotta head north. Danger.

Chase looked down at his hands and then over at the man shuddering in fear. As Chase stepped toward him, the man recoiled. He ripped the shirt from the man, dipped it in the ditch, and wiped the still-wet blood from his hands.

The gun. Chase saw it. He bent down and picked it up. As if in a trance, he turned it slowly to see all its brilliant facets, admiring the sun's reflection in the bright stainless steel. He wasn't sure what compelled him, but he brought the gun to firing position and slowly aimed with one eye. He lowered the barrel ever so slightly until the sights were centered on the head of the man squirming across the ground to find cover behind his dead compadre. Just as he'd been taught, Chase drew a deep breath, let it out slowly, and inched the tip of his finger onto the trigger.

"No, please, please."

He was ready—just another two pounds of pull. He hesitated; his concentration was broken. He looked skyward, scudding clouds, a bright sun. A calm settled over him. He lowered the weapon.

Chase picked up a cell phone and brought it to the man's face. "What's the code?"

"31881."

Chase turned and walked away.

Chapter Sixty-One
Nido del Cuervo Ranch

The Ochos had good intelligence on El Cuervo, but even better on his wife and son. They were easier to tail, even with their bodyguards. They were much more public in their daily activities—Serena with her incessant shopping, and Ramon with his school and fútbol. But it was through Serena's passion for riding they learned of the ranch.

* * *

Honoring his end of the deal, Comandante Guerra called his most trusted man—El Halcón a man whose career Guerra had cultivated with great care. If anyone could find them, it was El Halcón.

When he was a boy of fifteen, Guerra had arrested Guillermo, Billy, in Tijuana as he attempted to smuggle drugs across the border for his South LA gang.

During the interrogation, the kid proved he was not only tough, but also smart and resourceful. Guerra let him off with a warning. A few weeks later, Guerra showed up at the gang leader's house and offered him a deal. He needed "cleanskins," literally young gang members without any criminal records and especially without any gang tats. Billy fit the bill. Guerra recruited actively from the gangs—they knew the turf and the language. They weren't as ruthless as his homegrown vatos, but they had another advantage—many were US citizens.

* * *

With his parents' signature, along with a hefty signing bonus, Billy joined the US Army at the age of seventeen.

It was something Guerra had learned from the gang's leader—cleanskins were sent to the military. The lessons they learned and skills acquired would prove valuable when they returned. It was a free apprenticeship for the gang and a gateway into local armories.

After boot camp, Billy chose infantry school for his advanced individual training and, after that, jump school. As in all his training, he excelled. On graduation, he was assigned to the 82nd Airborne Division and was deployed to Tikrit, Saddam's home turf. He finally had some real action, but not enough. He needed more. He applied for Ranger Battalion and qualified for sniper school.

By the time he was discharged after one more tour in Iraq and two in Afghanistan, he had the experience Guerra sought.

Billy, now a civilian, flew to Mexico City, where Guerra met him.

"It's time we put your training to a productive use, El Halcón," Guerra said with a laugh, wrapping his arms around Billy in a full bear hug.

In a large isolated ranch outside Monterrey, Billy became the Ochos' own Special Operations trainer.

Billy never lost his edge. He loved combat, the fight, the finality.

When Guerra told Billy of the new mission, he jumped at the chance. His reconnoitering skills needed honing and this was it. He had grown tired of training guards to haul and protect shipments across the desert.

* * *

Guerra had not given him much time, so Billy felt his preparations were incomplete. He would have preferred to study the topographic maps more, but none were available. Instead, he relied on a two-year old satellite image from the internet. Harkening back to his sniper days, he scrutinized the landscape looking for high ground and clear fields of fire.

Getting in unobserved was his goal and also his problem. There was only one road and a car would be easily detected. There was also the problem of ditching the car. He thought about an ATV, but the noise would be too great. Maybe a mountain bike? He finally settled on man's most reliable transportation since the last Ice Age—a horse.

He could ride overland for twenty miles off the highway and be undetectable at night. He would ditch the horse and cover the last mile or so on foot. With any luck, he'd be done within twenty-four hours and the horse would still be around.

One of his men drove the small truck to the main highway. At around 10:30 p.m., they pulled onto the shoulder. Billy waited for the traffic to clear before he opened the horse trailer. In less than five minutes, horse and rider were off, along with Billy's favorite partner—Mitzi, a five-year-old highly trained German Shepherd.

The driver closed the trailer and drove away with instructions to return to the same location the next night.

Even with the horse, he packed light, a habit he developed in Afghanistan, where extra weight meant earlier fatigue as he scaled steep mountain passes. He needed water, his scope and tripod, MREs, a radio, and a little dry kibble. Everything else he would wear—the pistol, knife, flashlight, and compass. His fatigues were black for night travel.

Unsure of the terrain, he walked the horse at a slow pace. Billy's nerves tingled; it'd been some time since he had felt such an adrenaline rush. He was alone and had to make it on his own.

It took about three hours to reach the dry arroyo he'd pinpointed on the image. He unsaddled the mare and removed her halter and reins and stashed them under a chamise shrub. He shooed her with a swat to her hindquarter, and she ambled off in the direction they came.

Billy walked the draw for about thirty minutes before he turned and headed west. He reckoned the ranch about a mile away. Mitzi, as always, stayed fifty feet ahead, ever vigilant, sniffing the air constantly for danger and looking back to see that her small pack followed.

They came to the rise he'd seen on the satellite image. A gnarled live oak commanded the peak. Billy scanned the surroundings. This will do just fine, he thought. He settled for a spot just below the ridge to avoid being silhouetted against the sky.

He set up the spotting scope and small tripod from his pack. The sightline was perfect and the 3,500 feet to the ranch house and barns was an easy chore for his optics. Even in low light, the seventy-power scope had an effective range of over a mile. He might not be able to read a license plate, but he could tell the make and color of the car. He was accustomed to less powerful riflescopes and at this distance consistently made the eight-ring shot and often the nine.

He needed the extra power for another reason. He had a special mounting bracket to attach to his cell phone. It gave the cell phone camera the equivalent of a 1,000-millimeter telephoto lens. He could photograph everything with the cell phone and send it to Guerra. A ten-dollar app imprinted the date, time, direction, and geographic coordinates of the photo taken from the phone's GPS chip. If anything happened to him, the intelligence would get through.

Billy constructed a small hide with branches and brush, his home for the next day. He rolled onto his side and tried to get some sleep before sunrise.

Mitzi was still sniffing every nook and cranny of their lair, looking for food, danger, and painting a landscape with the palette of strange odors.

"Mitzi, *liggen.*"

She went down immediately. Now she knew it was her time to rest too. She lay on her side, extended her limbs forward, and arched her back. Her stretching done, she let out a long, slow, satisfied sigh—a good day, her pack together, a job well done.

Billy smiled. Though he spoke perfect English and Spanish, and conversational Arabic and Urdu, when he purchased Mitzi, he also had to learn Dutch commands.

A distant howl of coyotes captured Mitzi's attention in the silent darkness. Both ears, like hairy radar dishes, rotated asymmetrically to triangulate the sound. She raised her snout, sniffed a few times, and settled back down. Threat abated.

"Cousins?" he asked. Mitzi just released a long, guttural sigh.

"Guess not."

* * *

He positioned himself with the morning sun at his back. It would be the best light, and also less chance for a reflection from the lens being detected. Later in the day, the wind would whip the ground, and a dusty haze would hang in the canyon. He figured by three p.m., conditions would be bad with backlighting from the western sun. Also, he expected more activity in the cool morning than the hot afternoon.

Billy fed Mitzi a cup of kibble and a full bottle of water. It would suffice until noon.

Mitzi's growl was deep and almost inaudible. Billy felt it more than he heard it. It was her low-level warning.

He looked around but saw nothing. Mitzi's agitation grew, she bared her teeth. She had not yet isolated the danger but was on full alert. Her tail was erect, both ears shifted to pick up the sound, and she panted rapidly to draw in more air to analyze.

She turned and leapt to her right. She made two quick yelps and froze like a pointer. Billy stood and walked to her side. He searched the distance for signs of someone approaching, and out of the corner of his eye he saw the slight movement. A six-foot-long red diamondback rattlesnake was laid out, fully extended on a rock. Still lethargic from the cold night, it barely moved. It was warming from the rock.

Billy approached the snake. Even though it had a full complement of deadly hemotoxin, it didn't have the strength to strike. It just lay across the warm rock recharging. Billy knew it was no threat now, but he wasn't taking any chances.

With a narrow branch, he pinned the snake's head against the rock. He reached down with his right hand and grabbed it by the neck. It would have been easy to break its neck or sever its head; instead, he walked a few hundred feet from the knoll, found an exposed boulder, and put the snake down, reversing the hand-to-stick maneuver. He then backed away.

The snake never rattled. It sensed no threat from Billy.

The snake raised its head and slowly turned from side to side, it's forked tongue darting in and out tasting the air. While Mitzi imaged her world through smells, the pit vipers sensed theirs through tiny infrared detectors located under each eye. These detectors were the snake's long-distance data acquisition system. They could sense the heat produced by creatures in the environment; they could discern a small mouse as prey and a cow as a threat. This one seemed secure and continued to heat up for the day's hunt.

Boredom was Billy's problem with long-range patrols and surveillance operations. Even though he had always had a spotter, they had to stay hidden and quiet, yet always on full alert. It was draining. Overseas, Billy dreamed of the things he would do when he got back home—what new car to buy, where to R & R, the parties, his family, and friends. But now, he was almost home. He just hoped this recon would be short.

At around six a.m., he adjusted the eyepiece to sharp focus and scoped the ranch. His sightline was clear. Not much was happening but there was enough light to get some photographs. He attached the cell phone to the scope and shot a ten-photo panorama of the property from north to west to south. He zoomed in for details of the individual buildings—doors, windows, vents, and chimneys. To his surprise, he was able to make out the license plates of the vehicles. There were a couple of cars and two pickup trucks, one hitched to a four-stall horse trailer.

He released the cell phone from the scope and attached the photographs to a text message. The large file size took a few minutes to transmit.

His phone vibrated. He opened his message box. It was from one of his men: "Message received." That should help, he thought.

A half hour later, a few of the ranch hands began to stir. Most were milling outside the house, having a smoke while waiting for breakfast. A couple of the men headed to the stable, one carrying a tray.

Fifteen minutes later, one of the men exited the stable, leading a huge black horse followed by a young boy.

The man boosted the boy onto the horse and led him around the corral.

A few seconds later, a young girl walked alongside the older man.

Billy sent another series of photos.

Three minutes later, confirmation.

Mission accomplished. Now he had a long wait in the hot sun before heading back.

Chapter Sixty-Two
Eastern Tropical Pacific off Ensenada
31°50'08"N, 117°08'22"W

Nico saw El Cuervo swallow hard and slowly shake his head as he viewed the photos. Nico's men had spied Cuda leaving the café in Mexicali, followed soon after by a couple of Ochos goons. That, along with Cuda's phone records, was too much.

Nico didn't have the stomach for such things, but he set it up.

Cuda met Nico at the wharf, where Nico's men were readying the speedboats for another pickup.

"You don't need me for this," Cuda protested. "I don't like the ocean and it doesn't like me."

"You want to call El Cuervo and tell him?" Nico asked. "He insisted you come along for extra security. We've lost two shipments already."

Nico knew a heavily armed Cuda would be a problem, even if he was outnumbered three to one—those were barely even odds. Nico needed an advantage.

He checked the weather and surf reports for a couple of days and delayed until conditions were right. He instructed the driver to hit every wave head-on, to make the ride miserable.

Almost before they left the calm of the breakwater, Nico could see the pallor in Cuda's skin and his labored breathing.

After another thirty minutes, Cuda was retching over the rubber gunwale. The service boat had been stable and calm compared to the pitching and yawing of the much smaller and lighter speedboat. Soon, Cuda was laid out on the deck, incapacitated. Nico reached over and fired the electrodes into Cuda's neck.

Cuda instantly straightened and then arched backward as the electrical current short-circuited his nervous system. He mouthed a scream, but it was lost in the waves smashing against the boat. Cuda was motionless when Nico's men removed his weapons and tossed them overboard. They cinched thick cable ties around Cuda's hands behind his back and tethered the big man's ankles.

Even temporarily paralyzed and tightly bound, Nico felt unsafe around Cuda.

Cuda moaned quietly and began retching again. The electrical shock had only temporarily relieved the nausea. He vomited once more, this time in the boat.

He struggled to sit upright but failed. He cast a confused glare at Nico, and then his mind cleared and realized his situation.

"There is no shipment," Cuda said.

"No."

"Who sent you?"

"El Cuervo. He wanted to be here."

"Why didn't you shoot me when I was out?"

"I need some information," Nico explained. "I had an interesting talk with your friend Jonny."

"Jonny? He's no friend of mine. You hired him."

"Jonny says you think you could do a better job than El Cuervo, that you and he would make a better management team."

"Jonny says a lot of things—only a fool would take him seriously."

"Yet you were pretty close to him."

"What do you mean?"

"We checked your phone records. You seem to be in regular contact."

"He calls to taunt me, laughs that I haven't been able to catch him or find the lost shipment."

"But you talk at curious times, when our boats were jacked at the harbor, while the sub is at sea...and how did that skinny little runt overpower you at the warehouse? But what interested El Cuervo was when you started working for the Ochos and how much they know of our operation."

"The Ochos? No way are the Ochos involved. Where did you get that idea?"

"We saw you in Mexicali, at the café."

"I was trying to catch Jonny. I needed the information on the lost sub."

"What was in the bag you got?"

"Jonny sent it to prove he had the coke. He even had one of the transmitters."

"How did the Ochos get the bag?"

"I didn't give it to the Ochos."

"No, the Ochos gave it to you."

"What?"

"The taxi driver, he's one of their men."

Cuda, now sitting upright, threw his head back. An expression of confusion fell over his face.

"I think this is part of the big plan you and Jonny dreamed up to take over La Hermandad, but Jonny got cold feet and wanted out."

"Me and Jonny?" His laugh boomed over the roar of the sea.

"What's so funny?"

"It was Jonny."

"Meaning?"

"He played us all. I was supposed to meet him in Mexicali. Yes, he wanted me to help take over La Hermandad, but I just wanted to grab him. He said he had all the coke we needed to get started, and he knew how to get more shipments through. He knew La Hermandad's distributors were pissed about the recent shipments being lost and they didn't care who provided it as long as they had product to sell. Then Jonny sets me up with you with all those phone calls—like I was involved in the hijacking of the sub. You see it? Me against you, you against me."

"Jonny ain't that smart. What does he get out of it?"

"Everything. We take each other out, and he's the lone man standing."

"But we have the hostages. Is he playing Brenner too?"

"He could give a shit about the hostages, but Brenner is his insurance policy. Jonny says if anything happens to him, Brenner can dump on the entire operation."

"Well, your story is hard to believe."

"But you believe Jonny over me?"

"We've made a certain arrangement with Jonny; unfortunately, you were part of the bargain for the shipment."

"Why would Jonny give up the coke for me? It doesn't make any sense."

"He's also moving up the ladder, or so he thinks. El Cuervo is concerned about his loyalty."

"You all are in for a big surprise. Jonny was never going to be my partner, and the Ochos had no chance. I had planned on teaming with someone even better, someone closer, but I realized I could do it alone."

* * *

Cuda thought back on his betrayal of El Cuervo. It began unexpectedly.

It had been midmorning when he arrived at El Cuervo's home to deliver a package and was immediately waved in by the front guard.

He walked through the foyer into the kitchen. It was empty. He peered through the glass patio door. Serena, lying on her stomach with her head turned from the house, was sunning herself on a float in the pool.

Cuda stared. He couldn't help himself. Droplets of water shimmered on her long sun-bronzed legs. Her firm rounded butt was barely covered by the thin coral-colored bikini bottom, revealing just a hint of the pleasures beneath.

The large patio door screeched as Cuda opened it.

Startled, Serena turned her head and lifted her tortoise-framed sunglasses with one finger.

"Oh, it's you," she said. "I thought Estrella had returned."

"I have a package for El Cuervo," Cuda said.

"He's not here. He went to the ranch to play cowboy." She rolled sideways off the float and into the cool aquamarine water.

She swam to the side of the pool and placed her glasses on the tile coping. She shook her fury of black hair and a fine mist, refracting a thousand tiny prisms in the morning sun, haloed her. Rubbing her eyes clear, she asked, "Can you bring me a towel?"

Cuda stepped onto the gray slate tile deck and walked to a chaise draped with a thick pastel-stripped towel.

He stood at the edge of the pool, towel in one hand, the other extended to Serena. She smiled at the towering figure and clasped his hand.

In a single motion, she was effortlessly lifted from the pool.

Cuda caught himself looking again.

Serena noticed too and bent down slowly and deliberately to dry her legs, a motion she rehearsed a hundred times in the mirror. Cuda stared as the full fall of her breasts strained against her thin Lycra top.

She continued drying until she stood erect, then gently arched her back until her chest jutted toward him.

She turned away from Cuda and swept her hair over her right shoulder. "Please do my back." She handed him the towel.

He dabbed her soft, flawless skin as she slowly backed into him.

She was bored, he was aroused.

Cuda dropped the towel, grabbed her shoulders, and roughly turned her.

Serena yelped a faux surprise and looked into his eyes. "What would El Cuervo say?"

Cuda was silent, carefully assessing the gravity of his next move. He tilted his head slightly, ingesting her nearly naked body. His fingers slowly slid from Serena's shoulders to her bikini straps. He gently lowered her top.

She stood, vaguely smiling, as he cupped each exposed breast. With his thumbs and index fingers, he pinched each nipple, not hard but enough for Serena to rise on her toes and shudder a deep breath through her nose.

She backed away two steps and folded her arms over her breasts.

"We should go inside," was all she said.

Their lovemaking was hard and satisfying, but empty of emotion—a transaction. Cuda knew Serena had no deep affection for him, but he didn't care. Like him, he realized, she wanted power, and El Cuervo had that power. They became determined partners.

* * *

Nico hit Cuda with everything on the vessel trying to get information about Cuda's plan. But Cuda went into a trance, absorbing every blow, ceding nothing.

"One last chance, there's no need to suffer. I can make this quick. How were you going to take us down?"

"It's already happening," Cuda said with a smile. In a final gesture of defiance, Cuda stood by, propping himself against the side of the boat.

He looked at Nico and said, "Tell El Cuervo adios."He bent at his knees and leaped with a half-turn toward the smaller man. His bound hands clutched Nico's belt and the two men bounced once against the inflated gunwale before Cuda's momentum propelled them over the side.

The cold water assaulted Nico as he grasped at Cuda's massive hands in a frenzy to escape, but his strength was no match. In the struggle, he inhaled a lungful of water. As he gasped for air, he took in even more. Choking in panic, he clawed at Cuda's throat and eyes, tearing the flesh from the big man's face, but the men continued to sink. Cuda kicked his bound legs with a fury as the two descended as one. Finally, Nico's body went limp, but Cuda maintained his hold.

The driver and the crewman tried to reach the men but were too late. Both disappeared into the black depths. They searched slowly in a widening circle for a few minutes before giving up.

Bound and helpless, Cuda didn't panic. He knew he was dying, and fear drained from him. Instead, his face contorted into a grudging smile. Jonny, he thought, as he inhaled for his last time.

Chapter Sixty-Three
Nido del Cuervo Ranch

The truck hauling the horse trailer rambled down the long road to the gate at the ranch.

The ranch hand on duty rose from his chair under a pinyon pine to open the gate. It was the white Ford pickup with the dualies Tomás always drove.

He tried to peer into the cab, but the windows were tinted a smoky black. Instead, he unbuckled the chain securing the gate and opened it all the way.

The truck pulled forward a few feet into the entrance and stopped next to the guard. The rear door window behind the driver opened about four inches and the 11-inch barrel of a Heckler Koch 416 protruded just beyond the glass. Two shots were fired from the silenced rifle. One tore through the man's sternum and penetrated his aorta and thoracic spine at the third vertebrae, while the second blew out the back of his skull.

A third man in the front passenger seat exited and the truck continued through the gate. The third man dragged the body of the guard behind the pine, closed the gate, and began his own watch.

The truck and trailer continued down the road, past the ranch house and into the barn. The shooter got out and closed the doors at both ends of the barn. He went to the horse trailer and released the lock on the pull-down ramp, lowered it to the ground, and opened the rear trailer door.

As he did so, eight men, all in black fatigues, leather boots, and black bandannas, ran down the ramp, along with a large German Shepherd dog. They assembled at the rear barn door.

The driver and a fourth man from the truck joined them and were handed their weapons.

With practiced hard gestures, the driver signaled four men to follow him out the barn door to the left, and four others to the right, and two to stay with the rig.

The two teams ran silently toward the ranch house. Group Two, led by the driver and his dog, entered the rear door, and Group One through the front. Two men remained outside, one to disable the communication system, the other to guard against anyone wandering into the kill zone

Group One went room by room. At the last bunkroom, two men were sleeping in the dark shuttered room after the night watch. Neither ever awoke, and each made only the slightest jerk as the bullets found their marks.

Two men were sipping coffee at the table in the kitchen when the rear group entered. More confused than startled by the intruders, both were dead in seconds and without a sound. Neither had even tried to reach their holstered handguns, which would have been particularly difficult for the bearded man in the sling. The group leader opened the door to the basement and walked down. It was empty.

* * *

Manny watched Tomás's pickup truck approach from the remote video cameras. He hadn't worried until he saw the video feed from barn. He radioed his men, but no one responded. He reached for his cell phone and called El Cuervo.

"El Cuervo, we're under..." The line went dead.

"Check the door," Manny yelled to one of the technicians. The man ran to the door and rotated the steel handle.

"It's locked tight."

"Try to get a message out."

The technicians tried the computer and the satellite phones but could get no signals.

"Just stay quiet. They don't know we're here," Manny said.

* * *

The leader of Group Two walked over to the cabinet and swung it open to reveal the vault door and keypad. The intelligence from Ensenada had been accurate.

He banged on the door a couple of times with the butt of his rifle, although he never expected anyone to open it. He just wanted those inside the bunker to know they had visitors.

A second man brought over a small welding set and turned on the acetylene and oxygen valves. He let the vapors mix for a few seconds and then ignited the flame. It would take far too long to cut through the steel. Instead, he began welding. The thin one-foot-long bead of molten steel formed and then hardened between the steel door and frame. He repeated the weld at two more points and then turned off his equipment. He covered the remaining space between the door and frame with plastic tape.

The team left the basement.

"Did you find them?" the Group Two leader asked the Group One leader over his radio.

"Negative. We will check the barn and the outbuildings."

Group Two exited the ranch house and began a search of the grounds.

It was well hidden, but if you knew what you were looking for, there were only a few possibilities.

"Over there." Group Two leader pointed to a hand-operated well pump.

The men ran over, and the leader pumped the long steel handle a few times, but no water emerged from the spout.

He placed his hand over the spout and felt a slight suction.

"This is it," he said.

The bunker needed an external air supply duct for the ventilation. It didn't need to be huge because the space was small. But it had to be hidden so as not to give away the location of the bunker. But if you knew the bunker existed, well, it was easier to find the air supply.

"Move it," he ordered his men.

They began clearing the dirt and vegetation growing at the base of the old rusted pump.

After a few minutes, the concrete base securing the pump was uncovered, as were the four bolts holding the pump. These were removed with a large wrench and two men lifted the pump from the base.

A four-inch aluminum duct was visible just inches below the concrete base. The Group Two leader examined the pump closely. A series of horizontal slits had been cut into the pump. Those, along with the spout, provided a sufficient opening to draw in the needed air. In the bunker, the air was filtered as a ventilation pump drew it in.

With a hand signal from the group leader, a commando reached into his pack and withdrew a large plastic bottle. He poured the contents down the air duct and waited a couple of seconds. He lit a match and tossed it down the duct, where it ignited the mixture of gasoline and diesel fuel.

He then stuck a rag into the duct and covered the top of the vent with a plastic cap.

The burning of the fuel quickly depleted the oxygen in the bunker, which in turn extinguished the flames. The group leader figured the men would suffocate in another five minutes.

"He called on his radio to the Group One leader.

"Any signs of them?"

"No."

"Okay. You cover the barn, I'll check the stables."

The Group Two leader, along with two men and the ever-present dog, headed to the stables.

One man opened the heavy wooden doors, while the others trained their weapons on whatever threat lurked inside.

"Zoeken!"

The dog charged into the stables and began her search. With her nose almost dragging the ground, she ran into each open stall. At the closed stall, she sniffed the perimeter of the door and stood on her rear legs to peer over the half door. She saw the large black horse and sensed the disquiet in his labored breathing before she moved on.

The stables were a hodgepodge of odors, but she knew precisely what she was looking for. It may have been the needle in a haystack, but she could pick out the scent based on just a few hundred molecules, and there was no mistaking it—the odor was unique, as it was for the horses and other animals at the ranch. But she was only after this scent—the human scent.

With a practiced and methodical pattern, she made her way to the rear corner. She had it. She sniffed under the door, took two steps back, and sat quietly. Not a bark or a whimper, just as she had been trained so as not to alert her prey.

"Goed meisje," the Group Two leader said, tossing her a well-worn tennis ball as her reward.

The door was padlocked. The men again trained their weapons. With a single blow from a hammer, the lock with the hasp went flying.

One of the men stepped in and, with his back to the wall, swung the door open. Simultaneously, two others jumped in front of the doorway. One stood, the other knelt, and both were ready to release a fusillade at any provocation. But it was silent. The group leader walked in cautiously. He heard a quiet whimper. There, behind the bed, crouched in the corner, the mother was doing all she could to shield her two children.

"Please don't hurt us," Maria said with tears welling in her eyes, her arms wrapped tight around her children.

"That's not why we're here."

"Who are you?"

"Call me Billy." At that moment, Mitzi heeled at his side.

* * *

A small minivan pulled up next to the stable. A man bound, gagged, and blindfolded was led into the stable, where he was directed to sit.

Maria and the children were escorted into the van along with the driver and two commandos. Within five minutes, they were gone, but not before Maria pleaded, "Please don't hurt him. He was very kind to us." She pointed to the bound Tomás—the man whose horse trailer had been hijacked by Billy's men.

Team One unsealed the bunker door. As they had suspected, there was no need to cut through. The men entombed inside had desperately tried to get out as the choking smoke spread and unlocked the door, but it would not budge. Manny and the two technicians were atop one another, where they died vainly trying to draw air through the sealed doorframe. The bodies were moved and all the equipment from the bunker was placed in the horse trailer, along with the antennas and satellite dishes from the roof.

The rest of the men entered the horse trailer and the entire assault team was off the property in fifteen more minutes.

* * *

An unbound Tomás roamed the ranch in shock but alive, shaking his head slowly at the sight of the bodies of the men he knew so well. It would be his duty to tell El Cuervo—a task he truly regretted. At least he could tell his cousin El Diablo was unharmed.

Chapter Sixty-Four
Near Tecate, Baja California, Mexico

Estrella stood in the kitchen busily preparing a tray for Serena. She looked out the archway into the dining room. El Cuervo was sitting at the table with his back to her awaiting breakfast after having just seen Ramon off to school.

It was the morning routine and seldom changed until the call from Cuda.

"Estrella, more coffee, por favor," Cuervo said, still concentrating on the morning newspaper.

"Yes, Señor Cuervo." She walked briskly into the dining room.

It took almost no effort for Estrella to fire the two bullets from the blue-steel Beretta 9 mm into the back of El Cuervo's skull. The half-load ammunition lowered the entrance velocity and decreased blowback, but also made it difficult for the bullets to exit. Instead, both ricocheted around El Cuervo's cranium, causing maximum damage. Muffled by the DeGroat silencer, the shots were heard only by the maid.

El Cuervo jerked back ever so slightly as what remained of his nervous system transmitted conflicting signals to his muscles. But, finally, reflex was overcome by inertia, and his head slammed hard onto the polished mahogany table. Estrella suppressed the urge to sponge the blood flowing from the table and onto the floor. It was a chore for another person—she had one more task. This one would be much easier. She looked down and checked her light blue dress and frilly white apron—there was no splatter.

She walked back into the kitchen, placed the weapon on a silver serving tray, covered it with a large linen napkin, and walked to the master bedroom. She didn't bother to knock because Serena was still asleep—it was only eight a.m. Her daily chore was to place the tray with coffee and toast onto the chair next to the bed, open the drapes wide to awaken the señora, and leave.

Estrella broke routine. She placed the tray on the chair and grabbed the Beretta. She walked to the side of the bed, pressed the silencer against Serena's right temple, and said, "Time to wake up. You have a big day, señora."

Serena stirred. Estrella took two steps back as she savored the moment. El Cuervo had been difficult—he'd always showed her respect and kindness. The señora hadn't. She was imperious and treated Estrella as an inferior, often with open disdain.

Serena stretched slightly and removed her sleeping mask. She squinted tightly to accommodate the morning sun blazing through the window. She turned her head toward Estrella and was about to say something when her eyes moved to the barrel pointed at her.

Estrella remembered Cuda's instructions: shoot sure and fast, then leave.

As Serena's mouth gaped in confusion, surprise, and defiance, Estrella squeezed two rounds from the magazine. A wisp of smoke snaked to the ceiling as Serena's half-sitting body bounced against the soft yellow satin headboard. Her eyes were still staring directly at Estrella but registering nothing.

"Cuda says two can be a troublesome number also." A grim smile overtook her face.

Estrella returned to the kitchen and placed the weapon into the handwoven bag in which she brought home the daily groceries. She wrapped her shawl around her shoulders and put on her large sunhat. She checked herself one more time in the mirror before stepping out the front door. She nodded to the guard as he opened the gate for her daily walk to the market.

She did not look back.

*　*　*

Donte stood beside the small car parked at the market.

As Estrella approached, he opened the trunk. She placed the bag in the trunk along with her shawl, hat, and apron, and closed the lid.

"Any problems?" Donte asked as they drove off.

"No. Did you take care of Ramon?"

"I gave Father Simon the note he is to call Tomás if I'm late."

* * *

Cuda had been much more influential than anyone had imagined. He vetted everyone El Cuervo hired. And Cuda had been very selective when it came to domestic staff; he could not afford any mistakes, El Cuervo's security was at stake. But, more importantly for his plan to work, he needed the best intelligence—he needed to know El Cuervo's every move, his family relationships, and what he said when no one else was around. He needed more eyes, but he also needed strict loyalty. Taking a note from La Hermandad's own playbook, Cuda kept it in the family, although El Cuervo would never know. Estrella was Cuda's aunt and Donte was a cousin from another aunt. No one needed to know this, and if it were ever discovered, Cuda would insist to El Cuervo he only felt comfortable entrusting the safety of Serena and Ramon to people he trusted the most—his own family. And through his liaisons with Serena, he knew every move.

As instructed, Donte called the number Cuda had given him to confirm El Cuervo and, regretfully, Serena were dead. Cuda would then begin the purge.

Donte looked up at Estrella. "He is not answering. I'll try again later."

About a hundred miles southeast of them, Pescadero Baja was having similar problems contacting El Cuervo.

Chapter Sixty-Five
Near Tijuana, Baja California, Mexico

Chase hailed the first bus heading north. The passengers averted their eyes as he stumbled down the narrow aisle. His face was still caked with dirt and his clothes were a combination of mud and dried blood. He collapsed into an empty seat. His mind and his body were exhausted. His neck flopped back against the seat and in seconds he was out.

He was floating and looking down from a distance. Below, a man was on his knees, begging, pleading, but his screams were garbled as he coughed frothy blood and spat broken teeth. His nose was a bloody pulp and his eyes swollen shut, but still the two fists kept pounding with a fury. Chase tried to reach down to help the man, but his arms weren't long enough. He was frozen and helpless. He tried shouting at the assailant, but his voice was mute. He tried to move closer to see the man, to get his attention, but the man remained in the shadows. Help him...help him...

Chase snapped awake, his body shaking from the nightmare. He gasped and looked around. The other passengers were twisted in their seats staring at him. He lowered his head, trying to disappear.

His mind soon cleared of the nightmare and reality returned. He was on a bus, heading north, and was safe for a while. He remembered Cuda's man said the other crew was concentrating to the south, and the north crew wouldn't be contacting anybody because he had their phones. Chase slapped both pockets to make sure he still had them. He pulled one out and tried the access code. It failed. He tried again. Nothing. He tossed it through the open window. He pulled the second phone. The code worked. He had his line to Cuda.

He felt the hard bulge in his waistband. He lifted his shirt. He still had the gun too. He drifted off again, this time without the nightmare.

"Señor, this is where you catch your next bus," the driver said quietly, waking him at the Highway 1 stop. The driver looked down at his watch. "It should arrive in thirty minutes."

Chase thanked him and got off the bus. He was in El Sauzal just north of Ensenada. He walked across the highway overpass to a bus shelter on Highway 3, the Ensenada-Tecate Road. It was a bleak industrial zone. The only trees were commercial citrus orchards south of the highway. Traffic at this time of day was mostly produce trucks and semi-rigs hauling their cargos to the border.

He sat on the splintered wood bench shaded from the sun by the aluminum cover. Even for late spring, it was very hot; even this close to the ocean with the offshore breeze, the temperature was near ninety degrees and the air thick with exhaust.

He took the phone from his pocket. He'd set the ring volumes on low and checked to see if he missed anything during his sleep. No calls. He wanted to call Jonny; he needed to call Jonny. He had to know about his family but didn't have the number.

Sitting there, in the middle of nowhere, a sense of hopelessness descended on him. Jonny deserted him for the money. He was a smuggler, a lifetime criminal. Why should he care above me or my family? Hell, he doesn't even know us. What else would explain why he wanted to do it alone? It didn't make sense then and it didn't now. He used me to give himself enough time to get away. Make Cuda tie up his men holding his family and chasing him.

Alone, in the blistering heat on a nearly deserted highway, Chase broke down. Inconsolable tears flowed as he realized he had lost everything that meant anything to him: Maria, the kids, Gus, his crewmates. He had devolved to a person he would never recognize, a drug dealer, possibly a murderer; he was beyond redemption.

The bus arrived, and the driver opened the door. Chase just sat there, staring at the driver.

"You want this bus?" the driver asked.

Chase was silent.

"Okay," the driver said as he pulled the door lever.

As it was about to close, Chase leapt to his feet.

"Sorry," he said to the driver when he reopened the door.

He wasn't sure what compelled him to get on the near-full bus, maybe it was one last chance to find his family.

He paid the driver and found a seat.

The bus took a full three hours to make the less than hundred-mile trip over the steep foothills and valleys in the Sierra de Juárez range. There were numerous stops, some scheduled, others not. It gave Chase a chance to grab some food and water. He was nearly dehydrated from the heat. The only relief the bus provided was the breeze through the side windows, but it exacted a price in dust and noise. Still, Chase told himself, it was better than the melon truck or a net skiff, and he had no other place to go. Something told him Gus wouldn't be happy about his complaining.

"You think that's tough, you little shallow-water weasel. Try spending your eternity in the cold, dark ocean. Oh yeah... and being dead."

"I thought by now you'd have made it to hell."

"Hey, they took their good time in purgatory, but I made the cut, wiseass. But I'm quitting if they make me your guardian angel."

"Pretty loose standards up there, huh? A Gus with wings? That's too much."

"Yeah, and I ought to fly down and kick your malingering butt..."

He ignored the pain of his sun-blistered lips as the memory of Gus brought his first smile in three days.

* * *

Around 8:30 p.m., Chase entered the lobby and headed to the front desk.

"May I help you, sir?" the receptionist asked. She eyed Chase with suspicion; his filthy clothes were not in keeping with the hotel's standards.

Chase stared down at the crumpled note he unfolded from his pocket and tried to interpret Jonny's squiggles. "Yes. Could you call Mr. Nemo's room for me?"

"Certainly," she said with a slight smile. "You can speak with him on one of the house phones in the lobby. It will ring when Mr. Nemo is on the line."

"Thanks."

Chase sat in a plush red leather chair next to the end table with the white house phone. It was pure comfort, a step up after the hard aluminum and plastic bus seat.

This is stupid. Chase shook his head. Jonny split a long time ago, and I bet he's diving on the sub right now and the note was just a ruse. He probably set me up for Cuda.

Chase was about to run when the phone rang.

"Mr. Nemo?" Chase asked in surprise.

"Room 325."

Chase hung up and headed to the stairs. A mix of anger and trepidation roiled within.

As soon as the door opened, Chase jumped Jonny, threw the slight man to the floor, and gripped his pencil-thin throat. "Where's my family?" Chase shouted.

"Chase, Chase, get off me. Let me talk," he squeaked through a constricted throat.

Chase released his grip but still pinned the smaller man beneath him.

Jonny caught his breath. "Look, I know I deserted you, but I had to. If we were together, it would've been too easy for Cuda's men to find us."

"What about Maria and my children?" Chase was close to tears, but the only emotion he wanted Jonny to see was rage.

"I haven't talked to them, but we should know more in the morning." Jonny coughed and rubbed his throat. "We need to leave early. I don't want anyone tracking us here. You have to trust me one more day, that's all."

"What choice do I have? Where are we going?" Chase lifted Jonny to his feet.

"Outside Tijuana. It's about an hour's ride. I got a cheap rental. You need to clean up. Get in the shower. You hungry? We can go out or call for room service."

"I need sleep. Go ahead and order something. I'll eat anything."

* * *

The next morning, Jonny roused Chase from a deep sleep. Chase still couldn't believe that the little man was still there. He'd half expected Jonny to desert him again.

"Chase, we best be going, big day ahead." There was a calm in Jonny that Chase hadn't seen the night before. He smiled easily.

Chase followed Jonny from the room. He turned toward the elevators, where three men were just exiting. The recognition was instant. The man with the bandaged eye had been begging Chase for his life two days earlier. Now, his face was fixed in pure hate.

Chase grabbed Jonny by the collar and threw him back into the room, careful not to slam the door.

"What the hell—"

"Shhh, it's Cuda's men, by the elevator." Chase bolted the lock and hooked the flimsy night latch. He ran to the side of the room and began shouldering the bureau. "Help me with this."

Jonny grabbed the edge and began pulling. "How'd you know?"

"The guy with the bandage, he's one of Cuda's men who chased me down. I think I killed his partner."

"What? How'd they find you?" Jonny was wide-eyed and straining under the weight of the furniture.

"Oh shit." Chase patted his pants pocket. "I took his phone."

"Nice move. And you didn't remove the battery?"

"I...uh—"

"Never mind. We gotta get out of here." Jonny ran to the sliding door to the balcony. "It's three floors down. We can climb it."

"Here, move this first." Chase was already shoving the sofa across the room to barricade the door along with the bureau.

Jonny turned. A loud thud reverberated through solid wood as Cuda's men tried to kick open the door.

"Hurry. I've got a white Civic in the parking lot." Jonny scrambled over the wrought iron railing and clambered down to the second balcony before leaping and rolling onto a thin strip of lawn beside the parking lot.

Chase flinched as two gunshots rang out. The door lock exploded, propelling fragments of steel and chrome across the room.

Chase vaulted the railing and swung onto the second balcony. A moment later, one of Cuda's men flung his leg over the balcony. Chase reached out, grabbed the man's leg, and pulled with all he had.

The man hurtled past Chase with limbs flailing as he swam in midair before landing with a muted thump, straddling the pavement and grass.

Chase leaped from the balcony, the man's back breaking his fall. The man issued a guttural wheeze from his crushed rib cage.

A bullet whizzed past Chase before thudding into the sod beside him. He rose and ran to the side of the building. To his right, Jonny laid on the horn. Chase ran the fifty feet, weaving and ducking behind any vehicle he could find.

Jonny reached across and opened the passenger door. Chase dove in headfirst. Jonny accelerated, squealing tires and laying a black and smoky skid, before rounding the building and zooming out of range of their pursuers.

Jonny straightened the wheel and Chase bolted upright, bracing for the ride ahead.

"I thought you said they wanted us alive," Chase said, gasping and looking out the rear window.

"You must have pissed someone off big time. What good are we dead? They'd never find the sub. We gotta get the hell out of here. What did you do with the phone?"

Chase reached into his front pocket and pulled it out.

"Toss it, now!" Jonny yelled.

Chase lowered the window and hurled the phone. In the rearview mirror, Jonny saw the phone careening off the pavement in bits and pieces. "Why the hell did you keep the phones? You knew better!"

"I wasn't thinking straight when I left Cuda's men. I was in a daze. I thought if I never saw you again, it was a chance to contact Cuda, maybe I could deal with him."

"What, and leave me out? Thanks, man."

"I didn't know if you were dead or alive. I thought you deserted me and my chance to get my family. But I wasn't gonna do nothing until I came here. If you weren't here, I knew for sure you ditched me. I didn't have a whole lot of options, you know."

Jonny jammed the gas pedal as they entered the highway. The rear end swerved, pinning Chase against the door. Jonny steered furiously to gain control.

"Thanks for all your faith in me," Jonny said. "But we're in this together now and we got Cuda's boys after us."

It was just past dawn and the low sun cast an orange glow over the brown arid landscape. They sped through the hotel district to the residential beltway, and on to Federal Highway 2 with its patchwork of agricultural fields and industrial and commercial properties.

Jonny floored it and turned sharply into the left lane to avoid a line of trudging semi-rigs. The diesel exhaust fumes were thick, forcing Chase to close his window.

Cut off by Jonny's move, a small sedan blared its horn in protest, its driver gesturing indignation at the affront.

Chase looked over at Jonny, whose eyes were locked on the rearview mirror. "Dammit," Jonny said.

"What?"

"Look back. You see that black Suburban?"

Chase turned just as the SUV veered around the small sedan. It was gaining fast.

"This thing go any faster?"

Jonny's eyes tightened as he studied the road ahead. "We gotta outrun those guys for another ten miles. Hold on."

The car surged forward for a quarter mile but screeched almost to stop as a small pickup truck blocked the fast lane. Hemmed in by the pickup and a semi in the slow lane, Jonny laid on the horn.

The pickup driver sped up and Jonny slipped inches in front of the semi.

The pickup slowed again just as the black SUV tried the same lane change, but this time the pickup driver was mad and ceded no territory.

Jonny and Chase pulled ahead a quarter mile.

Chase faced rear. "The Suburban got around the pickup."

"They gotta have 500 horsepower in that beast."

The window of the Suburban opened and a man extended a .357 Magnum.

The first bullet struck pavement in front of the Civic but the second hit the trunk lid. It was the third that shattered the rear window, rocketing shards of glass through the passenger compartment.

"Duck!" Jonny shouted to Chase.

Another round slammed through the rear window and driver's seat, grazing Jonny's right arm.

"Damn, I've been hit." Jonny swerved between lanes to avoid the next round.

Chase looked over. Blood was spurting from Jonny's arm. "Can you drive?"

"Yeah, I think." His faced grimaced in pain. "Man, it burns."

Chase ripped a strip of cloth from the bottom of his shirt and tightened it around Jonny's arm.

Ahead of him another semi was rolling in the slow lane. "We got another half mile," Jonny said. "Hold on."

Chase's arms locked against the dash.

Jonny pulled up even with the semi and waited for the Suburban to catch up.

"They're gaining on us." Chase's voice broke in panic.

Jonny accelerated as fast as the little Honda could handle, passing two lengths in front of the semi. He jerked the steering wheel right and swerved into the path of the semi, missing the truck by inches, careening onto the gravel shoulder.

Jonny hit the brakes and slowed enough to turn onto a narrow two-lane road.

The Suburban saw Jonny's maneuver, but was boxed in by the semi. The driver slowed to let the semi pass and pulled onto the shoulder a quarter mile past the road. He shifted into reverse and slammed the accelerator, kicking up a plume of gravel and dirt that ricocheted like shrapnel against the SUV. He continued in reverse until he reached the side road, jammed the car into drive and sped toward the distant Civic.

Chase looked around. The area was deserted, nothing but desert scrub. "Where the hell we going?"

Jonny's face was tortured in pain. "Almost there."

The faster Suburban was now a few hundred yards behind.

Chase saw the outline of the warehouse in the distance. As they approached, the high perimeter fence surrounding the building came into view.

Jonny slowed as they took the turn into the driveway, then hit the gas as they approached the ten-foot-high chain link gate.

Chase covered his face and Jonny slammed through, knocking both gates from their hinges.

Jonny floored the accelerator again and the car lurched through the gravel parking area toward the front entrance. Twenty feet short, he slammed the brakes, locking them into a skidding stop. The air was ripe with hot oil and burning brakes.

"Run for the door," he told Chase.

Chase opened his door and was about to jump out when he saw Jonny struggling to move with his injured arm. He grabbed Jonny by his shirt and jerked him over the console and passenger seat, and out the door. Together they limped toward the entrance.

The Suburban swerved to a stop and the passenger rolled from the door onto the ground, wrestling his gun into firing position. In the same instant, a guard in black military fatigues burst through the door ten feet in front of Chase and Jonny.

All Chase really saw was the barrel of an M-16 rifle aimed at his head before the guard unleashed two seven-shot volleys.

The concussion deafened Chase as the bullets whizzed past his head. Pain sent him tumbling to the ground and Jonny along with him.

Chase was sure he was dead until an arm reached down and lifted him to his feet. The guard, a black bandanna obscuring his face, asked, "You okay?"

Chase shook his head. "I can barely hear you."

"The hearing will come back," the guard said.

Chase watched as a second guard helped Jonny up. Chase shook his head to clear his vision. Behind them, a dead body was sprawled on the gravel and another hunched over the steering wheel of the Suburban, the bandage still taped over his eye.

Fear welled in Chase and he was about to panic when he felt a gentle pat on his shoulder and saw Jonny. "It's okay."

Jonny turned to the first guard. "They here?"

The guard nodded. "At the other end."

Chase and Jonny followed the guard into the empty warehouse.

Chase blinked in the dark interior and thought the place deserted until he heard a dog barking. As he approached, he could see two children playing with a dog at the far end of the building

The kids looked up.

"Daddy," they shouted and ran full speed toward Chase and Jonny, the dog in hot pursuit.

"Oh my God," Chase yelled, turning to Jonny with a mix of shock and joy lighting his face.

The kids tackled Chase and they all fell to the floor in raucous delight.

"Oh, I have missed you so much. Look how big you've grown. I love you guys more than you will ever know."

"What about me?"

Chase looked up. Standing over him, looking disheveled and tired with her arms crossed in a defiant hipshot pose, but more beautiful than he'd ever seen her, was Maria.

He stood and hugged her, but her sweet scent tipped his emotions and the tears flowed freely now.

"I never thought I would see you again. I, I—"

Maria laughed and cried at the same time. "I know, Chase. I love you that much and more."

Chase looked at Jonny. "How—?"

"Your arm, what happened?" Maria asked.

"We will have plenty of time for explanations, but we gotta get you out of here. There is a car on the other side."

"Other side of what?"

"Follow me."

They walked to the end of the warehouse, where two other men dressed in the same commando gear were waiting.

The taller of the two men took control. "We have guards on the other side. Follow Carlos and Mitzi down the ladder."

Kevin took Chase's hand. "Come on, Dad. I'll show you."

They descended the ladder and into the tunnel. Kevin laughed with glee as he ran at a full sprint. Mitzi followed, barking and nipping playfully at his ankles. He stopped and kneeled to pet her. Mitzi returned with a face licking that got Kevin laughing even harder.

Chase looked over to the guard. "That's one hell of a dog you got."

The guard nodded. "She's a good girl."

The others soon caught up.

"Dad, can we get a dog like Mitzi, please?" Kevin asked.

"Please, Dad," Denise said.

"Yeah, Dad, how about it?" Jonny asked.

"I guess I'm outnumbered, but you have to ask the boss," Chase said, glancing to Maria for approval.

They arrived at the end of the tunnel and climbed the second ladder.

A small car was waiting; its motor running.

The guard walked them into the vehicle and told Chase to drive.

"Take the first left after you leave the parking lot. Go six miles and turn right, it will lead you to the interstate. You'll know the way from there," he said. "Now. Go."

Jonny stood behind him.

"Wait, Jonny, get in," Chase said.

"Not now, Chase. I gotta get this arm checked out. But I'll be in contact real soon." He looked directly at Maria. "I'm looking forward to a home-cooked meal. You do Cajun?"

"I'll learn. It's the least I can do."

"Okay. I'll be in touch. Take this envelope. It has instructions on what happened. You can pull it off, you'll be safe now."

"Thanks Jonny. You saved us."

"You did the same for me, buddy. Now, go."

Chase accelerated through the gate.

Chapter Sixty-Six
Point Loma, San Diego, California, USA

His miraculous survival made all the local stations. Even the networks carried the story.

Chase explained how he had survived the explosion when he was working on the net skiff. He drifted in the skiff but got thrown out during a storm and floated on a small raft. He washed up on the Baja coast and was taken in by a fisherman and his family, who nursed him back to health. He made it home as soon as he could.

There were holes a mile wide in his story, as in most of Jonny's plans. Any intrepid investigator could have found them, but the world loved a feel-good story, particularly after the sinking of the *Bella*. Everyone wanted to believe in miracles.

The Brenners kept a low profile after the initial flurry and were bothered little afterward. Nothing is as stale as last week's news. They settled into a new normal, appreciating life and each other like never before.

But his nightmares continued. Some nights were sleepless, and he paced trying to purge the images from his head.

Maria had enough and got Chase to a psychologist. The doctor diagnosed his memory loss and frightful dreams as dissociative rage. Chase's mind couldn't handle the trauma of killing Cuda's man and buried it deep. He was told it would take years of therapy, but he would heal.

* * *

Months had passed when Jonny showed up unexpectedly. He carried two suitcases. They would have never made it through Customs, so they came by tunnel.

"Where have you been?" Chase asked.

"I had to help some guys find a submarine, then they asked me to give them a hand in Colombia. Seems our old friends, El Cuervo and Cuda, along with many of their associates, decided to leave the business. I'm helping the new ownership iron out the wrinkles. It was part of our contract. Once it's up and running smoothly, I'll be heading back to N'Orleans. I've seen enough of this ocean for a while. But I know I'll be back at sea. It's always been my salvation, first from my stepdaddy, then the law. Can we take a little walk?"

"Sure, Maria and the kids will be home soon. They'll want to see you." Chase grabbed Jonny's luggage and put them in the house.

It was a perfect San Diego day; sunny, eighty-five degrees, just a hint of wind, and the sky a patchwork of white clouds against azure. Jonny rolled up his shirtsleeves, pulled his sunglasses from his shirt pocket, and snugged them around his ears. "Let's go."

"You have to tell me, how did you do it?"

Jonny gave his full hundred-watt smile. "I just threw the meat into the cage—they devoured themselves. What's the term they use? Yeah, triangulation. I offered La Hermandad, Cuda, and the Ochos a deal. The Ochos were just more motivated. They had the better meal."

"The Ochos?"

"Yeah, they run the cartel out of Juárez. It's short for 'Tres Ochos.' It was a prison cell at the Centro de Rehabilitación Social in Juárez, where the head of the Ochos, Comandante Guerra, was once held. The cartel brands all their products with a stamp of E-3-8 on the body of a cheetah."

"What's it mean?

"Block E, Tier 3, and Cell 8. Everyone knew when a letter arrived with that return address, you'd better pay attention. After he got out, the label stuck. He liked it because it reminded him he could endure anything. Now, it's just the 'Ochos.' At least, that's the story I heard. He is now just an old man waiting to die, all he wanted was a reckoning with El Cuervo."

They approached the corner and Chase turned right toward the small neighborhood park where the kids spent most of their free time in the summer. "Will you be safe?"

"As much as anyone in this line of work. But I feel some gratitude from these guys—El Cuervo is gone, and as long as the Ochos get rich, they will leave me alone. Besides, I have some new ideas to pitch them. The current operation can't last forever."

"I get a feeling you're not telling me everything. Things worked out a little too smoothly."

"Actually, my plan totally failed, at least Plan A."

"How so?"

"Well, if I can't trust you..." Jonny raised his sunglasses and gave Chase a conspiratorial wink. "I had planned for months to hijack a load, even before we delivered the first shipment. I'd have enough money to escape and live forever without La Hermandad threatening me every day. I was sick of putting in all the work and getting paid squat. Besides, they had no respect for me. I'd been a junkie, I was nothing. I was going nowhere with them. Fear and money bought loyalty in La Hermandad, and I had neither."

"How were you going to do it? I mean, you'd still have to sell it—you'd need a distribution network."

"Hey, if you got ten tons of coke, you can find a buyer. Hell, you did."

Chase shrugged and nodded in approval. "Yeah, if you can manage to stay alive. But you'd have to get it to land. You'd have to hide it and transport it."

"I had that worked out."

"Where?"

"I think you already know."

Chase furrowed his forehead in concentration, then arched his eyebrows. "No way, not the colony at Colonia Vicente Guerrero."

"Yup, and I'm Mr. Beaton. It was my cottage where we stayed."

"What happened? Why didn't you go through with it?"

"Cuda happened. It was gonna be my next boat, but he was tipped by one of my crew that I scuttled the boat on purpose, and that changed my plan. I wasn't gettin' another boat, I was gettin' dead."

"I don't get why you sunk the boat. It screwed your plan." Chase raised his palms in mock surrender. "What was the point?"

"I wanted them to think there was a flaw in the design. I got lucky the first time and got the bales out. On the next cruise, I wouldn't be so lucky. The entire boat, shipment, and crew would be lost at sea. That way, I'm gone forever. Adios El Cuervo and La Hermandad. And no lookin' over my shoulder the rest of my life. But I also wanted to see how well the bales worked. Because, not only would I be selling the coke, but also the technology—boat and bales. But, well, the plan changed."

"You still could have escaped with it all, but you didn't. You rescued me; you saved my family. Why..."

Jonny laughed. "Ha. Don't think it didn't cross my mind, but I'd had enough." His expression saddened. "I'll never forgive myself for what happened to your crewmates. I'll be haunted forever. Maybe something good can come out of this."

Chase stared at Jonny, unable to comprehend how tragedy so tightly weaved their fates. He just nodded to his friend. "Let's get back home. I know three people who can't wait to hug you."

* * *

Jonny left the next morning without his suitcases, and without waking anyone. Only the new puppy, Bella, pawed a farewell from her crate.

Chase opened the suitcases. There had to be ten million dollars in cash, along with a short note.

Dear Chase,
This is for you, but knowing you, you will probably refuse it. Too late, I'm gone and can't take it back. If you don't want all of it, there are some families who could use it. My redemption begins.
Jonny

Chase stared at the note in silence.

Over the course of the next few weeks, anonymous envelopes were delivered by courier to the families of *Bella's* crew. Each came with the same simple note: From Friends of the *Bella*. Even Garza's family, who would never know the depth of his treachery, received a share, but this time, they were all equal.

Chase had two shares remaining. He sat at his desk and took out his wallet. He pulled out the photograph of Maria and the kids, wrinkled and fading from all the endured travails. Time for you to take a rest. He taped it gently to the wall next to the desk.

He reached into his wallet once more and took out the photo of Gus from his personnel file in Nico's office. The grizzled face smiled back at him.

"You old son-of-a-bitch. I know what you would want me to do with your share, but I'd probably get arrested." Chase laughed as he returned Gus's photo to his wallet.

Lightning Source UK Ltd.
Milton Keynes UK
UKHW040741160223
417122UK00005B/526